What Alfred Hitchcock did in **The Birds** . . .
What Peter Benchley did in **Jaws** . . .
Kenneth McKenney does in the newest, most
exciting excursion into plausible terror yet,

THE PLANTS

The Plants

Kenneth McKenney

BANTAM BOOKS
TORONTO · LONDON
NEW YORK

🅱

THE PLANTS
*A Bantam Book | published by arrangement with
G. P. Putnam's Sons*

PRINTING HISTORY
Putnam edition published February 1976
Bantam edition | February 1977

ISBN 0-553-02976-2

Published simultaneously in the United States and Canada

*Bantam Books are published by Bantam Books, Inc. Its trade-
mark, consisting of the words "Bantam Books" and the por-
trayal of a bantam, is registered in the United States Patent
Office and in other countries. Marca Registrada. Bantam
Books, Inc., 666 Fifth Avenue, New York, New York 10019.*

PRINTED IN THE UNITED STATES OF AMERICA

*for Virginia
and her plants*

The
Plants

Other echoes
Inhabit the garden. Shall we follow?

—T. S. Eliot

Chapter

One

It was an amazing summer. The countryside flourished. From the beaches in northern Scotland to the cliffs of Cornwall the land was rich and green and fulsome. In living memory there never had been growth as luxuriant. There had never been such fruitfulness.

Long hot days were followed by endless evenings. As the land cooled, showers fell, consummating a twenty-four-hour growth cycle which made every leaf or petal, root or blade flourish as never before.

Suburban gardens overgrew wildly. Indoor plants spread lushly. Cities and towns and villages became encircled with growth. The countryside was tropical. Parks and pathways were mazes of leaf and cluster.

No one could explain the growth. No one could explain the weather. But both continued. The sun shone. The gentle rain fell. England flourished.

In bars and on the streets, in offices and on the beaches, people talked about the lovely sun, their gardens, the size of roses. Everyone wondered how long it would last.

It was unusual, they said. It was freakish.

The rest of Europe was normal. There was nothing strange about the weather in Canada or Australia. There was no alteration in America. Russia had nothing unusual to report.

But wasn't it nice, for a change, they said.

Jokes were made about forecasts. Complaints were frequent about cutting the grass. One of the more sensational London newspapers proposed a theory about biodynamic interference from outer space. Hayfever and allergies were frequent, and the pollen count was abnormally high. But by and large the weather was enjoyed.

People relaxed, barriers were lowered, they talked to each other more often, more easily. They hoped the weather would continue.

After all, they said, it's about time we had a decent summer.

So the days continued.

And when the Events in Brandling, as they came to be known, began, few suspected what they would unfold.

Brandling is a tiny village in the English county of Somerset, tucked between low folds in the Mendip Hills. It lies, quiet and serene, almost unchanged by time or technology; even its population has remained more or less constant. There never were more than forty villagers at any one time.

Later, after the Events in Brandling were made public, or as public as they ever became, there were many who found nothing surprising in the fact that Brandling had been chosen.

After all, it was said, the place is less than ten miles from Glastonbury, and everyone *knows* how mysterious that area is.

Glastonbury? Oh, yes, where they say the Holy Grail is buried.

And King Arthur.

What, however, was perhaps less well known about Glastonbury were two facts which could have had a great deal to do with the events themselves.

Legend has it that on the slopes of St. Michael's Tor, that lone ruined tower on a sculptured hillside, Joseph of Arimathea came after the crucifixion, thrust a thorn staff into the soil, and it immediately took root. It blossomed, survived, became famous as the Glastonbury winter thorn, and the tree itself was only finally destroyed by Roundheads, who cut it down because of the power of the beliefs surrounding it.

Also, it was said, Glastonbury was the place where the first conversion to Christianity took place in the British Isles.

2

All this, of course, came out later. Little of it was suspected as the amazing summer continued and the sun shone and the beaches were crowded and the plants grew. Although there were a few, from the beginning, who suspected that the long summer days were significant, that they heralded deep, unavoidable change; that they were symptoms of a sickness attacking mankind.

Chapter
Two

One Wednesday morning, late in July, in the village of Brandling a group of men stood outside The Bunch of Grapes, the only public house in Brandling. The men stood beside a small truck on which lay a huge marrow squash. They stared at the squash, at the size of it and murmured admiration.

It was a breathless day. The air was like milk. The high clear sun shone as it did on the rest of the country.

One of the men, Charlie Crump, was talking excitedly. The truck was his. The squash had come up in his garden. It was all he had ever grown.

"It came up overnight," he said. "Just like that. Overnight."

"Just like that?" repeated someone and laughed.

"Overnight." Charlie's voice rose. "I didn't plant it. I mean, not intentionally." He looked at the squash with pride. "It just came up, on its own."

The group admired the massive vegetable. Ted Wilkes, a man of eighty whose hands were rough with years of gardening, moved to the marrow squash. When he touched it his hands made a slurring sound.

"What d'you think of it, Ted?" Charlie Crump asked.

"It's no ordinary squash," Ted Wilkes said carefully.

"It's bloody enormous."

"But it's not natural," Ted Wilkes said. His voice was gentle, westcountry. "Not to come up like that, it's not."

"What's wrong with it?"

"It's not right for you," a man called Eric Bolton

4

said to Charlie Crump. He was a big man with a heavy face. "Not for you. You never grew anything in your life before."

"That don't matter," Charlie Crump replied quickly. He put his hand on his squash defensively.

"It does," said Ted Wilkes. "In its way." He shook his head at Charlie Crump. "You're no tiller of the fields."

"A squash that size don't come up overnight," Eric Bolton said.

"This one did." Charlie Crump looked at all the faces. "It wasn't there yesterday, I tell you. It came up overnight."

"You got anything else like that comes up overnight?" someone asked and laughed.

The laughter spread.

"It's a good size, Charlie. Didn't know you had it in you."

"Come up overnight again, will it?"

"If there's anything you're using, tell us the secret."

"Something you've been drinking?"

Charlie Crump touched the squash. He held it. They couldn't take it away from him. Whatever was happening, whatever else was going on, the huge vegetable was his. "I grew it," he said. "I tell you, I grew it."

"Never."

"That size?"

"What about them cabbages of Fred Clarke's?" Charlie asked, his voice uncertain. "The size of them? Their heads? There's been lots this year."

"Fred's a gardener," Ted Wilkes said softly. "He's been growing cabbages for years." He handled the squash again and listened to the sound it made. "Don't take on, Charlie," he said. "I know what a summer it's been. But overnight? Things like that don't happen."

"That don't mean they *can't*?"

Ted Wilkes nodded. He felt the life in the vegetable. "You're right," he said. "That don't mean it can't."

5

"See."

"But there's more to it than that," Ted Wilkes said. "This is a visitation."

"What you mean?"

"What I say."

"I bloody grew it, I tell you."

"Did you?" Ted Wilkes asked. "Or did it seek you out?"

"Come off it." Charlie Crump moved closer to the squash. "Don't give us none of your religious crap. Not about my squash."

Ted looked at Charlie's thin, disappointed face. "We're not trying to take it away from you," he said gently. "But maybe you hadn't noticed it before. The creatures of the fields move in strange ways."

"But it wasn't there yesterday."

"You wouldn't know what was there yesterday," Eric Bolton said roughly. He envied the marrow squash and Charlie's possession. "You was pissed yesterday."

"That don't make no difference."

Eric Bolton laughed. "Made all the difference to you."

"Come on lads," Ted Wilkes said. "This won't get us anywhere." He touched the squash again, feeling its massiveness. It seemed to be living beneath his hands. "But I'll say this for you, Charlie. It's the best bloody squash I've ever seen." He smiled. "You can almost feel it breathe."

The group of men nodded.

Ted Wilkes was right. It was the biggest, most massive marrow squash any of them *had* ever seen. It would take more than Charlie Crump to produce it.

Charlie Crump watched their eyes. Suddenly he hated them all. Eric Bolton, Ted Wilkes, the other brown faces lined by the sun. They hadn't the right to deny him the squash. It had come up in his garden. They all knew it.

"You're jealous," he said. "The whole fucking lot of you. Rotten bloody jealous."

He put his hands on the squash and held it.

6

From the beginning Philip Monk had questioned the progress of the summer. As it continued he became convinced it *was* a sign of something he did not understand, but that it *was* somehow, a key, a token.

At thirty-seven, Philip Monk had become a minor television personality. In the early sixties he'd arrived from Oxford with a degree in history and had gone into journalism, there to discover his talent, an ability to describe in simple terms highly complicated technological and scientific processes.

He had moved into radio and recently had completed a series for BBC television on what he lightly termed his "popular science thing." The series had been successful and another was planned.

On the program Philip had attempted to explain the effect science had on society. He talked about computer dating in order to explain the working of computers themselves and the control they had over so much that concerned everyday lives, from salaries to election results. He played with household detergents and plastic bags to illustrate how indestructible they were and how, slowly, they were clogging the world's lifelines.

Increasingly, Philip had become concerned not so much with pollution but with desecration. Every time he read or heard of the bacterial content of coastal waters or the overpopulation of cities and their squalor he felt anger. The slow decay of fine architecture due to industrial fumes was a sign of man's insanity; the increasing greed for energy and possessions a sign of man's shortsightedness.

Real or imagined shortages, the manipulation of markets, and panic buying were indicative, to Philip, of man's despair.

"We should know so much better," he said. "We have the brains but not the will. We have become greedy and shortsighted, and we deny our responsibility."

Sooner or later, he felt, some basic imbalance of nature would occur. Then, he feared, mankind would no longer have the power or ability to restore the balance as he knew it. It might be far too late.

7

Now, with the amazing summer baking the country and the weather fixed to produce maximum growth, Philip felt the change he feared was actually about to happen. He sensed that all mankind lay in danger, that every man, woman, and child could be affected. He wondered also how it would affect him, his wife, and his two children. He wondered how personal it could become.

Chapter

Three

Almost a week after the gathering at The Bunch of Grapes in Brandling a BBC announcer referred to Charlie Crump's squash.

"You'll all have heard enough by now," he reported, "about the Endless Summer. But we've received a letter from Somerset about an Endless Squash."

The announcer laughed.

"It's not that it doesn't have a front or an end, you understand. But apparently it hasn't stopped growing—and it's been picked for six days.

"It seems this squash measured about eleven feet when they took it from the vine and now, although it's been sitting on the back of a truck for six days, it's up to thirteen feet in length. And still growing. It's just a lad, they say.

"What's more, the grower claims it came up overnight."

The announcer laughed again.

"Take it all with a grain of salt, if you like, although you'd need more than a grain. But if this is what they mean by inflation then the more the merrier as far as I'm concerned. Could 'squash' depression, if you get my meaning.

"On the other hand, as we all know, they brew some pretty potent cider in that part of the world."

Philip Monk heard the broadcast and rang the announcer. They knew each other slightly.

"It'd take a lot of stuffing," Philip Monk said lightly.

The announcer, whose name was Alistair Rank, paused, not immediately understanding.

9

"The Endless Squash," Philip said. "The one in Somerset."

The announcer laughed. "Oh, that," he said. "We've had some pretty strange reports this summer but that marrow squash. . . ." He laughed. "If you believe it, that is."

"Where is it?" Philip asked.

"The squash? Somerset somewhere." There was a sound of rustling paper. "Here—a place called Brandling."

"Brandling?"

"Know it?"

"I live there," Philip Monk said, suddenly uneasy. "Liz and the children are down there now. I'm going down tomorrow," Philip went on, "for the weekend. Mind telling me who let you know about the squash?"

Alistair Rank paused. The paper rustled. "A Mabel Crewe," he said. "Rose Cottage. Do you know her?"

"Quite well."

"Is she sane?" Alistair asked. "I mean, could there be anything in this after all?"

"I don't know," Philip Monk replied. "She's a funny old duck and she's potty about her garden but I'd have thought—well, I'd have thought she was telling what she *believed* had happened."

"She doesn't go in for practical jokes?"

"No," Philip said.

The announcer thought for a moment. "You're not still doing that program of yours, are you?" he asked.

"My popular science thing?"

"Yes."

"No, but they're talking about another series. Why?"

"Well, it's just that there's been so much lately." Alistair Rank laughed to lessen the seriousness. "I know we're all bored with the Endless Summer bit, but something's going on."

"I know," said Philip, his voice serious. "That's why I called."

"We've had some very strange letters."

10

"Such as?"

"Well, I haven't got them with me, but I remember a chap in Yorkshire who— Well, it does sound absurd, but he said he couldn't get into his garden any more. The plants had shut him out."

"In what way?"

"Grown together. Formed a wall or something."

"Anything else?"

"Lots. Oversized this, oversized that. Records broken all over the country. People blinded by allergies. Old ladies short of breath." Alistair paused again. "You name it, we've had reports of it," he added. "I'm surprised you're not more involved."

"That's why I called," Philip said. "I've been talking to people for weeks about the weather."

Alistair sighed. "I know there's a silly season for everything," he said. "But this *is* becoming ridiculous."

"Could you let me have copies of the letters?" Philip Monk asked. "The really strange ones?"

"Well . . ."

"Come on, we both work for the same firm."

"All right, but you know what they're like." Alistair Rank hesitated. "No one wants to panic."

"Panic?" Philip's voice was sharp.

"Well, you know what they're like here."

"I'll be discreet."

"Of course." Alistair laughed more easily. "I'm becoming edgy myself," he said. His voice relaxed. "It's getting up at five in the morning that does it."

"Go to bed earlier," Philip suggested lightly. There was no point in showing the depth of his concern. "Get more sleep."

"Not easy . . . this time of year."

"Don't let it get you down."

Alistair Rank coughed. "If there *is* anything to this squash you *will* let me know?"

"One good turn deserves another," Philip said. "Don't forget those letters."

"Course not."

"Thanks, I'll call you after the weekend."

Alistair Rank put down the telephone. He wondered why Philip Monk had called him. The news-

11

papers were full of letters, and Philip had his own research team.

He shrugged. Perhaps the man was after all he could get. It was hard enough to dig out the truth at the best of times, and that squash didn't make sense. Mind you, he thought, it's not that unnatural. After all, a man's beard continues to grow after he's dead.

Philip, his wife and two children, lived in the tiny village of Brandling. But for the past year he had been aware that his marriage was altering, its magic beginning to fade. His wife, Elizabeth, realized this also, but neither had spoken of it, both appearing outwardly to accept the distance developing between them. As the summer continued they had moved farther apart.

Philip began to spend more time in London, blaming his work and the time it demanded. Elizabeth remained in the country cottage with the children, growing increasingly irritated by the long hot days.

As he spent his hours reading newspapers, looking for evidence to support his concern; as he talked to gardeners about growth and fruitfulness, he knew he was avoiding his own basic responsibility.

He knew also that the longer he let matters drift the harder they would be to remedy.

But the summer *was* a sign of something, of that he felt sure. He had to discover what it meant.

So far his success had been limited. There was nothing he could isolate or define, yet he felt that the right combination of time and place and individual would convey to him the message the summer carried.

Most of the people Philip talked to were skeptical, imagining him to be after something sensational for his program. Few took him seriously and, if they knew him well enough, they assumed the breakdown of his marriage had a lot to do with his obsession.

Philip ignored the rebuffs. Sooner or later he was certain he'd find the key he was looking for. But he never imagined it would be so close to home, that it would be in Brandling.

Nor did he suspect that there were forces at work drawing him back to the village, to his wife and children and his own mistakes. Slowly, inexorably, the red soil of Somerset and its rich, mysterious growth were calling him home.

Philip Monk was thoughtful after he put down the phone, more concerned than he had been prepared to admit.

"Panic," Alistair Rank had said. "No one wants panic."

There *are* others as worried as I am, Philip thought. I'm not alone in my apprehension.

Funny that the marrow squash should have come up in Brandling, he mused. Funny too that there was more information in the BBC than outside it. He'd have been better off talking to BBC staff than all those gardeners he'd questioned.

Philip shook his head wryly. There was a lot more than charity that began at home, he knew. There was curiosity and fear also.

He wondered what he'd find in his own home in the tiny village of Brandling where the oversized marrow squash lay, growing hourly.

But before he left for the country there was one other person Philip was determined to see. Michael Martin, an old Oxford colleague, was a senior research worker at London University. Philip had tried several times to contact him but Martin, it seemed, was totally involved in a new experiment.

However, Philip would try again. Before he went to Brandling and inspected the marrow squash himself he'd find out what Martin had to say about the whole phenomenon.

Chapter
Four

Later the same day Charlie Crump stood at the bar in The Bunch of Grapes, in Brandling. He held onto the bar with one hand and gripped his glass with the other, swaying a little as he swallowed. His nose was very red.

It was half an hour before closing, and the bar hummed with conversation. The air was hazy. Outside a gentle rain was beginning to fall.

In his corner, between the bar and a large open fireplace, Ted Wilkes sat with Eric Bolton, Police Constable Walters, and several other locals. Their pints of bitter, in dimpled mugs, stood on a scrubbed wooden table.

At the bar Charlie Crump emptied his glass and put it down carefully, to conceal the unsteadiness he felt.

"Another, please," he said to the barman. "Scrumpie."

The barman poured the pale flat cider. "Scrumpie'll be the end of you, Charlie," the barman predicted. "Rot your boots, it will."

"They're my boots," Charlie said carefully.

The barman laughed. "How's that marrow squash of yours?" he asked.

Charlie Crump didn't reply.

"I'm told it was on the radio," the barman said. "The BBC was talking about it."

"The BBC should mind their own bloody business."

"Everyone's business," the barman said, "a big 'un like that."

"No," said Charlie Crump. "It's not nobody's busi-

ness but mine." His voice rose. "If no one's going to believe me, then it's none of their bloody business." He
coughed. "Fuck 'em," he said.

"Talk like that and you'll be on telly next."

Charlie Crump lifted his glass and drank. The
rough cider ran down his chin.

The barman smiled and moved away.

At the table by the fireplace the group of men
turned their heads when Charlie raised his voice, and
watched him drink.

"He's getting worse," Eric Bolton observed.

"He's always been like that," Ted Wilkes said.
"When he's had a few."

"He's had more than a few."

"He's all right," said P.C. Walters. "He never
causes any bother."

Eric Bolton turned his heavy head. "I'll tell you
something," he said. "He's been quiet enough about
that bloody squash, the last couple of days." He
laughed. "Can't get a word out of him about it."

"Had enough of it, I shouldn't be surprised," P.C.
Walters said. "The way some people've been pulling
his leg."

Eric Bolton stopped laughing. "Deserves to have
his leg pulled," he said warily.

"I dunno," Ted Wilkes said slowly. "Maybe he was
telling the truth."

"What?"

"It's in all our mouths, somewhere."

"Don't be funny."

"I'm not," said Ted Wilkes steadily. "But that's
the trouble with us, isn't it? We don't face the truth
when we see it."

"You're bloody preaching again," Eric Bolton said
roughly. "Need a pulpit, you do."

"That squash's real," Ted said.

"Don't mean Charlie's got anything to do with it."
Eric Bolton turned to the constable. "What d'you
think?"

P.C. Walters shrugged. "It's nothing to do with
me," he said evenly. "Not till it commits a crime, that
is."

15

Eric Bolton laughed.

"There's something about that squash," Ted Wilkes said. "The way it's grown on the truck like that. You can feel it," he said. "When you put your hands on it, there's something."

"You and your *bloody hands*."

Ted Wilkes smiled. He'd lived most of his eighty years in Brandling, a man close to the earth and its seasons. From its early days he had suspected that this summer contained something personal.

As the long hot days led into each other and the evenings spun he felt it coming closer.

"It'll change us, William," he had said to his dog, a honey-colored labrador. "This'll be our reckoning."

In Brandling Ted Wilkes was somewhat of an oddity. The village accepted him the way they would a child or an invalid. Few took him seriously. His practices were strange, remote. He lived alone. He had inherited religion, and he often spoke of things natural and unnatural.

"What you mean, natural?" P.C. Walters had once asked him.

"Simple," Ted replied. "Things that are natural keep their place. They don't take more than they ought to."

"That all?"

"That's enough," Ted replied. "Being natural's what you can rely on."

P.C. Walters nodded slowly, wondering if Ted was as daft as people said.

Now, Ted Wilkes knew his world was about to change. The knowledge excited him. It was not altogether unexpected because this summer *wasn't* natural. Its demands were somehow beyond its needs.

He looked at Eric Bolton steadily. "It's got at you, that marrow," he said. "You can't abide it, can you?"

"Can't abide what?"

"The fact that Charlie's got it and you haven't."

"Bollocks," said Eric Bolton, but his voice betrayed him. He emptied his mug. "Load of bollocks."

"Is it?"

"Course it is." Eric Bolton stood, empty mug in his hand. His gaze went from Wilkes to Walters. "I'm having another," he said. "Want one?"

Both men shook their heads.

Eric Bolton shrugged. "Suit yourselves," he said and went to the bar.

Charlie Crump turned his head as Eric came up beside him, stared for a moment, then looked away. Very deliberately he lifted his glass and drank, put his glass back on the bar, and wiped his chin with the back of his hand. Each movement was slow, calculated, provocative.

The barman came over.

"Pint for me," said Eric. He paused, then added, "See what Charlie's having as well."

"Charlie drinks Scrumpie."

"Better get him one then." Eric laughed. "He can always use another."

The barman turned to Charlie Crump and reached for his glass, but Charlie's hand came out and held it. His palm was over the top, refusing.

"Eric's—" the barman began.

"Piss off," said Charlie Crump.

"What?"

"Tell Eric to piss off," Charlie said. "Him and his bloody drink."

"You don't want one?"

Charlie Crump shook his head.

The barman turned to Eric. The bar was quiet. In the warm hazy light the faces turned toward Eric, watching him, waiting. Outside the rain continued to fall softly. Something of the summer was about to break.

"Not like you to turn down something," Eric Bolton said uncertainly.

"Piss off."

"Didn't turn down that squash." Eric tried to laugh.

"What you mean?" Charlie Crump turned quickly.

"When it was dumped on you."

"Listen." Charlie Crump's thin face twisted. "I

17

grew that fucker. It's mine. I grew it on me own. So leave off about it. You hear me—just fucking leave off."

Eric Bolton grinned. "Sure you won't have a Scrumpie for old time's sake?" he said.

"Stick it up your arse."

Eric felt the eyes and the turned faces. He blinked and then laughed. "His loss," he said to the barman. "If he don't want one that's his hard luck."

The barman nodded.

"Course," Eric said loudly, "if he's too bloody proud that's a different matter."

"Charlie proud?" said the barman.

"Now that he's been on the radio," Eric said. He turned away from Charlie Crump and faced a group at the end of the bar. "Now that he's become Brandling's leading squash grower."

Someone laughed. P.C. Walters watched.

"Him and his bloody squash," Eric said. His voice was forced. "Lying there like a giant's prick. Can't stop it, either. Keeps on growing, it does."

Charlie Crump stood at the bar, swaying, his hand over his glass, his thin face sharp with anger. He picked up the glass and held it like a weapon, uncertain what to do. But P.C. Walters moved quickly and took him by the arm.

"Come on," Walters said. "Time you was off home, Charlie."

"I'm—" Charlie began.

"Off," said Walters firmly. "There's a good lad."

Charlie's face creased; for a moment he looked as if he was going to cry. "He's got no right," he said uncertainly, "keeping on like that. It's not—"

"You'll be all right in the morning," Walters said. "But you better be off home now."

Charlie Crump belched and turned toward the door. Walters let him go. Charlie pushed through the door and disappeared into the darkness and the gently falling rain.

Inside The Bunch of Grapes the conversation slowly resumed, moving away from the mystery. But they were men too close to the soil to remain unaffected by the squash and its size and the reactions it was beginning to cause.

They were beginning to feel its presence like fear.

Chapter
Five

Charlie Crump walked home in the dark, his hands in his pockets. Rain ran down the back of his neck.

He was sick of all the jokes, the remarks people like Eric Bolton made. It wasn't his fault the marrow squash had come up. They should either believe him or leave him alone. He didn't ask it to grow in his garden; he didn't want it. They'd no right to go at him like that.

Charlie turned a corner and slipped in the wet, staggered a little, lurched, regained his balance, and went on.

When he got to his cottage he paused to peer about. He could make out the shapes of bushes in the dark, the overgrowth, the lushness. It was a rotten bloody summer, he thought, and he was sick of it.

He walked around the side of the cottage where the truck was parked. The hump of the squash loomed in the darkness.

Charlie stopped and looked at the vegetable's bulk. It's all your bloody fault, he thought. Why'd you come up like that?

"What'd you pick on me for?" he suddenly said aloud.

The squash was silent in the dark.

Charlie belched and spat. Then, with the drunken cunning of someone who has nothing left to lose, he knew immediately what he had to do.

"I'll do you, you bugger," he said. "I'll bloody stop you growing."

He lurched past the truck and into a shed behind the cottage. Switching on a light, he poked among pieces of timber, dirty sacks, and worn tires. He found

the ax he was looking for. Taking the ax he turned
and went outside again. The huge squash glistened in
the light from the shed.

"You got no fucking right," he spat out.

Charlie Crump, the ax in his hand, climbed onto
the back of the truck and stood for a moment looking
down at the marrow squash. It extended from between his legs, enormous and shining.

He swung the ax, lifting it high above his head,
then stopped suddenly, listening.

About him he heard the sudden, sinister sound of
the rustling of millions of leaves.

The sound froze Charlie Crump. He paused, the
ax held high above him, and turned his head and
listened. The sound rose. It was as silver as the sound
of tiny Christmas bells. It bristled, as though every
plant or bush or tree within earshot had lifted a voice
in protest, dismay, outcry.

Suddenly Charlie Crump was afraid.

"What?" he stammered, moving his head around,
listening, allowing the ax to swing slowly down to the
truck. "What's that?"

About him the plants continued to rustle.

"Who?" Charlie asked, but the night was still.

The rustling persisted for a while longer, then
began to die away. Charlie Crump swallowed. His
throat was dry, his heart raced, his palms were wet.
He listened, seeking the sound. But it was dying,
falling away, becoming untraceable.

"What's going on?" he whispered.

The rustling died.

For a moment it seemed Charlie Crump's fear
would overcome him. For a moment his hand loosened
on the handle of the ax, and he turned to jump from
the truck. But anger replaced his fear, and he halted,
lifting the ax with a grunt to plunge it into the squash.

"There!" he shouted.

A frenzy overtook him. He lifted the ax again and
again, its wet blade catching the light, and smashed
the huge vegetable to pieces. Hacking and cutting,
he swung the ax until there was nothing left to cut.
Then he stopped, exhausted, rain and sweat soaking

him, gasping for breath in the middle of the mess he had created.

"There," he gasped. "That'll teach you."

He threw the ax away and, slipping, clutching at the sides, climbed down from the truck. He switched off the light in the shed and went into his cottage where, without removing his clothes, wet and covered with pulpy slime, he fell into bed and slept.

When Charlie Crump woke the sun was high.

He went outside into the hot day. The back of his truck was a mess of pulverized vegetable. It was beginning to dry, changing now to a deeper shade. Before long all that would remain of the huge marrow squash would be a dry, thin crust in the back of the truck.

Charlie Crump looked at it and shivered.

Chapter
Six

While Charlie Crump stood and shivered, Mabel Crewe bustled and hurried. She was an active spinster of seventy-four. She lived in an overgrown cottage off Brandling High Street, where she spent all her waking hours tending her roses. Most years they filled her garden; this summer they overran it wildly.

Rosebushes, their branches heavy with bloom, crowded round the small thatched cottage where they climbed the cottage walls and entered the windows.

From a distance her home looked like a bouquet, festooned and garlanded.

The Friday morning after Charlie Crump destroyed the marrow, Mabel Crewe decided that, as much as she loved her roses, the time had come to reduce their number.

"Sorry, my loves," she apologized gently. "But there just isn't the room." She spoke aloud to the bushes, as she always did. "Some of you will have to go."

The Endless Summer had begun by delighting Mabel; now it was beginning to disturb her. Like Ted Wilkes she felt it, instinctively, to be wrong somehow. This was one of the reasons she had written to the BBC about Charlie Crump's marrow squash. They should have taken her letter more seriously. There was more going on than they knew.

Standing in her overgrown garden, she examined her roses. The tall bush with the heavy, overblown blooms by the window could come out, she decided.

"Sorry about this," she said as she opened her pruning shears. "But it happens to us all in the end."

Grasping a branch of the rosebush, she moved it

23

and then, suddenly, let out a small gasp and quickly pulled her hand away.

On her thumb appeared a bright red spot of blood.

"Now that wasn't very nice." She sucked the blood, then waggled the pruning shears at the rosebush. "That wasn't very nice at all."

Very carefully Mabel Crewe took hold of the branch again, avoiding the thorns. But once again as she moved the pruning shears close she gasped and once again blood appeared on her thumb.

"That's funny," she said in a different tone, no longer addressing the rosebush, but talking to herself. "I could have sworn—"

Mabel was reaching for the branch for the third time when there was a movement behind her. She turned quickly and saw a blond, bright girl of seven.

"Oh—Deborah!" Mabel said. She frowned, disturbed by the child's silent entrance. There was something about the little girl that was different, penetrating. Not for the first time Mabel Crewe wondered about the child and what went on behind her simple, innocent eyes. "You did give me a start," Mabel admitted.

Deborah Monk laughed. "You were talking to your roses again."

"I always talk to them, you know that."

"Do they ever talk to you?" the child asked.

Mabel smiled. "Quite often. In fact, I think one of them just bit me."

Delighted, Deborah laughed. "Plants don't bite," she pointed out.

Mabel sucked her thumb again. "This one did."

"But they *do* talk," Deborah went on. "I've heard them."

"Have you now?"

"Yes."

There was a pause. "You've never mentioned that before," Mabel said carefully.

Deborah's face wore an innocent expression. "You've never asked about it," she said simply.

"Perhaps not," Mabel agreed. "Tell me, what do they say when they talk to you?"

"Oh, they never talk to me."

"I thought—"

"They talk to each other," Deborah explained. "And sometimes I hear them." She smiled and turned away, her interest fading. "I don't know what they're saying. I don't understand them. But sometimes I hear *them* talking."

"Tell me—" Mabel Crewe began but Deborah interrupted.

"Daddy's coming home today," the child reported. "He's coming home this afternoon."

"That'll be nice."

"Yes, it's a long time since he came down."

Mabel nodded. She liked all the Monk family; she regretted that Philip and Elizabeth didn't appear to have a more successful marriage. And it was obvious that both the children missed their father.

"How's Jacob?" Mabel asked.

"He's all right."

"You haven't been fighting again?"

Deborah laughed, uncaught. Bending to sniff a rose, she cupped it in her small hands, her face bright above the rose's pale color.

"What are you going to do?" she asked Mabel Crewe, staring at the pruning shears.

"As a matter of fact I was going to prune this monster."

"Is that when it bit you?"

Mabel nodded, her gaze on the tall bush by the window.

"Perhaps, it didn't want you to cut it." Deborah moved closer. "If it really did bite you, perhaps it didn't want you to cut it with those."

Mabel hesitated. "I was only joking," she said, "when I said it bit me. You mustn't take me too seriously."

"But you *were* going to cut it."

"It has to be done." Mabel Crewe shook her head briskly. "We all know that. If they weren't pruned the whole place would get out of hand. It's quite good for them, you know. They benefit from a good cutting back."

25

"Doesn't it hurt them?"

"Well, no. I mean, not in the way it would hurt us." Mabel paused and studied the steel of the shears. "It gives them a bit of a nip, I imagine, but that's all."

"Is it?"

"Oh, stop it, Deborah! You know as well as I do how much I love these roses of mine."

Mabel Crewe hefted the shears in her hand. Her thumb had stopped bleeding. She turned back to the rosebush. Deborah Monk watched her steadily, her hands behind her back, her face serious.

Mabel Crewe took hold of the rose branch again, carefully, avoiding the thorns, feeling the child's eyes and something beneath her own fingers also, a strange resistance, a defense.

This is absurd, she thought. What could this child know?

"I don't think it wants to be cut," Deborah said in a firm voice.

Mabel turned from the bush, feeling something amounting to relief. The child's interruption had been timely.

"I don't think *you* want me to prune them," Mabel pointed out.

"I don't either."

Mabel Crewe shook her head. "You're a determined child, Deborah. I'll say that for you. Once you get an idea in that little head of yours—"

Deborah laughed her bright, sharp laugh. "You're not going to cut it, are you?"

"Well . . ."

"I can tell you're not."

"Perhaps I shan't," Mabel promised. "Not now, anyway."

"That's good," said Deborah. She quite disarmingly took the old lady's hand. "They really don't like it at all," she added.

Mabel Crewe nodded slowly. Deborah's words sank in. Perhaps there *was* more to it than she was prepared to admit; perhaps all the signs of the summer demanded a special understanding.

Chapter

Seven

On Friday, before Philip Monk left London to drive to Brandling, he consulted his colleague, Michael Martin, the research worker in biology at the London University.

Martin suggested they meet in a corner of the laboratory where he worked. Philip found the humidified air of the laboratory to be refreshingly cool after the hot, diesel-smelling atmosphere of London's streets.

Philip Monk pulled his shirt away from his back where sweat had plastered it. "I see why you suggested this place."

"I seem to live here these days," Martin said.

"You could do worse."

Martin nodded. "Tell me about this marrow squash."

Philip told him what he knew. "I'm going down there now to see if it's really all they say."

"Why are you interested?" Martin asked. He stared down at his hands. "I mean, apart from the fact it might be a good item for a program of yours sometime?"

"I was curious when I heard about it on the radio," Philip explained carefully. "I became even more interested when I knew it was next door, so to speak."

"How can I help?"

Philip shrugged, uncertain how much of his concern to reveal.

"You're the only person I know working on plants at the moment," he said. "Measuring their responses, that sort of thing."

27

"I see. . . ." Michael Martin looked at his hands again. "Have you any theories about the marrow?" he asked.

"None. I mean, I suppose some growth continues after a vegetable is picked. And the bigger it is—well, the more it's likely to occur. But, well, it's unusual to say the least."

"There's nothing more to your inquiry than that?"

Philip wondered what Martin was getting at. There was something the scientist was trying to say, something he wanted to talk about. It was just a matter of pushing the right button. Philip understood suddenly that Michael Martin could tell him a great deal.

"I mean," Martin continued, "you're not likely to get excited by one squash no matter how big it is— or what it's doing."

Philip took in a deep breath. "All right," he said slowly. "I won't deny it. Forgive me for a wild idea, but I believe that some sort of change is taking place in the balance of nature."

Martin listened with interest.

"Between man and his environment," Philip continued. "I think something is happening. It shows in the weather and I believe this squash, and all the other odd little things that have happened this summer, might be part of it. I think something very big is about to occur."

Michael Martin nodded. "It is," he said crisply.

"What?" Philip, aware of a precognition, sensed that Martin's thoughts preceded his own. "You think—"

"Something *is* happening."

"You believe it, too?"

"I know it." Michael Martin leaned forward and began to speak urgently. "It's happening to the plants. They're just about ready to rebel."

"Rebel?"

"Yes. For years we've been manipulating them, creating new species, killing off others. We began with cross-pollination and now we're transplanting genes. Scientists are even talking about changing, recoloring, and disciplining nature. Have you ever heard anything more arrogant? *Disciplining nature?* It's insane."

Philip nodded. "Mankind's a bit like that," he said, watching the intensity in Martin's face. "The things that've been done to guinea pigs and fruit flies. . . ."

"But we've never interfered with a whole *king-dom* before. Don't you see? We're attempting to alter the greatest body of living matter on the entire planet. Do you realize what that means?"

"I hadn't thought of it that way," Philip said. The button had been pushed. Nothing would stop Michael Martin now. "I mean—I felt something was happening. That nature could protest somehow. But I never thought it would begin like this."

"We assume so much," Martin went on rapidly. "We assume that because we are able to communicate with each other that's all the communication there is. I know, other groups do intercommunicate—some apes, ants, dolphins, for example. But we don't credit them with great intellectual powers and we certainly never imagine they have moral values."

"Moral values?" Philip wondered what deep well he had tapped. His fears were suddenly intensified. The air seemed cooler. Martin's concentration was total. "Did you say moral values?"

"Yes, *moral* values." Michael Martin spread his hands to gesticulate what he wanted to say. "Don't call me crazy. But what would you say if I told you I believe that the plant kingdom morally disapproves of what man is doing to the world?"

"You think that's possible?"

"Yes—I think it's possible." Michael Martin shook his head. "I only *think* it's possible, mind you. There's no way of proving it—yet."

"That plants can actively disapprove—"

Martin paused. "Just exactly how much do you know about plant life?"

"The usual basic—"

"Ever heard of the Backster Effect?"

29

Philip Monk paused. "He's the American," he said slowly, remembering. "He put some plant through a lie detector test or something."

"That's right. He linked a plant in his office to a polygraph. And he got a reaction. Then, and this is what's so amazing, he wondered what he could do to provoke a more intense reaction. So, knowing that pain works best in man, he thought—just *thought*, mind you—of burning the plant's leaves. And the reaction he got was so intense that the plant freaked out. Needles jumped all over the place."

"You mean just by thinking it?"

"He never lit a match. Well, he did later, and got a reaction which, in fact, wasn't quite as intense as the first one."

"Just by thinking of doing it?"

"That's all."

Philip Monk let out his breath. "So he measured fear on his lie detector; not pain but fear."

"Yes."

"But—"

"I know." Michael Martin turned away. "I know what you're going to say; that's why I was reluctant to talk to you in the first place. You're going to say, 'So what? If it's been proved then why aren't we doing something about it?'" Michael Martin faced Philip again. "Isn't that what's going through your mind?"

"In a way."

"I suppose you think I'm crazy, too. A lot of people thought Backster was off his head. Oh, he got a few small grants and went on a couple of television interviews, but most established scientists thought he was nuts. He's not, Philip. He's probably one of the sanest men alive."

"I don't think *you're* crazy," Philip admitted.

"Everyone else I've tried to talk to does."

Philip looked around the laboratory.

"Oh, they'd have me out of here if they could," Martin said. He shook his head. "They probably will in time. But they'll regret it. They'll be bloody sorry about it afterward."

30

Philip nodded. "If the plant kingdom does have an—intelligence," he said, watching Martin's face, "and they do disapprove of what we're doing, then they could be about to—what was it you said? Rebel?" He tried to keep his voice even.

"Yes. That's what I said."

"Could that account for the weather we're having?"

"Hard to say," Martin said quickly. "That's a bit like the chicken and the egg. Maybe the plants were able to bring about a climatic change in this country just to see how much control they had. Maybe something else caused it and they're just taking advantage of the situation."

"Either way it's frightening."

"Of course it is."

"Is it possible they could control the weather?"

"Why not?" Martin looked at Philip. "They produce all the oxygen we breathe, don't they?"

"Yes."

"We look at the millions of miles of plant life and we think how good it is they produce all that oxygen for us. But that's only our conceit, isn't it? What if it was actually the other way around?"

"What do you mean?"

"I mean, for instance, what if the plant kingdom decided, ages ago, that they were running short of carbon dioxide and that the best way of solving the problem was to encourage the growth of animal life in order to turn the large buildup of oxygen into carbon dioxide? What if they decided that, eh?"

"They would then be considered our creators," Philip said simply.

"Creators, encouragers—something like that." Martin's voice rose a decibel. "But if you look at it that way, you begin to see just how much we depend on *them* and how little they depend on *us*—mankind, that is." He tapped his chest. "This animal. The fact of the matter is that they'd be a lot better off with just about anything else in the animal kingdom except us."

31

"And now"—Philip kept his voice steady—"now you think they might have decided we've gone too far and it's time something was done about it?"

"Yes, I do."

Philip shivered.

"I think they realize how irresponsible man is," Michael Martin went on. "My God, they've seen enough of it in their own terms. Think of the defoliation in Vietnam, for example. Or what some of the large industrial laboratories are doing." Martin moved closer. "You must know something about that? Work's going on today to develop a pea plant mutant that's got nothing on it except peas. No leaves. No unnecessary growth. Just peas. No flowers even. It's like—like turning a woman into one bloody great womb. Nothing but a breeding organ."

"I've read about that sort of thing. But I've never thought of it exactly that way."

"It's happening all over the world. Us. The Americans, everyone. The Russians have been working on plant mutations for years. Their long-term goal is the control of all plant growth." Martin put his hands together. "My God, talk about disciplining nature."

"Nature may turn out disciplining us," Philip said quietly.

"It's about time something did. We'd run this planet down to nothing at all if we had the chance. Then we'd push off somewhere else, leaving the husk behind."

"I've had that thought also." Philip nodded. "It's one of my nightmares."

Michael Martin rubbed his face. He looked tired. "I suppose you wonder what I'm doing here?" he asked abruptly and, continuing before Philip had time to reply: "It's a question I ask myself often enough. But this is one of the few places where I might find answers to all those questions. Something here might tell me how long we have left."

"You think it's as immediate as that?"

"I don't know."

"What *are* you working on?" Philip asked.

Martin eyed Philip shrewdly. "Do you know anything about plant memory?" he asked.

Philip shook his head.

"It's possible, you know," Martin said. "Experiments have already been carried out. Look at this."

He led Philip toward a series of shallow trays which contained hundreds of tiny bean sprouts. Wires led from the trays and the innocent-looking sprouts to sets of dials and batteries of tape recorders. Above the plants small lamps flashed intermittently.

"This is one of the programs I'm working on," Michael Martin said, his voice calm now. "It has to do with plant memory." He pointed to the arrangement of lights above the trays of pale green sprouts. "They remember the pattern it makes."

Philip bent over the trays, looking at the sprouts.

"The Russians have worked on plant memory," Martin explained. "Short-term memory mainly. My stuff is longer—collective memory. The body of knowledge plants work from."

"Have you got anywhere?" Philip asked carefully.

"I don't know yet. I'm not sure." Martin glanced at the plants and then at a set of dials. He watched the light. As the light blinked the dials responded. "The plants are recording," he went on. "I'll have to wait and then run them through a printout. To see how long the knowledge is retained. But it's there," he said quietly, to himself. "It's there."

Philip nodded. "Do *you* think this marrow squash I told you about has anything to do with all this?"

"Yes." Martin's voice was sure. "I think it's their way of beginning to tell us what they think of us— how much they disapprove. It's part of their early warning system."

"By showing how *independent* they are."

Martin's face was serious. "Yes," he said quietly. He lifted his hands and touched the flesh of his cheeks, softly, as if to convince himself it was real. "We'd better take their warning. Because if we don't, if we ignore it, they could just—wipe us out."

Philip Monk felt the chill the words carried. He watched the rows of tiny plants, the flashing lights, the dials and the tapes. He was tensely aware of the cool, conditioned air.

"You believe that?" he said.

Michael Martin nodded.

"I didn't know you had such a conscience," Philip told him.

"Is it a conscience?" Martin asked. "Or is it fear?"

There was a silence between them. Philip thought fleetingly of the world outside, where the sun beat on pavements and tar melted and people walked and sweated and tanned.

Michael Martin took a deep breath and ran his hands over his hair. "Is there anything else you wanted to know?" he asked crisply, changing moods. "Any more questions?"

"Not just now," Philip said.

"Good, I'll get on with things here then. I'm sorry, but I must get ahead. I've no time—"

Philip paused at the door. "Tell me," he said casually, "any idea of when you'll know something about those?" He pointed to the sprouts under the light.

Martin shrugged. "Who knows? A few days, a few weeks—it depends on them really."

"Mind if I call you in a day or two?"

"Not at all. But I wouldn't wait a couple of days," Martin said. "I'd call daily if I were you. The rate things are going even an hour's important."

"I'll call tomorrow."

"Do that."

"And thanks," Philip said.

"Think nothing of it," Martin said in a tone of dismissal. Then he added, "It *is* just possible that I'm wrong."

Philip watched Martin for a moment, bent over the plants, turning dials, waiting. Then he left.

After the isolation of the laboratory the London streets seemed overwhelmingly crowded and hot.

Philip breathed deeply, feeling the hot air in his lungs, wondering what had led him so surely to Michael Martin, deciding their contact could not have been more timely.

Chapter
Eight

Elizabeth Monk ironed Jacob's T-shirt. It was four on Friday afternoon and the worst of the sun's heat was over. Outside the sky was a clear blue and in the garden bees and butterflies moved, dappling the heavy air.

Later, the long evening would begin and rain was again predicted.

On the radio an announcer's voice said, "The outlook continues fine. A series of related highs remain steady over the British Isles. Tomorrow's temperatures should be in the vicinity of thirty-two degrees centigrade, which is abnormally high. Towards evening showers are expected. The outlook for Sunday and Monday should be similar." The announcer's voice faded and music replaced it.

My God, Elizabeth thought. How bored can you get with fine weather?

She folded the T-shirt, put it to one side, and picked up another as Jacob came into the kitchen. In contrast to his sister Deborah, Jacob, at eleven, was a dark, serious child.

He carried a book with him as he came in and dumped himself into a chair.

"Hello," Elizabeth greeted him. "What have you been up to?"

"I've been reading about pollen count."

Elizabeth smiled. "I thought I'd banned the weather as a topic of conversation."

"Pollen count is very important," Jacob told her. "Did you know it's reached the highest ever for this part of the world? It's a record. It's more than doubled this summer."

"You don't have to tell me. Half the village is down with some sort of allergy. There're more runny noses and puffed eyes this summer—"

"It's very puzzling, though," said Jacob.

"What? Pollen count?"

"No, the allergies. After all, it's not as if we're not used to pollen and things. We've grown up with them. You'd think we'd all be used to them by now."

Elizabeth listened to the small, serious voice. He's too like his father, she thought.

"Don't you think so?" Jacob persisted.

"You'd better ask Philip about that sort of thing," his mother replied. "I don't know much about it." She wondered if she should have taken a greater interest. Perhaps it would have helped. "He'll be down this evening."

"I wish he came down more often. There's so much I want to ask him these days. After all, I can't go on ringing him up all the time."

"He's extremely busy."

"What's he doing now? He hasn't been on the telly for ages."

"I think he's getting another program together," Elizabeth suggested evasively. "It takes quite a bit of doing, you know."

"Will it be the same sort of thing?"

"I should think so."

"I hope so," Jacob said. "Even if he is my father I like watching him quite a lot."

Elizabeth smiled. "That's a relief."

"I think I'll be a scientist when I grow up."

"You're quite grown up now," Elizabeth pointed out. "Anyway, Philip's not really a scientist. He just reports on that sort of thing."

Jacob picked up his book and Elizabeth continued her ironing. The radio music played on.

"Tell me," Elizabeth asked after a while, "exactly how *do* they count pollen?"

Jacob smiled, delighted to be able to inform. But as he opened his mouth to speak, Deborah ran into the kitchen.

"Do you know what?" Deborah asked excitedly.

37

"One of Miss Crewe's roses bit her! It bit her on the thumb. I saw it. It was bleeding."

"Plants don't bite," Elizabeth said lightly.

"Some of them do," Jacob said. "Venus's fly-traps for example."

"That's different."

"No, it's not."

"Well, Miss Crewe got bitten," Deborah repeated.

"I'll bet she didn't."

"I'll bet she just pricked herself," Jacob said, scornfully. "On a thorn."

"That's not what *happened*." Deborah's face revealed sudden anger. "It's not. And anyway, Miss Crewe *said* it bit her."

"You know what she's like."

"Children—" Elizabeth scolded, putting the iron down gently. "Tell me what this is all about, Debby."

"It's like I said," Deborah said, her face softening. "I saw her pull her thumb away and it was bleeding. She put it in her mouth and sucked it and when I asked her what happened she said the rose had bitten her. It *did*," she emphasized to Jacob. "It really did."

Jacob didn't reply.

"Why do you think it did that?" Elizabeth asked.

"Because she was going to cut it. She was going to cut it with—with those big cutters she has—and it didn't want to be cut so it pricked her. In fact it bit her twice," she added, her voice reflective. "She didn't take any notice the first time, and she was going to cut it again, *so it bit her again.*"

Elizabeth looked at her daughter, at the small bright face, the little feet tightly together.

"Really," Elizabeth said lightly, "there are times when I'm not sure that even you believe the stories you tell."

"But I do."

"She does," Jacob said quickly. "That's one thing I'll say for her. She might have fantasies, but she doesn't tell lies."

Elizabeth nodded thoughtfully.

"It *is* true," said Deborah. "You must believe me."

"Well . . ."

"Miss Crewe believes it," Deborah said quickly, watching her mother's face. "I know she does. Because in the end she didn't cut the rose at all."

"I beg your pardon?" Elizabeth said.

"Miss Crewe didn't cut her roses. They didn't want to be cut—so she didn't cut them."

"I see." Elizabeth looked at her daughter's confident face, then down to the T-shirt she'd been ironing. The smooth white surface seemed to her uncomplicated. "How odd."

"It's true, I saw it," Deborah persisted.

"She can hear plants talking," Jacob put in quickly. "At least, that's what she told me. Especially sunflowers."

Deborah's face clouded. "You said you wouldn't."

"Wouldn't what?"

"Tell about the sunflowers talking."

"It's nothing to be ashamed of."

"But it's secret," Deborah said, furious. "You promised."

"I did not."

"You did."

"Stop it!" Elizabeth's voice cut through. Her head was beginning to ache. "Stop yelling at each other," she said, her voice calmer. "Now, Debby—what's this all about?"

Deborah sighed and turned away.

"Well?"

"It's just as I said," Jacob said. "She told me—"

"Let her tell me," Elizabeth said. "Well, Debby?"

"It's nothing," her daughter said quietly, dismissing her mother. "Nothing really."

"*Deborah.*"

"Oh, Mummy, it's nothing at all." Suddenly Deborah smiled at her mother, her small, young face innocent. "Really, really, Mummy—it's nothing at all. You mustn't worry about it."

The girl turned and ran from the kitchen. Before her mother could speak again the child had disappeared.

"Deborah!" Elizabeth called, but there was no reply.

Elizabeth sighed. She felt forlorn and out of touch. She looked at Jacob and recognized the guilt on his face.

"I don't think you should have mentioned that."

"Why not?"

"Well, wasn't it a secret?"

Jacob shrugged.

"You should keep secrets," his mother told him quietly.

"I'm sorry."

"Never mind."

Elizabeth picked up another garment and laid it on the ironing board. Outside the shadows lengthened as the sun sank. She felt tired and alone. She wished Philip could help but knew she would be unable to confide in him.

They were just not that close anymore.

Chapter
Nine

On Friday, the day after Charlie Crump smashed the marrow squash, he was subdued and nervous. It was as if he were hung over from the effort. He rose and looked at the marrow in the early sun, then went to the farm he worked on and slaved all day baling hay, expiating, feeling the sun and the muscles in his arms.

During the day he barely spoke and, after a few attempts, was barely spoken to. His companions put his mood down to alcohol.

Charlie Crump completed his labor late in the day. In the early evening, his face browned by the sun, he trudged home, slowly, avoiding The Bunch of Grapes. He felt no need to go to the public house or any desire for alcohol.

As soon as he returned to his cottage he examined the remains of the marrow. It was drier now and yellower. Flies buzzed about it. When he saw the flies Charlie Crump suddenly thrashed at them furiously with the jacket he carried over his arm.

They rose, buzzed, and returned.

He went inside, and a little later fried a slice of bacon and a piece of white bread.

He ate from the frying pan, sitting on a wooden chair in his dirty, overcrowded kitchen, watching the shadows and feeling the heat begin to die.

For a long time after he finished eating he sat, barely stirring, watching the evening descend.

As a rule he was in The Bunch of Grapes by this hour, a glass of Scrumpie in front of him, several others inside. But tonight he had no desire to move and perhaps would not have gone out at all if it hadn't been a Friday night.

There was something about the tradition of going out on a Friday evening he was unable to deny. The week's work was over and the habit too entrenched to break.

Charlie Crump picked up his jacket and went out into the twilight. He walked toward the center of the village, pretending there was nowhere he intended to go, but knowing that finally he would arrive at The Bunch of Grapes.

On the way he paused once by the village church to lean on the crumbling wall and survey the tombstones surrounding the church.

A bit overgrown, he thought, as if seeing the growth for the first time. Something should be done about it.

He approached The Bunch of Grapes from the far side of the road, slowly, reluctantly, aware of the inevitability of his destination.

He stood a moment looking at the white-plastered building with its beams and its thatch. The large green sign hung still in the evening air.

Charlie Crump crossed the road and entered.

"Evening, Charlie," the barman said. "Better late than never, as they say."

Charlie nodded.

"Scrumpie?"

Charlie shook his head. "No," he said hesitantly. "Not tonight. I'll just have a glass of lemonade."

"*Lemonade?*"

Charlie nodded. "That's right." He glanced around to see if anyone had overheard.

"You feeling all right?"

"Course I'm bloody feeling all right." Charlie wiped his mouth with the back of his hand. "Just get it for me, that's all."

The barman raised his eyebrows significantly, poured a glass of lemonade, and was about to pass it over the bar when he paused. "Ice and lemon?" he enquired, smiling.

"Get fucked."

"A straw perhaps?"

Charlie Crump took the glass roughly and went to a table where he sat alone, the glass in his cupped hands, defying comment.

Ted Wilkes watched from his corner.

Beside Ted, Eric Bolton grinned. "Charlie's lost his marbles," he said softly.

Ted Wilkes did not reply.

"The heat's got him," Eric added. "Bloody lemonade?"

"Leave him be," Ted Wilkes said.

Eric Bolton shrugged. "His business what he drinks," he said off-handedly, lifting his pint to empty it.

Charlie Crump drank his lemonade. No one spoke to him. Two men sat at his table with glasses of Guinness. They nodded at Charlie and Charlie nodded back, but that was the only exchange.

Later Charlie pushed his empty glass away and stood, the ritual of Friday night over. He looked slowly around the bar and left.

All eyes watched him go.

"He all right?" Eric Bolton asked seriously. "I mean, he's—well, he's gone soft."

"He's had some funny things happen," Ted Wilkes explained. "That old marrow. The way it keeps on growing."

"You reckon that's real?"

"You can feel it," said Ted. "It's real enough all right, even though it's not natural."

"Not natural for Charlie to drink lemonade either."

"That's what I mean," Ted Wilkes agreed. "There's a lot round here not natural."

Outside, Charlie Crump paused. The night was dark, almost purple. Cloud hung below the ample moon. A little rain fell, and the air was clear and cool.

Charlie Crump hung his jacket over his arm and began to walk slowly down the High Street, the gentle rain dampening his shirt.

Turning off the High Street, he walked past Mabel Crewe's cottage. He stopped by the cottage gate, overcome by the heavy scent of roses, their odor suddenly enveloping him.

A bit strong you are tonight, he thought.

The air about him moved quietly, imperceptibly, and suddenly, without knowing why or where it came from, Charlie Crump felt fear.

A chill went over him as he turned to peer into the purple dark. As he did he heard the rustling of the plants. The sinister noise was all around, pervading, threatening.

"Who's there?" he whispered, the words catching in his throat. "What you want?"

"Come on," Charlie whispered. "What's—"

The rustling rose and fell in waves, like no other sound he had ever heard.

Terrified, Charlie Crump thrashed out suddenly, beating the air with his coat, impotently striking at the invisible sound.

"What you bloody want?" he cried.

The rustling continued.

His eyes wild with fear, Charlie Crump bolted. His throat was dry and he held the coat in his hand, still beating the air as he ran, clumsily.

He ran five paces, accelerating in terror, pushing the ground from him, his mouth open, clawing his way through the sound. Then a rose branch appeared suddenly in front of him, catching his leg, tangling him, and he fell, tumbling toward the garden wall.

Charlie Crump felt the rose thorns bite, heard the beginning of a cry, deep inside, felt himself fall, twisting. He hurtled forward toward the rock wall at the end of Mabel Crewe's garden and crashed, head-first, against it.

He felt blackness surround him, cover him, possess him. The last thing he heard was the rustling of the plants, and somewhere within the sound, lost and forlorn, his own voice sobbing.

Charlie Crump lay still, dead by the side of the road.

Around him the plants grew quiet and the gentle rain continued to fall.

Chapter
Ten

The Friday sun was going down as Philip Monk drove out of London. The sky was a pale translucent lemon, the sun a huge orange ball. Philip drove west along the M4, into the eye of the sun. From Bristol he continued south through Bridgewater and Taunton and from there to Brandling.

The rolling fields were lush, heavy with wild flowers. Clumps of bushes and small trees were overgrown, tangled with vine and creeper. It was all as Philip knew it, lusher perhaps, heavier, but nothing about it appeared sinister or threatening.

He recalled Michael Martin's voice and the words which so closely reflected his own fear. Man's disregard for his environment *was* one of Philip's nightmares. It *would* lead to an imbalance of nature. He shrugged, wishing the subject didn't absorb him quite so completely, wishing he were able to give more time to Elizabeth and the children.

Philip drove into Brandling and parked the car by the cottage.

Elizabeth and the children had finished supper and the remains of the meal littered the table. As he came in the children ran to him and he kissed them on the cheek.

"Are you hungry?" Elizabeth asked. "There's salad and cold meat."

"No, thanks."

"Sure?"

"I'll have a beer."

"I'll get it," Elizabeth said, a little too quickly. She went out, leaving Philip with the children.

Philip looked at his son and daughter.

"Well," he said. "What've you two been up to?"

"Nothing much," Jacob answered.

"I've got a new guinea pig," Deborah reported. "Mr. Snuffles died. You know that, don't you?"

"I know," said Philip. "Liz told me."

"I don't know why he died," Deborah said. "He was all right in the morning, but when we went out at night he was dead."

"It was old age," Jacob explained knowingly. "He was nearly five."

"Mr. Wilson's got one that's nine," Deborah argued. "Five isn't old."

"Mr. Wilson's guinea pig is senile," her brother said with some scorn. "He's almost blind and he can hardly move."

"He's not dead."

"He might as well be."

"How can you say that?"

"It's true."

Philip listened to the children's chatter. "All right," he said, interrupting. "Apart from the guinea pig, what else is new?"

Jacob smiled and looked at Deborah.

Deborah looked away.

Philip, aware of the hesitancy, leaned forward. "What's going on? Secrets?"

Both children turned as Elizabeth reentered. She carried a tray with bottles and glasses, put it down, poured a lager, and handed it to Philip. "Will you be down for long?" she asked, and something in her voice betrayed her. "Or is it just the weekend?"

"I don't know," Philip replied. "I may be down some days."

"How privileged we are."

"Don't—" Philip began but Deborah interrupted. "Can we go for a walk?"

"Of course," Philip told her. "Where?"

"Lots of places," Deborah said.

"I want to talk to you about allergies," Jacob said.

"What's an allergy?" Deborah asked.

"Allergies are when a person reacts badly," her

46

brother replied, looking at his sister critically. "Sometimes I think I'm allergic to you."

"What happens to them?"

"It brings them out in spots," Jacob said smugly. "Or their eyes swell up. Or their noses run."

"Then you're not allergic to me," said Deborah. "Those things don't happen to you."

Philip looked at Elizabeth, seated on the far side of the table. She seemed absorbed, remote.

"What *about* allergies?" Jacob was saying. "What do you know about them?"

Philip turned to his son. "What do you want to know?"

"Why they happen." Jacob's face was serious. "It seems a bit odd that they happen at all."

"It is, I suppose." Philip paused. "Has there been a lot of hay fever down here?"

"Masses," Elizabeth said quietly.

"Miss Crewe's rosebush bit her," Deborah interjected suddenly. "On the thumb."

"That's not an allergy," Jacob said.

"It made her bleed."

"Miss Crewe's roses did what?" Philip asked.

"It's a story of Deborah's," Elizabeth said. "She was there this afternoon."

"It's true," Deborah interrupted.

"It's not," said Jacob.

"It *is*," Deborah said with great emphasis, the words tumbling out. "Just because you don't believe me—" She turned to her father. "She was going to cut it with those nasty cutters she's got and it bit her because it didn't want to be cut. I was there and I saw it. It bit her on the thumb and it bled." She moved closer to her father, seeking reassurance. "You believe me, Daddy, don't you? You know about things like that."

"Well . . ." Philip began, aware of the urgency on his daughter's face, the need to be believed. "Well . . . it does seem a strange thing for a rosebush to do. . . ."

"But I saw it."

"Yes . . ."

47

"It was just a prick," Jacob scoffed.

"You weren't there," Deborah said, turning on him.

"Children—" Elizabeth said. The tiredness in her voice penetrated. "Stop it—we've been through all this before."

"But it's *true*," the girl insisted.

"I'll tell you what we'll do," Philip said, reaching for Deborah and taking her by the shoulders. "Tomorrow we'll go and see Miss Crewe and her old rosebush and ask it a few questions."

"No"—Deborah's voice was quick—"no, you mustn't—"

"What?"

"—talk to them. You mustn't."

Philip regarded his daughter's determined face. Beneath his hands he felt her young strength. He looked at his wife, surprised by the concern in her eyes.

"All right then," he said to Deborah, his voice easy, reassuring. "We won't talk to them. We'll just go and have a look at them." He smiled, and saw the relief on his daughter's face. "Is that all right?"

Deborah nodded.

"Good. That's settled. Now it's time for you both to be off to bed."

"My God," Elizabeth said, an edge to her voice. "You're back five minutes and they're eating out of your hand." She watched the children leave the room. "What it is to be a celebrity!"

Philip didn't reply; he felt if he did something might snap.

Chapter
Eleven

Mabel Crewe sat in her cottage watching *The News at Ten*. On the television screen a helicopter view of the New Forest was vivid, green, and dense.

"Amazing," she said quietly. "Quite amazing."

The trees were entangled with vines, creepers, and lush flowers; the growth splendid and exuberant. An entire carpet spread beneath the helicopter in a rich maze of vegetation.

"—these wild ponies," a voice was saying, "are well fed and seem to have plenty in store. But they're cut off, and proving very difficult to contact on the ground. As you see, only by helicopter have we been able to locate them. The Department of the Environment . . ."

The voice continued as Mabel watched the helicopter circle over a dozen or more shaggy ponies. They grazed peacefully in several acres of rich grassland. The helicopter moved to the edge of the clearing and the wall of vegetation enclosing it. The growth appeared thick and impenetrable.

"Several attempts have been made to get through to the ponies," the voice continued, "but each has failed. There is no cause for concern yet, in fact the ponies seem well content. But it is felt they will have to be liberated soon as their food supply may run short or the clearing itself may become overgrown."

The camera on the helicopter zoomed into a close-up of one of the ponies. Its expression was relaxed as it chewed with contentment.

"I'd leave them where they are," Mabel Crewe

told the announcer. She got up from her chair to switch off the television set. "They seem all right to me."

Switching off the light in the sitting room, she went upstairs to bed.

She opened the bedroom window to look out at the night. Low clouds moved slowly across the face of the almost full moon. Rain fell lightly and beneath the window her garden grew in profusion.

Just before she fell asleep Mabel Crewe felt her thumb. It twinged a little but that was all.

I must do something about those bushes tomorrow, she promised. They'll be all over *me* if I let them go much longer.

Chapter Twelve

Later that evening Philip Monk and Elizabeth sat opposite each other. The children were asleep and the house was quiet.

Philip picked up his glass. It was empty and he put it down again.

"Would you like another?" Elizabeth asked quickly.

"I'll get it," Philip offered.

They rose together, bumping into each other clumsily. Both stopped, realizing how eagerly they'd fallen upon an excuse to move.

"We've got to stop this," Philip said.

Elizabeth nodded. "It's—it's this damned weather."

"It's more than the weather."

"Yes." Elizabeth's voice was small. "Oh, Jesus," she whispered. "I feel so alone."

Philip touched his wife's arm gently. "There's a bottle of scotch in my bag," he said. "I'll get that, you get some ice. Then . . . we'll . . ." He let the sentence drift away.

Elizabeth went into the kitchen and Philip poured the whiskey. When they sat facing each other again, in spite of the small ritual, both remained uneasy. Neither knew how to begin.

Philip took a deep breath. "There's something you've got to understand, Liz," he told her uncomfortably.

Elizabeth put her hands together and stared at her white knuckles. "Don't." His wife's voice was a whisper. She had closed her eyes.

"I mean—"

"*Stop it.*" Elizabeth's voice grew harsh. "Don't be so damned reasonable." She stared at him. "You're not on television now."

"I'm—"

"And don't say you're sorry," Elizabeth went on. "Hit me if you like, or scream, but don't, just please don't, sit there and be reasonable saying you're sorry."

Philip Monk wondered if his wife was going to cry.

"I'm—I'm not that sort of person," he said lamely. "I don't hit people."

"Perhaps you should." Elizabeth unlocked her hands and picked up her drink. Her glass shook as she put it to her lips. She drank deeply, savoring the whiskey in the back of her throat.

"You'll never be that sort of person, Philip. Neither will I, I suppose."

Philip shrugged.

"So, what do we do?" Elizabeth asked.

"What do you want to do?" Philip asked carefully.

"I don't know," Elizabeth answered. "Except to change this uncertainty. I can't go on like this. There's nothing to believe in."

Philip was silent.

Elizabeth stared at her husband. "You do *care*, Philip?" she asked. "You do care about us?"

"Of course."

"I don't think you do. I really don't. You're not—you don't seem involved."

Elizabeth was abruptly interrupted as Deborah screamed.

Somewhere in the cavern of her mind Deborah saw a man lying in the dark by the side of a country lane. His head was bleeding and he lay very still.

All about, Deborah could hear the angry, threatening voices of the plants as they whispered and rustled with fury. Rosebushes thrashed and the great golden faces of the sunflowers glowered.

Deborah screamed, her body wet with perspiration. Her small, matchstick arms beat at the bedcovers. She could not see who it was that lay in the country lane. All she knew was that something terrible had happened.

Deborah woke as Philip and Elizabeth ran into her bedroom.

"What is it, Debby?" her mother asked. "What's wrong?"

Deborah began to cry.

"A nightmare?" her father asked. "Did you have a bad dream?"

Deborah pushed her face into the warmth and comfort of her mother's neck.

Philip asked again, "What was it?"

"Shhh," Elizabeth comforted. "It's all right now. Shhh, we're here."

Deborah's sobbing abated as she clung to her mother.

Philip opened his mouth but Elizabeth prevented him from speaking. "Later," she said. "Talk to her later." She stood with the child in her arms. "Come on, Debby. Come along into my bed."

Elizabeth carried the child out of the room. Philip paused for a moment before he followed. Her parents remained with Deborah, comforting her, until her small body had stopped trembling and she went back to sleep. Then they returned downstairs.

Philip poured more whiskey.

"It's us," Elizabeth said quietly. "She's sensitive. She knows."

"It's more than that."

"What?"

"She's in touch with something."

"No." Elizabeth shook her head. She remembered her daughter's voice chastising Jacob for betraying a secret. She remembered a reference to a sunflower. "No. It's quite normal for her to be upset by us."

"Listen," Philip said. "There's something I've got to tell you."

"We've tried—"

"This isn't about us."

Elizabeth put her glass down. "What is it about?" Her voice was uneven.

Philip began carefully. "I went to see Michael Martin today. He—"

"Who's he?"

"We were at college together. You've met him, although you may not remember." Philip sipped his drink. "He's at London University, doing advanced research in biology."

"What did he have to say that's so important?"

"Michael doesn't think this wonderful weather we've been having is an accident," Philip explained slowly. "He doesn't think it's happened by chance."

Elizabeth blinked. "I don't understand."

Philip watched his wife carefully. "You've noticed nothing? Nothing strange . . . about the children?"

"What—what sort of thing?"

"Small things? Changes?"

Elizabeth felt her hands tremble. "I don't know. It's hard to tell. Everything's been so strange lately. I don't know what to think."

"Are you sure there's been nothing particular?"

"Well . . ."

"Tell me."

"There *was* something," Elizabeth said, her voice distressed. "With Deborah."

"What happened?"

"It was this afternoon. She was strange." His wife twisted her hands. "You know how she is," she said. "Always making things up. Well, this afternoon she said she . . . could hear things."

"What sort of things?" Philip came closer. "Tell me, Liz. It might be very important."

"Well, it wasn't her exactly. It was Jacob. He said she could hear . . . plants talking."

Philip felt his scalp prickle. He heard Michael Martin's voice. He saw the tiny rows of bean plants; dials and tape recorders.

"I know it sounds absurd," Elizabeth continued. "But it did upset me."

"What did Deborah say about it?"

"Nothing. She just laughed and ran away."

"Listen," Philip said, trying to keep his voice under control. "There *is* something I have to talk to you about. Something important." He recognized the doubt in his wife's eyes. "I don't know how you're going to take this. But I think we're all in some danger."

Elizabeth's head moved.

"Not normal danger," Philip went on. "But something else. Something new, something strange."

"What—what do you mean?"

"I'm not sure. But it's something to do with the plants."

"*Plants?*" Elizabeth's voice was fearful. "What do you mean, plants? What's Deborah got to do with plants?" She pressed her hands together. "What on earth's going on?"

"I'm not sure."

Philip cleared his throat. "Michael believes that nature, and the plant kingdom in particular, disapproves of what man has done to this planet. He believes that all this wonderful weather, all this fantastic growth, is part of some early warning system."

Elizabeth sat very still. The words seemed personal. "What are they warning us of?" she asked.

"Ourselves."

"Philip"—Elizabeth's voice was suddenly critical—"if this is one of your pet theories."

"I mean it," Philip said. "I think he's right. In fact I went to see him because of what's been going on. Little things, all over the country. What finally made me go was that marrow squash that grew here in Brandling. That finally made me do something. It seemed so close to home."

"Home?"

"Yes, home," Philip said.

Elizabeth closed her eyes. There was the greenery in the garden. Charlie Crump's marrow squash. Mabel Crewe's roses. Deborah's voice screaming.

"Listen," Philip continued, his voice quieter. "As a race, as people, we don't seem to have any regard for anything on this planet. Not even ourselves. We're overbred. We've fouled the air. We've congested our own movement. The centers of our cities have been reduced to squalor. We've torn resources from the earth with no thought of replacement." Philip shook his head. "We don't even show any regard for ourselves anymore."

"Lots of people love nature," Elizabeth pointed out gently.

"Lots of people aren't enough." Philip's voice was cutting. "Don't you see? A lack of respect for the world we live in in the end indicates a lack of respect for ourselves."

"It's not like that."

"It is." Philip pointed a finger. "We're quite unique in our contempt for ourselves. No other creatures soil their nests the way we do. No other society rapes the earth as we do." He paused. "Nothing else slaughters its own kind as regularly and as despicably as we do."

"No."

"Yes. We've probably concentrated more money on killing one another than anything else. Do you realize that? We've become specialists in self-destruction. It's no wonder anything from outside shouldn't actively assist us in our own suicide."

"Suicide?"

"What else?"

Elizabeth stared down at her clasped hands; they seemed very frail in her lap.

"We're going through some sort of awful moral vacuum, Liz," Philip told her. "Somewhere along the way I think we've lost control of ourselves."

"But what can we *do?*" Elizabeth asked, clinging to the world she understood. "In the meantime we've got to live, we've got to do things." Her eyes were pale with fear and confusion. "What will happen to . . . us?"

"I don't know."

"You don't *know.*"

Philip shook his head sadly.

"Then it's just words, isn't it?" Elizabeth asked, hoping to reduce her confusion and her fear. "It's just talking, isn't it? It's not *real.*"

"No, Liz, there's more to it than that."

"I don't believe it." Elizabeth's voice was firm. "It's all very well to talk about the state of the world, and the plants, and all that, but it doesn't concern us, does it? It doesn't help us."

Philip stared at his wife; her evasion was sad, distressing, isolating.

"It doesn't stop Deborah waking in the middle of the night, screaming," Elizabeth went on, her voice rising. "It's got nothing to do with that."

"Liz—"

"Anyway, what has Deborah got to do with all this?" Elizabeth demanded.

"A lot, more than most of us, perhaps."

"What do you mean?"

"I mean, I really believe she's aware of something we're not. She may even be in touch with . . . the plants."

"No. That's absurd."

"Listen—"

"No, I don't want to hear it. I don't believe it." Elizabeth clenched her fists. "You're making all this up. You're dramatizing."

Philip didn't reply. He studied the pain and fear etched on his wife's face and realized that at that moment they were as separate as they had ever been.

Chapter
Thirteen

Michael Martin looked at his watch. It was almost midnight. He should have left the laboratory hours ago but he'd not been able to leave the tiny rows of bean sprouts.

The responses of the plants had kept him in the laboratory all day. He had not eaten since morning, nor had he thought of eating. He had lost all regard for time.

When he looked at his watch he was surprised how late it was. He stood and straightened his back, alone with his fear.

The fear had begun in the early part of the afternoon, unobtrusive then, easily ignored.

It had begun when he'd run a check on the tapes he'd made of the patterns the plants remembered, playing the memory tapes against the plot of the light flashes. Both records were then fed into a computer. In every case the memory tapes were accurate, the plants recalling everything that had been played to them no matter how far back in time the records went.

Then, Michael Martin noticed a new factor beginning to emerge. A time squeeze was beginning to develop. The plants were beginning to play back at a faster rate than the light impulses were received. They were beginning to catch up with the impulses, even moving ahead of them in time.

And that was when Michael Martin first felt fear.

At first he refused to accept the evidence and reprocessed the material, every centimeter of tape. But the results were the same. Over the past thirty-six hours a change had been clearly established.

Michael Martin switched his programming from

58

main voltage to constant voltage batteries, to eliminate any voltage fluctuations which might have occurred. Again the results were the same. The plants were beginning to catch up in time with the information they received.

Michael Martin knew what that meant.

It was only a matter of time before the plants would not only catch up with the information received, but could, in fact, surpass it.

They would not only be able to remember, they would be able to see into the future as well.

Michael Martin shivered as the enormity of this discovery hit him.

He knew the light-signaling system was a random response system. It followed neither program nor pattern. There was no formula to be worked out. If the plants were developing foreknowledge of the signals they were to receive, it was pure prescience. It had nothing to do with the materials around them.

Michael Martin thought of the Backster Effect. Not only were plants capable of knowing what he thought, they knew now what he was thinking before the thought had actually formed.

He felt his spine go cold. A tic on his cheek jumped. He was at a loss as to what to do, shocked by the knowledge that very soon, if not already, the plants would know what was forming in his mind.

He stood for a long time staring at the rows of tiny bean plants, innocent and fresh in their containers. He stared at the wires and the dials and the flashing lights.

Then, very slowly, dreamily, like a man underwater, he began to move forward toward the bean plants, clicking off switches as he went, shutting off his experiment.

He must stall, he must delay the process of acceleration until he had time to think, to consult, to establish help. Once the process got out of hand it would communicate itself to every living leaf, branch, or root in the kingdom. There would be no stopping it. There would be no control.

He reached for another switch, and as he did so

a bean shoot seemed to brush his wrist. Instinctively Michael Martin pulled his hand away, horrified. He rubbed his wrist with his other hand and stared at the shoots. They were still, unmoving, innocent.

I'm going mad, he thought. I'm losing my mind.

I must talk to someone, he told himself. Philip—there's Philip Monk. He understands.

"Calmly," he whispered, "calmly."

Michael Martin reached forward again and turned the switch off. This time nothing touched him, nothing gave him reason for fear. He exhaled in relief and moved to another switch.

He would turn everything off. He would hold the preknowledge the plants were forming. If necessary he would destroy his experiment before it destroyed him. Then he would call Philip and inform him what he'd discovered.

Michael Martin reached for another switch.

In the gentle hum emerging from the air conditioning he failed to hear the tiny rustling sound from the rows of bean sprouts, nor did he detect the small, whispery note of menace it contained.

Chapter

Fourteen

Ted Wilkes walked his dog, William, each morning before the sun came up, while the sky was a pale, pre-dawn pink and simple freshness hung over the land.

He found Charlie Crump's body early Saturday morning, and as soon as he realized Charlie was dead, he called Police Constable Walters.

"I thought he was drunk at first," Ted told Walters. "But then I remembered. Last night he only drank lemonade."

When they lifted the body they found the rose branch twisted around Charlie's ankle. Ted had to cut it away with a pocketknife before Charlie's remains could be taken away. Together they removed the body and took it to a room in Walters' cottage, which served as a police station.

"That's funny," Ted commented.

"Probably what he tripped on," Walters replied.

"Cut right into him. Look at that." Ted lifted the trouser leg, showing the thorn marks in the flesh. "Dug in deep."

"Does seem strange."

"It's not natural."

P.C. Walters grunted.

When they arrived at the cottage and laid Charlie's body out, Ted Wilkes began to examine the corpse systematically, working from the ankle upward. Walters objected, pointing out that the work should be carried out by the police, but Ted Wilkes brushed aside his objection.

"We haven't got the time," he said, examining

61

Charlie's hands. "It's Saturday. You won't get anyone down today."

"There's no hurry."

"Isn't there?"

Ted Wilkes turned to Walters. The old man's face
was excited. "Don't be a bloody fool, Percy," he said.
"Can't you see there's something funny going on?

"What you think killed Charlie?" Ted asked quickly.

Walters paused. "Well, tripped, I suppose. Hit his
head. You can see that."

"You think it was an accident?"

"Don't you?"

"Look at this." Ted Wilkes held up one of Charlie's hands. The palm was scraped. "The other's the
same. He was running, Charlie was. Running away
from something that scared the daylights out of
him."

"Scared him?" Walters came closer. "You can't
be sure of that."

"He looks scared enough."

"That could have happened after—after he was
dead."

"Well, how do you account for that, then?" Ted
pointed to the ankle and the thorn marks. He stared
at the policeman. "Can't, can you?"

"It's what he tripped on."

"Then he must've been going pretty fast to bash
his head like that." Ted's eyes were sharp. "Must've
been running to scrape his hands like that. Running
away from something if you ask me. Running for his
life."

P.C. Walters looked at Charlie's body for several
minutes. "I don't get what you're on about. I don't
see what you're making all this fuss about it for."

Ted Wilkes turned away. "I seen it coming for a
long time," he said. "There's more to this summer than
meets the eye."

P.C. Walters began to wish someone else had
found the body. "You're not suggesting this wasn't an
accident, are you?"

"Accident or no, it wasn't natural."

"Listen to me, Ted Wilkes—"

"No, you listen to me." There was a new authority in Ted Wilkes' voice. "There's been a lot that's unnatural round this summer." He looked at Charlie's remains. "That marrow squash of Charlie's. Now there's a thing. Coming up like that. Keeping on growing." He shook his head. "No, Charlie didn't grow that marrow, Percy. *It came to him.* It was a sign, it was. We shouldn't have joked about it the way we did. We should've give it more of a chance." He put his hand on the constable's arm. "Something's happening the likes of which we've never seen before."

Walters removed the old man's hand. "Don't be daft," he said, turning away. "You're making too much of all this."

Ted Wilkes began to cover Charlie Crump's body with a sheet. "And you're not making enough of it. I wonder what you did to that marrow, Charlie," he said. "I wonder how you offended it."

P.C. Walters was aware of the uncomfortable stillness in the room.

"You must've done something, Charlie," Ted Wilkes went on, "because now they've took their revenge."

"Charlie had an accident," Walters said firmly.

"Charlie's only the first of them."

Walters blinked.

"They'll get us all in the end," Ted predicted.

"Who will?"

"Them. The creatures of the field. We got to do something, Percy. We got to warn people."

"About what?"

"What's happening." Ted leaned forward. "Ever see a tiny plant push up through the footpath? Ever see the way it makes all that gravel and tar and cement bulge and give way? They got strength, the creatures of the fields. If they'd a mind to they'd push us out of the way."

"You're daft."

"Not a religious man, are you, Percy?"

"I believe."

"Not the way my mother believed," Ted said. "There was one passage she used to quote. Stuck in my mind. From the Apocalypse. Something about two olive trees, standing before the God of the earth." Ted Wilkes reached for the words. "And, if any man hurt *them* fire proceedeth out of their mouths and devoureth their enemies. And, if any man *hurt them* he must . . . in this manner be killed."

P.C. Walters sat and regarded Ted Wilkes. The old man's face was alive with certainty.

"If I was you," Ted suggested, "I'd get on to the phone to Taunton."

"Taunton?"

"That's where your chief constable is."

"Don't be mad."

"Be mad if you didn't. Things are happening here, Percy. We've had a sign and we've had a death. You can't ignore it. You got to pass the word along."

P.C. Walters looked at Ted Wilkes steadily. "You're enjoying this, aren't you?"

Ted nodded. "Always knew I'd be round for the end of the world."

"Listen." Walters spread his hands. "Perhaps Charlie *was* scared by something. Perhaps it *has* been an unusual summer. But that don't mean . . . anything more than that."

"Meaning is . . . what meaning is," Ted said cryptically, moving toward the door. "I'll go my way and you go yours. But if I was you," he repeated, "I'd be on the phone to Taunton."

"What are you going to do?"

"Look around. Ask a few questions."

"You won't go spreading any rumors?" Walters cleared his throat. "We don't want no panic."

"You won't get any."

"I hope not."

Ted Wilkes tapped the side of his nose with a forefinger, knowingly, with relish. Then he went out the door.

P.C. Walters sat, without moving, for a long time after Ted Wilkes had gone, staring at the body of Charlie Crump.

Chapter
Fifteen

When the sun was higher that Saturday morning Philip Monk and his daughter, Deborah, went to see Mabel Crewe. Jacob, absorbed in a book, had no desire to go with them.

Deborah had awakened bright and clear-eyed in her mother's bed with no recollection of the events of the night before.

"That must have been a very nasty dream you had," Elizabeth told her. "Don't you remember any of it?"

Deborah shook her head. "Is that why I'm here with you?"

"Yes," said Elizabeth. "We thought you'd been attacked."

"Do you often have funny dreams?" Philip asked from the other bed. "Or is it just when I'm around?"

Deborah laughed and her words tumbled out. "Sometimes they're awful," she said, making a game of the conversation. "Sometimes there are awful things with big teeth and eyes." She giggled. "They chase me and I can't get away and it's horrid. And once there was a big pussycat that thought I was a mouse and wanted to eat me up." Her voice sounded happy.

"Did that happen last night?"

"No."

"Are you sure?" Philip asked gently.

"Quite sure. Quite, quite sure," Deborah said as she ran from the room.

Philip looked across to Elizabeth but there was nothing in her face that he could read.

Later, as they walked toward Mabel Crewe's

cottage, Deborah took her father's hand, looking up at him.

"There's one thing I've just remembered."

"What about?"

"My dream."

"Oh."

"Want to know what it is?"

"Yes."

"Well, there was a man in my dream. I don't know who he was or what he was doing. But he was there, I've just remembered. He was lying down by the side of the road."

"That's a funny thing to dream," Philip said. "I wonder why it frightened you."

"I wasn't frightened. At least I don't *remember* being frightened." Her glance took in the stone wall of Mabel Crewe's cottage and the rosebushes bulging over. "It was somewhere like this," she said eagerly, her face revealing nothing at all. "I saw him lying there, all in a heap, by the side of the road. He wasn't moving—well, he wasn't moving when I saw him. He was just lying there all of a heap."

"Is that all you remember?" Philip asked gently. Deborah nodded.

"Sure?"

Deborah nodded again and skipped on ahead. She opened the gate to Mabel Crewe's cottage and led the way up the garden path, between the full, heavy-petaled blooms and their overpowering fragrance.

Deborah rang the doorbell and waited.

Mabel Crewe came to the door, her face serious. When she saw Deborah and her father, she smiled.

"Hello," she said. And looking at Philip, she added, "Stranger."

"Hello," Philip said. "Mind if we come in?"

"Of course not. I've just made coffee." Her eyes went from Philip to Deborah. "Have you heard—" She began and stopped.

"What?" Philip asked, noting her nervousness.

66

"Nothing," Mabel said, glancing at Deborah again. "We can talk about it later."

She led them into the house.

"I understand you've been writing to the BBC," Philip said after a while. He stood with a cup of coffee, looking out the window at the splendid roses, "Is that so?"

"What do you mean?"

"That report about a marrow squash? Wasn't it you?"

"It was," Mabel said. She glanced at Deborah, who had picked up a small china dog on the far side of the room and seemed absorbed. Mabel moved close to Philip. "You haven't heard?"

"I'm not sure I know what you mean."

Mabel lowered her voice. "About that man," she said. "The one who—who died last night."

"What man?"

"Charlie Crump. A harmless enough little man. The local drunk, I believe." She looked across to Deborah, but the child was playing with the china dog. "It was outside here, on the road, right outside here."

Philip put his coffee cup down and listened.

Mabel told him how Ted Wilkes had called earlier and informed her of Charlie Crump's death and the way his body had been found. Ted Wilkes had asked her if she'd heard anything but Mabel had been unable to help.

"What time was this?" Philip interrupted. "What time did the—the accident occur?"

"About eleven, they believe."

Philip remembered it was about that time Deborah had screamed. "That's odd," he said very quietly.

Mabel went on. "There's something else."

Philip waited.

"Ted Wilkes didn't think it was an accident." She shrugged, uncertain. "He, well, seemed to think there was more to it than that."

"What?"

"He—he and Police Constable Walters took

67

Charlie Crump's body down to the Police Station. He said he examined it and there, well, there was something unusual about the way he'd died."

"Unusual?"

Mabel Crewe nodded.

"In what way?"

Mabel shook her head, watching Deborah play. "I think perhaps we should talk about this later."

Philip nodded. "Very well. I'll come back on my own."

"I think that's a good idea."

Philip smiled and went to his daughter. "Come along," he said easily. "Let's go and see how the others are getting on."

"Oh, they'll be all right."

"Let's find out anyway."

"They're quite all right," Deborah said firmly. "I know."

"Well, let's go and see anyway," her father said, and took her hand.

They left Mabel Crewe by the door. Her brown, wrinkled face was more worried than usual, her eyes less bright.

As they walked down the sunny lane toward the house Deborah asked mischievously, "Miss Crewe didn't say anything about her roses at all, did she?" She looked up at her father, smiling.

"I didn't think you were listening."

"Oh, I wasn't. Not really . . . not really listening. But I always know what people are talking about . . . or anything really. I always know."

"Always?"

"Oh, yes. Well, almost always." She squeezed her father's hand. "Aren't I lucky?"

Philip did not reply.

Chapter
Sixteen

It was almost ten thirty that Saturday morning when Michael Martin rang the police station in Brandling. It was the quickest way he could think of to get in touch with Philip Monk. He'd tried the exchange but Philip's number was unlisted and in spite of his urgency the operator would do nothing until a supervisor came on later in the morning.

When P.C. Walters picked up the phone the first thing he was aware of was the edge of hysteria in Michael Martin's voice.

"Yes?" he said cautiously.

"I must have Philip Monk's phone number," Martin told him.

"This is the police station, sir."

"I know."

"Have you tried the exchange?"

"They won't give it to me. It's unlisted."

"I see."

"You don't. This is urgent."

"I could get a message to him, sir."

Michael Martin felt the pressure building up inside. "Is there no way I can talk to him?" he asked, his voice rising. "If you won't give me his bloody number can't you go down the road and get him?"

P.C. Walters paused. Martin's voice grated on his nerves. "I don't think that's possible, sir," he said carefully. He looked across at the covered body of Charlie Crump. "I can't get away for the moment."

"Jesus Christ . . ."

"Is there something I could do?" Walters asked.

"*You could give me the number.*"

"I don't think—"

"I'm a personal friend," Michael Martin explained. He could hear himself beginning to babble. "It's urgent. It's about something we discussed yesterday. It's —good God, man, it's important!"

P.C. Walters hesitated. Too much had happened that morning already. Charlie Crump was dead. Ted Wilkes seemed to think it was the end of the world. He was suspicious of the hysteria in Michael Martin's voice.

Walters picked up a pencil. "I could take a message, sir."

"You wouldn't understand," Martin said quickly.

"I'll write it down."

"Jesus Christ!" Something broke in Michael Martin's voice. "That's good, that's a lot of help. You'll write it down. Jesus Christ, what do you think that's going to achieve?"

"Sir?"

"Please give me his number," Michael Martin said, as steadily as he could. "I assure you it's very important."

"I'm afraid I can't do that."

"You must."

"Now just a minute," P.C. Walters said, his voice firm. "I can't spend much more time with you. I can't give you the number but I'll take a message if you like. There's been enough trouble down here for the one day as it is."

"What?"

P.C. Walters paused, aware that he had said too much.

"What trouble?" Martin persisted. "Tell me, man! It might have something to do with—with why I must talk to Philip Monk."

"There's—"

"*Tell me what happened.*" Michael Martin's voice grew hard, now under control. "Has it got anything to do with plants in any way at all?"

"Plants, sir?"

"Yes. Anything like that. Growth, movement— even that marrow squash you've got growing down there?"

P.C. Walters looked at Charlie Crump's body and swallowed. "Yes," he said, his voice a whisper. "It has, sir, in a way."

"In a way?"

"Well, sir, the man who grew the marrow, Charlie Crump, he's had an accident, sir. He's dead."

"Dear God."

"Sir?"

"It's started then."

"I don't understand, sir." P.C. Walters could feel the shock on the other end of the telephone line. "I mean, it *was* an accident, sir."

"Never mind," Martin said, his voice suddenly tired. "Please ask Philip Monk to ring me." He gave Walters a number. "As soon as he can."

"Is there any message?"

"Yes," Martin replied. *"Tell him it's begun."*

"Yes, sir."

P.C. Walters replaced the receiver and looked at the number he had written down. It was a moment or two before he realized he'd not even asked for Michael Martin's name.

But Martin's call was decisive. It was then that P.C. Walters made up his mind to ring his chief constable in Taunton.

Chapter
Seventeen

Even after Michael Martin's call it took P.C. Walters some time to bring himself to ring Chief Constable Parkhurst in Taunton. Parkhurst was an impatient man who had spent most of his life in various colonial administrations and still regretted the demise of the colonies.

He also regretted being called to the telephone on a Saturday morning. He had been practicing his golf swing in the garden. It was flowing and he objected to being called from it and the lovely sun.

This summer reminded him more and more of the climates he'd left behind half a world away.

"What's he want?" he asked when Walters' call came through.

"He didn't say," his wife replied.

"Have him call back later."

"He said it was important."

The chief constable grunted and went to the telephone, his golf shoes clattering on the floor.

"Yes," he said abruptly. "What is it?"

P.C. Walters hesitated. "I'm sorry to disturb you, sir."

"You've disturbed me already," Chief Constable Parkhurst pointed out. "Don't waste any more time apologizing."

"Well . . ." P.C. Walters wished he hadn't called. "There's been a death down here, sir."

"So?"

"Well, the circumstances are a bit unusual."

"Was he murdered?"

"No, sir."

"Did he commit suicide?"

"No, sir."

"Then what the devil are you bothering me for?"

P.C. Walters took a deep breath. He shouldn't have allowed Ted Wilkes near Charlie Crump's body. The man from London, whoever he was, had sounded panicky, but he could have been drunk. He couldn't, however, ignore him or the way the events seemed linked. Also there had been the grotesque fear on Charlie Crump's face.

"Come on, man," the chief constable prompted. "What's so special about this death of yours?"

"Well, I thought you should know, sir. He seemed very frightened."

"Frightened?"

"Yes, sir. The expression on his face—"

"What actually caused his death?" the chief constable asked in a more reasonable voice. "I mean, it wasn't just fear, I presume?"

"His neck was broken," Walters explained. "It seems he was running and tripped. He fell against a wall and cracked his head, and I think . . . his neck is broken. But—" Walters continued. Now that he'd come this far he might as well mention everything. "There's something odd about that as well, sir. The thing he tripped on, a rose branch, was wound tightly about his ankle. It had to be cut away."

"What do you mean, constable?"

"It was almost bound round, sir. Almost as if—"

"What?"

"—it had grown there."

The chief constable removed the telephone from his ear. He looked out the window at the endless sun.

"Are you there, sir?" Walters' voice asked.

"Yes, of course." The chief constable cleared his throat. "Now listen to me, Walters. I'm not quite sure I understand what you're getting at."

"Neither am I, sir. That's why I rang."

"What do you expect me to do?"

"Well, I thought I better report it," Walters said. "Especially after the man from London called as well."

"Who was that?"

"Well, he was trying to get hold of Mr. Monk, sir, who lives here. He was from London, sir, and he knew about Charlie Crump's marrow squash."

"I beg your pardon?"

"Charlie Crump. He's the man that died."

Chief Constable Parkhurst blinked. It could have been another country in another time. Something moved in his memory. "Perhaps you'd better begin at the beginning," he suggested.

P.C. Walters told the chief constable about Charlie Crump and the squash. He mentioned the way the village had mocked him. He explained how Ted Wilkes had found Crump's body. The marks on it. The expression of fear. He spoke of Michael Martin's call and the hysteria in his voice and how he had said "It's begun." As he spoke his voice became steadier. A sense of order was being restored. Walters was glad he'd rung. The responsibility was now shared.

When Walters had finished, the chief constable said, "I see why you're a bit confused, Walters. But I wouldn't have thought there was any need to involve me." He strongly felt the need for normality. "After all, there's no real evidence is there?"

"No, sir."

"Well then?" The chief constable shook his head. No one in their right mind could believe that anything out of the ordinary had occurred. "I appreciate your concern, Walters," the chief constable added, "and I think you did the right thing in ringing me. But I don't believe there's anything to be worried about."

"I see."

"There's a good chap." Chief Constable Parkhurst coughed a little guiltily. "It seems quite clear that this chap died of a broken neck. As far as the other details are concerned—well, anything could have happened. I'd just make out the normal accident report if I were you and leave it at that."

"Yes, sir."

"Thank you, constable."

Parkhurst sighed. A moment of aberration had passed.

P.C. Walters put down the telephone. He looked at Charlie Crump's body covered with the sheet. Just the shape of it was visible and the soles of Charlie's shoes. Walters opened a drawer of his desk, took out a form, and began to fill it in. He'd done everything that was necessary.

Chief Constable Parkhurst went outside into the bright sunlight, picked up his golf club, and began to swing it. But he'd lost the rhythm. Something had gone from his game.

He became aware of eyes watching him and turned to see his wife.

"Well?" he asked.

"I just wondered."

"What?"

"What that was all about?"

"That? Nothing." The chief constable swished his club across the grass. It needed cutting. "Some chap from—what's it called?"

"Brandling?"

"That's it."

"Is everything all right?"

"Course it is." The chief constable frowned. "Funny little place, Brandling. Bit of a backwater really. Quite cut off from the rest of the world." He patted the lawn with his club. "Seem to think the slightest thing that happens to them's of national importance."

"*Was* it important?"

"Eh?"

"Was it important?" his wife repeated.

"Not really. Some chap had an accident, that's all. Walters was making a bit of a fuss about it." He shook his head. "One of a dying breed, Walters. Few of them left in tiny places like Brandling. Most of that sort of thing's done by patrols nowadays." He peered at his wife. "You all right?" he asked.

His wife nodded.

"Thought you were crying for a moment there."

"It's my hayfever." His wife wiped her eyes. "It's been particularly bad this year. Hadn't you noticed it before?"

"Can't say I had." The chief constable straightened his back. "Don't get that sort of thing myself."

"I know."

The chief constable nodded. "By the way," he said after a moment. "Do we have the number of that chap who calls himself keeper of parks and gardens? What's his name?"

"Reynolds."

"That's right—Reynolds."

"We should have his number somewhere," his wife said. "Would you like me to get it for you?"

"Hmmm . . ."

"*Shall* I get it for you?"

The chief constable shook his head. "No," he said evasively. "Not at the moment."

The chief constable set his feet and swung his golf club carefully. The club bit into the grass and lifted a divot. He grunted.

His wife went indoors.

Chapter
Eighteen

When Philip Monk and Deborah left Mabel Crewe they returned to their cottage. Deborah went upstairs; Philip found Elizabeth drying the breakfast dishes in the kitchen and he mentioned Charlie Crump's death.

"Poor man," Elizabeth said. She picked up a cup and put it down. She looked at the sunlit garden and its profusion of flowers. There was something wrong suddenly; there was more to the man's death than the expression on Philip's face indicated. She faced her husband. "What happened to him?" she asked in a different voice.

Philip told her.

"But what's that got to do with—" Elizabeth's words hung; she could not complete the thought. "Good God, Philip," she added. "What is *happening?*"

"I'm not sure," Philip admitted. "But whatever it is, or however much you don't want to believe it, we must face it. Now, or whenever it comes."

"Stop it." Elizabeth's voice rose. "Stop it. I'm not going to listen to all that again. Once, last night, was enough."

"Very well," her husband said steadily. He moved toward the door. "I'm going out. And I'm taking the children with me."

"No."

"Yes. I can't just stay here doing nothing."

"Then go on your own. Leave the children behind."

Philip hesitated. "No," he said finally. "I think they should come too. They are part of it. Especially Debby."

Elizabeth closed her eyes. "I don't know what you're doing," she said softly. "You sat up half last night trying to convince me we're all doomed and now you want to take my children out amongst it."

"They're my children, too."

"Then for God's sake—"

Philip moved closer. "I may be wrong," he said slowly. "I may be totally wrong, but I know the plants are trying to tell us something. If we don't listen, if we don't try to understand, then we really are doomed."

Elizabeth bit her lip.

"You should come too," he said.

"No."

"Please."

"Never." Elizabeth's voice rose. "Go out if you insist. Take the children. I can't stop you taking the children. But if you think I'm going out there as well—" She folded her arms.

"Don't fight me," Philip said. "We're in this together." He should have put his arms out and held her, but he was unable to. He should have comforted her, but he didn't know how to begin.

Silently, Elizabeth watched him leave.

Philip Monk walked with Jacob and Deborah to the outskirts of the village. They climbed to the top of the low hills on the east and stood looking down at the stone houses, the slate roofs, the shape of the village in the arms of the little valley. Under the overhead sun the village lay flat and lush and contained.

"That's our place," Jacob said, pointing. "There."

"Where?" asked Deborah, then saw the white stucco walls. "Oh! I can see it, too. Doesn't it look little, down there."

"That's perspective," Jacob said.

"What?"

"The way things look in the distance."

"Isn't it funny," Deborah said, "how small they get."

They walked in the sunlight. Butterflies hovered among the wild flowers and bees swung in the heavy air. They could feel the heat rising from the valley. It shimmered, hanging about them like a veil.

They stopped on the edge of a small woods on the top of a ridge. Philip wiped sweat from his forehead and paused in the shade.

"Isn't it hot up here!" Deborah said.

"That's because heat rises," Jacob said.

"Did you know," Philip asked, "that long ago, ages ago, it used to be *very* hot in this part of the world?"

"How hot?" Jacob wanted to know.

"Quite tropical. There were real jungles." He looked across the landscape, trying to imagine it. "There were dinosaurs here then, Jacob. Great prehistoric monsters. They used to gather in swamps in places like this and eat the waterweeds."

Jacob looked into the valley. "In places like that, like our valley down there?"

Philip nodded. "And when they died their bones often sank to the bottoms of the swamps and became fossils. That's how we know they were there."

"I've seen pictures," Jacob said.

"Is that *all* they did?" Deborah asked. "Just stand around in swamps all day eating and then falling to the bottom when they'd finished?" She sighed expressively. "It doesn't seem *much* to me."

Philip smiled. "It was to them. They were so huge they had to eat all day in order to survive."

"Why did they all die?"

"No one knows really," Philip said. "Perhaps they forgot how to live."

"I find it quite difficult to picture them," Jacob said. "Down there, in our valley."

"I don't," Deborah said. She put her hands by her ears, forefingers raised, making horns. "I'll bet they're all over if you looked for them, all over everywhere, waiting to jump on you."

"They wouldn't *jump* on you."

"Course they would." Deborah jumped. "Jump, jump—they'd jump on you and eat you up!"

Deborah ran at her brother, who stood looking

at her impatiently, then turned and ran at Philip, who laughed.

"Jump, jump!" Deborah cried. "I'm going to eat you all up."

Philip moved out of the way and Deborah ran deeper into the woods. She was about to turn and run back again when she stopped, frozen, her eyes wide with concern.

"Ohhh," she exclaimed. "Poor thing!"

"What?" Philip ran to her.

"That—look—"

Deborah pointed to a net strung between the trees. On it, captured in the mesh, hung a chaffinch, its tiny yellow-brown body fluttering, pulling against its captivity.

"Poor . . . little . . ."

"It's all right," Philip said, relieved to find her concern was something he could handle. "It's not dead. I'll let it go."

"That one is." Deborah pointed to the body of a thrush hanging lifeless in the netting. "That one's dead. Oh, who did it? Who killed it?"

"The birdcatchers put them up," Jacob explained, coming closer. "They put them there to catch them so they can mark them."

"What do they do that for?"

"So if they find them again they know where they've been."

"That's awful." Deborah watched her father put out a hand and clasp the chaffinch softly. The bird struggled and tried to peck Philip's hand, but he held it, slowly releasing it from the netting.

"Is it all right?" Deborah asked.

"I think so."

"Poor little thing."

"It's not as cruel as it seems," Jacob told them. "If they mark them and find out where they go, then they can help to feed them and things like that."

"I think it's cruel." Deborah reached out and touched the bird's head. The chaffinch struggled, then became quiet beneath her finger. "It *must* be cruel—if it's not cruel why did the other one die?"

"Sometimes they do," Philip said.

"Why?"

"Fear, mainly. They're just frightened to death."

"That's awful."

"It happens quite often with birds," Jacob said with authority. "They die of fright."

"Well, this one's all right." Deborah ran her finger over the bird's head. "Are you going to let it go?" she asked her father.

Philip nodded. He opened his hands. The chaffinch sat a moment, not knowing what to do. Then, quickly, it leaped from Philip's hands and flew away. Where it had been, in Philip's palm, was a small brown dropping.

Deborah laughed. "It liked you," she said. "That's why it did that—because it liked you."

Philip smiled and wiped his hand. "A funny way of showing appreciation," he said lightly.

They walked back along the ridge and down toward the valley.

After a while Jacob said, "I do find it difficult to imagine dinosaurs down there." He lifted a hand and touched his hair. "Even in weather like this," he added.

"They were here all right," Philip said. "Anyway, it's always been hot here. That's why it's called Somerset. The early Saxon farmers thought it was the eternal summer land. That's what Somerset means."

"That's interesting," Jacob said.

"That's silly," Deborah said. "Everyone knows it's not summer all the time. Not even here. *Everyone* knows that."

They began to walk back to the village. About them the splendid sun shone and the fields hummed with life. Philip felt a slow, widening awareness. Whatever Martin had said, whatever had happened to Charlie Crump, nothing seemed to menace this morning. They were together in it; they were unified.

Perhaps, thought Philip, that's where the secret lies, perhaps that's what we're being told. To unify, to share.

81

Chapter

Nineteen

Under the same high sun Ted Wilkes walked to the small cottage Charlie Crump had lived in. It was the end cottage of a row of tied houses, small one-story dwellings on the edge of the village.

After he'd left P.C. Walters, Ted Wilkes had talked to Mabel Crewe. He wondered if she'd heard anything during the night but she reported she'd heard nothing.

Then Ted had gone to The Bunch of Grapes and, with a pint of bitter, sat in his corner for some time, listening to the early drinkers talking of Saturday, the weather, the weekend.

Ted Wilkes heard nothing further about the death of Charlie Crump, nor did he mention it to anyone. But all the time he sat, he could feel the excitement about him.

Something strange was happening, he was sure. Something unlike anything he had ever known. It had begun with Charlie Crump's marrow squash. It continued as the marrow grew, even after it had been taken from the vine. It was connected with Charlie Crump's death and the rose branch embedded in his flesh. It would go further, Ted was sure.

Ted Wilkes left The Bunch of Grapes and walked to Charlie Crump's cottage. He was not certain why he was going; he knew only that he must.

When he arrived at the little stone building he did not go around the side of it where the truck and the remains of the marrow were. He went instead to the front door and found it unlocked.

Inside the cottage the thin sour smell of Charlie Crump's life permeated. Ted Wilkes shook his head to avoid it and walked slowly through the few rooms of the cottage.

He peered into the bedroom, at the soiled bed and the blanket lying across it, then looked into the kitchen, which contained masses of dirty dishes and a filthy stove. The smell there was stronger. Ted walked through it, out the back door, and around the side of the house.

After the dimness of the cottage the sunlight was bright and it was a moment or two before he saw the flies buzzing over the back of the truck and the remains of the marrow squash.

As soon as he saw it he knew what had happened.

He stood looking at the dry, pulped marrow and the flies and he could understand something of Charlie's frenzy and his despair.

"Poor bugger," he said aloud. "Poor silly bugger."

He found the ax. It was rusted, and the faintly reddish stain reminded him of blood.

Ted Wilkes wiped the ax carefully and put it in the shed behind the cottage. There he found a spade and with it he dug a hole at the bottom of the small garden.

Carefully, like a man preserving something, Ted Wilkes lifted the drying, brown remains of the marrow from the back of the truck and buried them in the earth. He covered them gently, tapping down the soil with the flat of the spade.

When he had emptied the back of the truck Ted washed it clean, removing all trace of the marrow.

He did not know what it would do and he was not sure why he was doing it. It merely seemed to him appropriate.

Then he replaced the spade, closed the doors of the cottage, and walked back to the village. Under the high sun his shadow was a small black pool at his feet.

As Ted Wilkes buried the marrow squash, Mabel Crewe picked up her pruning shears. Her old, lined face was determined. It had gone on long enough, she

83

thought. It's becoming ridiculous. But she hesitated, wondering why she was afraid.

Twice that Saturday morning she'd picked up her shears determined to prune the roses on the front wall of the cottage. Each time uncertainty and a vague uneasy fear had stopped her. She found herself vacillating, wavering, finding other small tasks to do which prevented her going outside.

Twice she'd replaced the shears and avoided pruning the roses.

Now she realized that if she didn't act soon the fear would become so magnified in her mind that she'd never overcome it.

It's not that I'm doing them any real harm, she thought. It's for their own good. Surely they know *that*.

"You're being ridiculous," she said aloud, boldly. "It's got to stop."

She marched outside into the sunlight and walked toward the rosebush climbing the red-brick wall. It seemed even more overgrown, heavier than it had the day before.

"This will hurt me more than it will you," she said to the rosebush. "Just try to be brave."

Mabel Crewe grasped the rosebush firmly. She wore thick leather gloves, but nevertheless, as she took hold of the bush, she was aware of her own tension and the rapid beating of her heart.

Absurd, she thought. It's all in the mind.

Mabel Crewe raised the pruning shears and with a crisp and defiant movement cut a branch from the bush. She stepped away from the wall, the branch in her hand, and let out her breath.

Well, she said to herself. That wasn't as bad as you thought, was it? She put the branch on the grass carefully, smiling at her own foolishness, and took hold of the rosebush again. As she did so, she became aware of the rustling.

It grew suddenly out of the silence.

Mabel Crewe turned her head but there was nothing to be seen. Nothing moved. All the leaves she could see lay still in the hot air. But the rustling persisted; buzzing, threatening, warning.

She shook her head as if to drive the sound away.

"How odd," Mabel Crewe murmured, ignoring her fear. "Must be some sort of machine somewhere."

She increased her hold on the rosebush and raised the shears again, lifting them with a sense of determination as the rustling increased, knowing that if she did not persist now she would never again face anything.

She opened the blades, preparing to cut another branch.

Afterward, Mabel Crewe could never remember exactly how it happened. One moment she was standing firmly on the grass, the rosebush and the shears in her hands. The next she was lying on the grass, yards away, her body crumpled, her hands tingling as though they'd received an electric shock.

The shears lay below the rosebush, their shiny blades scarred as if singed by fire.

Around her again was the harsh rustling sound of the plants.

Mabel Crewe lay very still, hardly breathing. She felt if she were to move at all something else would happen.

She lay feeling the sun on her skin, hearing the menacing voices of the plants. Both the house and the garden seemed to reject her.

From where she lay she could see the bush she'd pruned. It was enormous suddenly, overpowering the wall on which it grew. The blooms were heavy, almost obscene in their vivid coloring, evil in their lushness. The thorns caught the sunlight and the roughness of the branches was harsh.

No, Mabel Crewe thought, it can't be like that. It can't be. What's happened to my roses? What have they done?

After a while she began to sob.

As Philip Monk walked back to the cottage with the children he heard Mabel Crewe crying.

At first he thought it was a child, but the sound was too old, too alien. Then Philip became aware of other noises mixed with the crying. A faint steady rustling sound, intermingled, incapable of separation.

He stopped in the road and the children stopped also.

"What's that?" he asked.

"Someone crying," Jacob suggested.

"No," Deborah said. "It's—"

"What?"

"It's the plants!" Deborah cried. "The plants—they're talking. Can't you hear them? I can hear them. They're talking to each other. Can't you hear?"

"What plants? What do you mean?" Philip knelt beside Deborah, putting his head beside hers. "What do you mean, Debby?"

"They're talking." Deborah's eyes were very bright. Words tumbled from her lips. "That's the way they talk to each other." She listened. "They're very cross," she announced suddenly. "They're very cross about something. Can't you hear the way they're shouting at each other? Can't you hear what they're saying?" She listened, her face curious. "I wish I knew why they were so cross. I wish I knew why they're so unhappy."

"Are you sure, Debby?" her father asked.

"Can't *you* hear?" Deborah turned to her brother. "Tell him, Jacob," she said. "Tell him that's the plants talking."

Philip looked at Jacob, who nodded. "That's what Debby calls that sound. She says that's what it is."

"Is it?"

Jacob shrugged. "I don't know. I can't listen to them the way she can."

"But—"

"It's true, Daddy," Deborah said. "Really it's true."

Philip listened. Here was more than he understood. Things he'd only suspected. Nothing Michael Martin had spoken of was in any way as close to this. This was deeper, more mystical, further-reaching than anything the biologist had mentioned. Philip listened, holding his daughter close.

"But there's something else, isn't there?" Jacob pointed out. "There *is* someone crying as well."

Philip nodded. "Stay here, both of you. Here—in

86

the middle of the road." He began to walk toward Mabel Crewe's cottage.

The children watched him go.

Philip Monk opened the gate and paused. The rustling was louder, filling the overgrown garden. The sound of sobbing was close by.

Philip found Mabel lying on the grass. The old lady lay with her head in her hands. The thin wailing cry came from her like something lost.

Philip walked toward her, uncertain of what else he would find. Nothing else moved in the garden. The rose blooms lay heavy on the branches and the sound of rustling continued to fill the air. But only Philip moved.

He knelt beside Mabel Crewe.

"Are you all right?"

She stopped crying but didn't move.

"It's me. Philip Monk."

Very slowly Mabel lifted her head and looked at him.

"What happened?"

She shook her head. "I don't know."

"Are you hurt?"

Mabel Crewe paused. "No," she said. "I'm all right."

"Come on then." Philip began to lift her. "I'll help you inside."

"No." Mabel Crewe drew back, shaking her head vigorously. "I'm not going back in there."

"Why?" Philip looked at the cottage. It seemed peaceful in the sunlight. "What's in there?"

"Nothing. I don't know. I'm not going in." Her face wore a determined look.

"All right," Philip said. "Let's get you to your feet."

Slowly he raised Mabel Crewe from the ground. She stood for a moment, swaying, her hands over her face.

"Are you sure you're not hurt?"

Mabel Crewe nodded.

"Come along then," Philip said. He led her slowly

through the rose garden. The rustling was dying, receding. Mabel allowed herself to be led. "Come over to the house. You'll be all right there."

Mabel Crewe nodded.

Philip led her out into the road while the children watched. Neither Jacob nor Deborah spoke. There was something in Mabel Crewe's face which prevented any comment.

Together they walked slowly toward the white stucco cottage where Elizabeth waited.

They were all acutely aware that something quite extraordinary had happened.

Chapter
Twenty

For a long time Chief Constable Parkhurst did nothing about P.C. Walters' phone call. He tried to dismiss it, but it nagged, lying uneasily on his mind.

After his wife went indoors he remained in the garden, poking the lawn with his golf club. It did seem extraordinarily lush this year. Old Harry, the gardener, was at it all day and it didn't appear to make any difference.

He swung his club and took the head off a daisy. Even they were larger than usual this year.

After a while he went inside and poured himself a whiskey and soda. He sat and sipped it, watching the sunlight burst through the windows.

"Do you have that number by any chance?" he finally asked his wife. "You know, the one I mentioned?"

"Reynolds? Keeper of parks and gardens?"

"That's him."

"It's by the telephone," the chief constable's wife informed him. "I imagined you'd want it sooner or later."

"Hmmm," said the chief constable, remaining where he was.

Later he went quietly to the telephone, dialed the number, and waited until someone answered. It was Reynolds' son.

"Is your father there?" the chief constable inquired.

"Yes, but he's not very well."

"Oh, I rather wanted a word with him. But if he's not up to it."

"I think he can make it to the phone." There was faint amusement in the son's voice.

Before the chief constable had a chance to reply the receiver was laid down. Then it was picked up by Reynolds, a slight, bald man who had a hangover this morning.

"Hello?" he said in a slightly throaty voice. "Reynolds here."

"Ahhh . . . Reynolds . . ." The chief constable hesitated. Harry Reynolds put a hand to his head and waited.

"I, ah . . . I'm not quite sure how to put this, Reynolds . . . but I, ah, had a strange call from Brandling this morning."

"Who am I talking to?"

"Oh, sorry. Parkhurst, chief constable."

"I see."

"Know Brandling, do you?"

"Vaguely."

"Bit west of here. Pretty little place."

Reynolds closed his eyes.

"Well, anyway," Parkhurst continued, "chap called Walters phoned this morning. Local bobby. Pretty sound. Quite levelheaded as a rule."

"Yes?"

"Well, he had this funny story, you see. Mind you, could be a lot of tommyrot, but . . . well, as I say, he's pretty levelheaded."

"I'm sorry." Reynolds' head thumped. "But I'm afraid I don't follow."

"Well now . . ." The chief constable took a deep breath. He wished he were back in Malaya or Fiji. It would have been easier there. "Well, he, Walters, has this funny idea that a chap down there . . . local drunk or something . . . had an accident. And there was something pretty odd about it."

"Go on."

"Hit his head. Broke his neck or something."

"What's odd about that?"

"Two things really. One, he seemed to have been pretty frightened. And the other, a . . . ah, rosebush was involved."

"A what?"

"Rosebush. Florabunda I think he said it was."

90

"Was he poisoned, anything like that?"

"No, I don't think so. Seems odder than that."

"In what way?"

"I'm not sure." The chief constable cleared his throat. "You see, it wasn't so much what this constable chappie said, but the way he said it. Reminded me of the sort of thing natives might get up to. It, ah . . . seems this chap, the one who died, was tied up by the rosebush in some way."

"*Tied up?*"

"Something like that. Seems to have bound itself around him. Thorns went in quite deep."

Reynolds sighed. "Why are you telling me all this?"

"Thought you ought to know," the chief constable said, piqued. "After all, it's your territory."

"My what?"

"You're keeper of parks and gardens, or whatever it is you call yourself."

Reynolds sighed again. His mouth was dry. "Where did you say this occurred?"

"Brandling. But London seems to be involved somehow. Some chap rang the local constable, the one who rang me. Seems he knew something odd was going on with the local vegetation." The chief constable paused significantly. "What do you think of that?"

Reynolds opened his eyes and closed them again. "Who called from London?" he asked.

"Some official, I gather."

"I see."

"Wouldn't want them, in London, to think we'd done nothing about it now, would we?"

"Listen—" Reynolds wondered how much longer the conversation would continue. "I don't actually think—"

"I *actually* think we should do something about it, old man," Chief Constable Parkhurst said forceably. "After all, there might just be something in it."

"What, for example?"

"You never know. It has been the damnedest summer. Anything could be happening."

"What do you suggest we do?"

"Thought you might go down and have a look around, actually. See for yourself . . . sooner the better."

"Today?"

"What's wrong with today?"

"It's Saturday."

"Goddammit, man!" The chief constable's voice rose. "Someone's got to go and have a look. Put a stop to all these rumors—that sort of thing."

"All right." Reynolds held his forehead. "I'll look into it. I may not get down there until tomorrow, but I'll look into it."

"Good." The chief constable sounded pleased. "After all, you must know for yourself how the weather's been. Your own records must show—"

"There's a great deal of difference between my records and this—what would you call it? Biological warfare in reverse?"

"That's putting it a bit strongly."

"All right," Reynolds agreed. "But if there *is* anything unusual, what'd you like me to do?"

"Do what you have to, old man."

Reynolds sighed. "Tell me," he asked tartly. "How *do* you arrest a rosebush? Florabunda or any other kind?"

Chapter

Twenty-One

Alone, Mabel Crewe stood in the front room of the Monks' cottage and listened. There were voices; she could hear voices which seemed to be whispering and singing all inside her head.

She shook her head vigorously, but the voices persisted; there was no avoiding them. This time she must accept their presence.

Outside, in the sunlight, the children played in the garden. Philip was not in the house. Elizabeth was upstairs. But the voices Mabel heard were not human voices; they did not belong to the Monks.

Mabel tilted her head as the voices beckoned, feeling suddenly exposed, isolated. She couldn't quite make out what the voices were saying, but she *had* heard them before, in her own house, in her own garden. And always, in the past, she had hidden from their presence.

It had taken Mabel a long time to admit, even to herself, that the voices were real. At first she had denied them, then when they became more insistent she had put them down to an aberration of hearing, an aspect of loneliness and old age.

But they persisted. They called from her garden, they raised their silvery, whispery voices and invaded her house. They were everywhere, and slowly, like a photograph developing, their sense began to take shape in her mind.

They needed her, they said. And she, in turn, would find that she needed them.

This was urgent, they said. Time was fast running out.

"What?" Mabel had whispered in return. "What need? What time? What do you mean?"

The voices consulted, their sense fading, their words indistinct. Then they returned to Mabel's ear.

"We need to breathe," they told her. "We all must share the air."

"Share the air?"

"Yes," they whispered back. "Share the air. Share the air. Share the air."

The sinuous phrase floated.

Mabel Crewe had turned, her heart fluttering, looking for something more than the soft, silvery voices.

But there was nothing else.

"Share the air," they repeated. "Share the air."

"But . . ." Mabel's voice faltered. "It's all right here. It's clean. In Brandling we—"

"It is clean *now*," the voices said. "But it will not be soon. Soon it will become soiled and used."

"But—"

"No buts. No buts. No buts."

Mabel turned her head. She put a hand to her chest and held the beating of her heart.

"Soon," they said. "Soon it will be impossible to breathe here. Soon it will have to stop."

"*Stop?*"

"Stop."

"What—what will have to stop?"

"Mischief," the voices said.

"Mischief?"

"We will answer filth with filth, ruin with ruin, destruction with destruction, death with death."

"No."

"We must. We must. We must."

"What do you want me to do?" Mabel Crewe had asked finally. Holding herself, feeling the fear and the presence. "What is it you want from me?"

"Tell them."

"Who? What?"

"Your people. You must tell them to stop. Tell them now."

"Why me?"

94

"You are one of the few who can hear, one of the few who are close."

Mabel's voice failed. "Must?"

"Yes."

Mabel shook her head, frightened, confused, unable to capitulate.

"You must. You must. You must. . . ."

The voices lifted and trailed, then faded and finally were gone.

Mabel Crewe stood a long time in the garden after the silence returned, staring at her roses. They seemed to be staring back. Nothing further was spoken on that first occasion. All that was needed had been said. Mabel Crewe wondered then if she would pass their message on and knew immediately that she would not. It was beyond her. However much she accepted the voices she had heard, she knew she could never tell another living soul about them.

Now she stood in the Monks' house, which suddenly seemed as close as her own, and heard the voices again.

They whispered, they sang, demanding.

Slowly their message became clear.

"Why have you not spoken?" they asked. "Why not? Why not? Why not?"

"I—" Mabel began, but her words stuck in her throat.

"We asked; we warned."

Mabel felt the rose thorn in her thumb. She saw the flash and felt the force which had thrown her to the grass and scorched the pruning shears. She understood why it had happened.

"I'm sorry," she said.

"It is not too late."

Mabel Crewe heard the words and wondered.

"It is not too late," they repeated. "It is not too late."

"I—"

"You must. Must. Must. . . ."

Mabel Crewe nodded. Perhaps it wasn't too late. Perhaps she could tell someone. Philip Monk, in spite of his remoteness, his distance, understood something of what was happening. Deborah, the child, knew more than she ever admitted. Perhaps it was possible to tell either of them what the voices warned of. Perhaps they would understand and not think of her as old or foolish or insane.

"Now," the voices repeated. "Now . . . now . . . now. . . ."

"I'll try."

Mabel Crewe paused. "I'll try," she said again, feebly. It was all she was capable of. "I . . . will . . . try."

The whispering rose and fell.

"*You must,*" they repeated once, clearly. Then they were gone, leaving their faint, silvery sibilance dying in the hot, closed air. "You must," echoed through the room.

Mabel Crewe looked across to her own cottage and the roses which grew there, wondering how she would ever be able to do what she knew she must.

The task was formidable. Demanding and exact, it stretched before her endlessly, requiring of her more than anything she had ever encountered in a long, lonely life.

Chapter
Twenty-Two

The events of the past hours had drained Elizabeth Monk. The things Philip had said, Deborah's screams, had been enough. But earlier, the sight of Mabel Crewe, pale with shock, had been final. Now Elizabeth stood in the kitchen of the cottage, facing her husband, her hands twisting in her lap. Her face was drawn, filled with fear. Tired lines ran from the corners of her eyes. Her mouth looked as if it had been cut from stone.

"We've got to get out of here," she said. "We've got to get away, now, while we can."

Philip shook his head. "That's not what they want us to do," he said quietly.

"*They?*"

"The plants."

Elizabeth's voice descended to a whisper. "You're mad. You're absolutely crazy."

"I'm trying to do what I think's best. What matters is—"

"Us," Elizabeth said firmly. "That's what matters: *us.*"

"I know."

"No, you don't." Elizabeth held herself. "You don't think about us. All you're concerned with is some theory about plants. If you cared about us you'd get us out of here."

"We must stay," said Philip, watching her. "We must face it. That's what they want."

"No." Elizabeth's voice was low, vibrating with emotion. "Never." She shook her head. "When you talked to me last night," she said, "when you told me of your theories, I almost believed you. I went

97

along with it. I listened, because then it was only something we were talking about. But now it's happened. Don't you see? My God, don't you see the difference? We're—" Elizabeth's shoulders shook. "I don't know what we are, all I know is we must get out of here."

"Running away won't help." Philip's voice was level. "You know that, Liz. Running away never did anyone any good."

Elizabeth closed her eyes. There was nothing she could relate to, nothing sane in her small world.

"I'm sorry," Philip went on. "But I believe this is the only chance we'll ever get."

"Chance? What do you mean by chance? What are you talking about?" Her voice wavered. "What sort of chance did Mabel have? Look what happened to her! And Deborah—my God, what's she become?"

"Deborah's got more chance than any of us."

"Don't be absurd."

"She's in touch with them," Philip said. "She's listening. I only wish I could hear the things she hears."

"Listening?"

"Yes," said Philip. "I believe she can actually hear the plants . . . communicating."

"No," Elizabeth said, sounding unconvinced. She remembered Deborah's bright face, recalled the conversation about the sunflowers. "No," she repeated, but the word lacked force.

"It's true," Philip said. "We need her now. She may be one of the few who will save us."

Elizabeth put her hands to her face and wept, silently, desperately, her body shaking. She was close to collapse. When she spoke her voice sounded trapped. "Stop playing your little games," she told her husband bitterly. "Stop pretending you understand."

Philip put out his hands.

"You're playing games with our lives," Elizabeth went on. "Stop it, Philip. Please, please, stop it."

Philip took her by the elbows.

"Leave me alone."

"I need you." Philip held her.

"No."

"Yes," Philip said. "Help me. Don't shut yourself off. Don't be so bitter." He looked at her. Tears ran down her cheeks. "I need you—really. Believe me, Liz, I do. We all need you."

Elizabeth lifted her head.

"I'm not playing games," Philip went on, gently. "I'm really trying to understand what's happening to all of us."

Elizabeth shivered. "I'm so frightened."

"I know," Philip said softly. "I'm afraid too. If I wasn't afraid I *would* be mad."

Elizabeth leaned her head forward and put it into the hollow of his shoulder.

Philip held her. "But being afraid's not going to help."

"What is?" asked Elizabeth.

"Understanding."

Elizabeth sighed. But the emotional outburst was waning now. She sought comfort, consolation, warmth. She did not know whether Philip was right or wrong, only that he was now closer to her than he'd been for a long time.

"What are we going to do?" she asked.

"Listen . . . understand . . . hope," Philip told her. "Find out what they want. Try to understand what they have to say."

"It—it just seems so crazy."

"No," said Philip steadily. "For years, all through history one way or another, people, certain people, have believed that plants are more than just vegetables. They've believed in some sort of plant intelligence or communication, biosignals, whatever you like to call them, and they—those who believed—have often been called crazy. I'll bet some have even paid with their lives for their beliefs. Society has always been against them."

Elizabeth listened.

"Now," continued Philip, "now it looks as if they might have been right."

"In *communicating* with plants?"

Philip nodded. "Some of them even believed that plants had a natural affection for mankind," he said. "That they really wanted to help us."

"But—"

"I know, you wonder about the violence."

"Yes. It's—" Elizabeth shuddered.

"I don't know why," Philip said. "It's hard to know what they think of us. Perhaps they think we communicate through violence," he said. "There's so much of it. Perhaps they think that's all we understand."

Elizabeth Monk breathed deeply. "Is that *really* what we are?"

"It's what we're becoming. It's what we express best. All the things we build, all the changes we make, are so much less expressive than the bombs we've dropped. Or the vast numbers of our own kind we've slaughtered."

Elizabeth lifted a hand to touch her husband's cheek. "Poor Philip," she said softly.

"Why, do I sound—"

"—sincere," Elizabeth said. She rested her cheek against her husband's. "Thank you," she said softly, calmer now. "Thank you very much."

Philip held his wife and waited, grateful for the comfort he'd been able to give. He hoped his words were as confident as they sounded.

After a while he said, "Liz—"

"What?"

"We're together now, aren't we?"

Elizabeth hesitated.

"We've got to be. There's no other way."

"Do you really believe the children—Deborah—will be all right?" Elizabeth asked. "Really all right?"

"Yes. They'll be all right."

"Very well," Elizabeth said quietly. "I won't fight you anymore. If you believe we must stay, and that the children will be safe, I won't resist."

Philip tightened his arms about his wife. Nothing seemed to him to be more important at that moment than their togetherness. Together, he believed, they would survive. It was the only way.

"Thank you," he whispered. "Whatever's going to happen is going to happen to us all. The least we can show them is that we care."

"We care." Elizabeth's voice was soft. "That's the trouble, really. If we didn't care nothing would matter, would it?"

Philip smiled. "Thank God we do," he said.

Elizabeth stepped away and pushed her hands through her hair, recovering. Then she paused, suddenly remembering something she had meant to pass on to Philip earlier.

"Oh," she began, a little guiltily. "There was a message for you. While you were out, Walters, the policeman, called."

"What did he want?" Philip's voice was eager.

"I'm not sure. He'd had a telephone call from someone in London."

"Who?"

"He didn't know. He forgot to ask." Elizabeth felt her calm dissolving. "But it did sound like that man you saw yesterday. Martin somebody."

"Michael Martin?"

"I think so. There's a number he wants you to call."

"Did Walters say anything else?"

Elizabeth nodded. "There was something about it being—the beginning," she said. Fear was returning to her voice. "What does that mean, Philip?"

Philip kept his voice steady. "We're going to be all right, Liz."

"My God, I hope so."

"Believe that we will."

Elizabeth nodded slowly. "I'll try," she said. "I will try."

Philip Monk tried to contact Michael Martin immediately.

It took some time to get the call through.

There were delays at the switchboard, and once Philip was cut off completely, but he persisted and in the end a male voice answered the laboratory phone.

"Michael?"

"Whom did you want?" the voice replied.

101

"Michael Martin. Dr. Martin."

There was a small pause. "I'm sorry, sir. He's not here," the voice said finally.

"Who is that?" Philip asked.

"The janitor. I'm the janitor, sir. There's no one else here at the moment."

"Are you sure Dr. Martin's not there?"

"He's not here."

"What's going on?" Philip asked impatiently. "I've had enough trouble getting through as it is. Kindly connect me with Dr. Martin or tell me where I can get in touch with him."

There was silence on the other end of the line.

"Come along," Philip said. "I haven't got all day."

"I'm sorry, sir." The janitor sounded confused. "But it's a bit difficult, sir."

"Difficult? What do you mean difficult?"

"Well, sir . . ." The janitor's voice trailed away. Then he had a sudden thought. "Are you by any chance a personal friend of Dr. Martin's, sir?"

"Yes, I am," Philip said quickly. "In fact he asked me to call him. I'm surprised he's not there."

There was another pause. Philip Monk could hear the janitor deciding. "Well, sir," he said, "I'm afraid there's been an accident . . . sir."

"Accident? What on earth do you mean?"

"To Dr. Martin."

"Is he all right?"

"I'm afraid he's dead, sir."

Philip Monk held the telephone tightly, aware of a small buzzing tone in his ears. For a moment he could think of nothing to say.

On the other end of the line the janitor's voice went on. "Are you still there, sir?"

"Yes." Philip coughed, clearing his throat. "Of course I'm here. What happened? Do you have any details?"

"Not much."

"Do you *know* what happened?"

"I don't really know, sir. I'm not really sure, sir, but I was told that Dr. Martin had an accident . . . sir."

102

Philip put a hand to his forehead and closed his eyes. "When did it happen?"

"This morning, sir."

"Do you know anything more?"

"No, sir." The janitor's voice went on. "Except that it's an awful mess here, sir. It seems that something quite strange happened—happened to Dr. Martin."

"What?"

"I don't know, sir. I'm told he was doing some experiment with some plants, but I don't know what. But it seems he went berserk or something. Everything's smashed to pieces. There's nothing left. It's a right mess, sir. It'll take days to clear up."

"I'm sorry." Philip's voice was dry.

"It's in a shocking state."

"Yes."

"Is that all, sir? Is there any message?"

"No, no message."

Philip replaced the receiver and stood staring at the plastic of the telephone. In spite of the heat, the room felt clammy and piercingly cold.

Chapter
Twenty-Three

After Ted Wilkes buried the remains of Charlie Crump's marrow squash he walked back to the village center. Brandling was almost empty beneath the high Saturday sun. The Bunch of Grapes had closed for the afternoon. The Brandling Stores & Post Office was shuttered.

A dog sniffing restlessly about a rubbish bin was all the movement Ted Wilkes saw until Eric Bolton swung round the corner.

Eric Bolton walked heavily, moodily, his head hanging. When he saw Ted Wilkes he approached him.

"What's this I hear," Eric asked, "about Charlie?"

"What'd you hear?"

"He's had an accident or something. There was talk about it. There's been gossip."

Ted Wilkes scratched his old gray head and said nothing.

"They say you know something," Eric probed. He stood heavily, uneasily, crinkling his eyes against the sunlight. "That true?"

"Charlie's dead," Ted said simply.

"What happened?"

"What'd you hear?"

Eric Bolton stood squarely in front of Ted Wilkes, feeling anger rise. Ted was mocking him, avoiding the question. "Don't muck me about, Ted Wilkes," he warned stolidly.

"Well, now." Ted smiled, his knowledge separating him, giving him perspective. "Well, now, it all depends what you mean by mucking about, doesn't it?"

"I mean about Charlie Crump. You was there, I was told. You know what happened."

"I found him, if that's what you mean."

"I mean more than that." Eric Bolton's face was determined. "I want to know what happened to him."

"He fell over," Ted said easily. "Cracked himself on a wall."

"That's all?"

Ted Wilkes nodded. "What you so interested for? Didn't think Charlie was any special friend of yours."

"He wasn't."

"Well then?"

"What happens here concerns us all," Eric said doggedly. "I got the right to know."

Ted Wilkes nodded. "I suppose you have."

Eric Bolton moved closer. "It's true then?" he asked. "There *is* something funny going on?" He licked his lips. "Something that's not right?"

"We all got things to answer for," Ted said abruptly, appraising the bulk of Eric Bolton. "You got *your* house in order?" he asked.

Eric's attitude became cautious.

"Charlie's wasn't," Ted went on, his voice crisp and direct. "His house wasn't in order. He'd offended, Charlie had. He'd offended the creatures of the fields." His eyes gazed steadily at Eric. "Hope you got nothing like that on your conscience."

"Now, look here—" Eric began.

"It's you got to look," Ted went on. The effect of his words was satisfying. "It's you who's got to face up to it."

"What you on about?"

"You know."

Eric Bolton took a step backward. "They said it's got to you," he said slowly, uneasily. "They told me finding Charlie'd upset you." He looked away, unable to face Ted's clear gaze. "They told me—"

"Don't listen to false gossip," Ted said quickly.

"Now wait a minute."

"Don't listen to false gossip," Ted repeated. "Don't waste time idling. There are things to do. There's work to be done."

"You're daft."

"No." Ted Wilkes shook his head solemnly. "I'm not daft. Charlie Crump offended and was repaid. It's up to us to hearken. It's up to us to be warned. His sins found him out."

Eric Bolton swallowed, moving away. He'd always thought Ted Wilkes was crazy. Him and his *unnatural* things. He could see now that whatever had happened to Charlie Crump had turned the old man's mind.

"All right," Eric said carefully. "Whatever you say."

"You'd better listen to what I say," Ted said levelly. "That's my advice to you."

"Course," Eric said, sidestepping the old man standing in the sunlight. "I'll see to it."

"While you got the time."

"Yes, while I got the time."

Ted watched Eric leave, then, his eyes twinkling, he called, "You haven't got no olive trees, have you?"

"What?" Eric paused.

"Olive trees," Ted repeated. "Standing about?"

"You're pulling my leg?"

"No, just thought I'd ask."

Eric hesitated a moment longer, then hurried away, his heavyset figure sweating in the heat.

Ted Wilkes waited until the center of Brandling was empty and still again. He watched the dog circle in the shade by the rubbish bins and flop down on the warm asphalt.

Ted Wilkes grinned and scratched his head.

Do Eric Bolton good to worry a bit, he thought. Keep his mind off his greed.

Eric Bolton went into his house. He could hear his wife, Edith, sewing in the back room on the shaded side. Eric walked through the house thinking of what Ted Wilkes had said. The old man was daft enough, but—

"You're late," Edith commented as Eric came in. "I expected you back after the pub closed."

"I was talking."

"Your dinner's in the oven."

"You haven't heard, then?" Eric asked cautiously, leaning against the windowsill. "You haven't heard the news?"

"What news?" Edith lifted the trousers she was mending and bit through a thread. Her arms were heavy. "What are you on about now?"

"Charlie Crump."

"Not him again."

"He's dead," Eric said quickly, enjoying the news, watching the expression on his wife's face, seeing the interest grow. "You know that? He's dead."

Edith opened her mouth but said nothing.

"That's right," Eric continued. "Died last night."

Edith swallowed, her eyes softening. "Poor old Charlie. I always knew it'd get him, in the end."

Eric frowned.

"Scrumpie," Edith went on. "You can't go on drinking it like that. Not the way he did." She shook her head. "Let it be a lesson to you," she added.

"It wasn't that."

"Don't you believe it." Edith went back to her sewing. "You can't fool me. Everyone knows what he was like."

"It wasn't the booze." Eric swallowed. Edith was always like this. She intimidated him, then took over. "He didn't drink nothing yesterday, I saw him. I was there—"

"—usually are."

"—he drank only lemonade. We had a laugh about it, but that's all he had."

"One night wouldn't make no difference," Edith murmured, unimpressed. "Not after the damage he'd done."

"It wasn't like that." Eric felt the need to convince her. He rubbed his hands on the sides of his trousers. "There's something funny going on. There was talk in The Grapes and Ted Wilkes knows something as well."

"What?" Edith demanded. She looked at her husband, noticing the perspiration on his forehead. "If

107

something is going on I'm surprised you don't know more about it. Not like you to be left behind."

"I been trying to find out all I can."

"All right," Edith said, resting her heavy arms on the machine. "Tell me what happened to poor old Charlie."

Eric hesitated.

"Well, do you know something or don't you?"

"It wasn't the Scrumpie," Eric said. "It was something else."

"What?"

"He fell, cracked his head or something. Ted Wilkes found him this morning. He fell over."

"Drinking lemonade?"

"That's got nothing to do with it." Eric folded his arms. "There's something else. They're trying to hide it."

"Who's that?"

"Ted Wilkes, Percy Walters." Eric Bolton saw gain somewhere; profit. "They're hiding something."

"Percy Walters? He's honest as the day is long. And as for old Ted Wilkes, he might be a bit barmy but I'd trust him with my life."

"Would you now?"

"Course I would," Edith said briskly. She picked up the garment she was sewing, shook it vigorously, and started the machine again. There was nothing further she wanted to hear. "You'd better get your dinner," she said, dismissing him.

Eric Bolton shrugged. It was all right for her to talk, he thought. What did she know? He went into the kitchen and took his dinner—a pork chop, cabbage, carrots, and potatoes—from the oven and sat at the table chewing slowly. He perspired a little as he chewed, the moisture running in lines down his heavy cheeks.

If there was something, he thought, he'd find out what it was. It'd take more than Percy Walters and old Ted Wilkes to keep it from him.

Eric chewed thoughtfully, then stopped.

Perhaps there was something to the marrow squash after all. Perhaps Charlie'd got onto some-

108

thing special. A new fertilizer, a new way of cultivation. After all, it kept on growing even after it had been taken from the vine.

You never knew, even a drunk like Charlie sometimes had a good idea. It might be worth his while, Eric thought, to go down to Charlie's place and have a look around.

He nodded, a little gravy trickling down his chin.

Ted Wilkes was right. He had envied the marrow squash ever since he'd seen it. There could be money in things like that. There could be profit.

Eric Bolton chewed, feeling better. When he'd finished his dinner he'd go down to Charlie's and have a look around. Before anyone else did. Before the word spread.

He wiped his chin with the back of his hand.

From the back room on the shaded side of the house the sound of the sewing machine hummed.

Eric Bolton lifted his head and listened. Edith didn't understand. It was a long time since she'd looked at him properly, with appreciation. No one did anymore, not even his son, Billy.

The last time their boy had been home was months ago. He'd come down from London almost unrecognizable. Hair long, a gold earring in one ear, nothing to say for himself. He'd remained one night and then gone back again to whatever he did in the city.

Eric Bolton belched, cut a piece of fatty pork, and chewed on it slowly with enjoyment. Later he'd go down to Charlie's and find what there was to be found. They couldn't make a fool of him. No, he was too clever for that.

On a bend in the main road, a mile out of Brandling, Peter's Elm stood. It had been there as long as anyone in Brandling could remember. It had been called Peter's Elm as long as anyone could remember, although no one was certain why.

Some said the land on which it grew once belonged to a farmer called Peter, and that was enough. Others in the village thought it had something to do with Peter, the apostle. That there was a rooster at one time which crowed each dawn and that was why the tree bore its name.

But however it came to be called, Peter's Elm was a landmark in Brandling, marking the last turn before the final run down to the village.

It told the inhabitants of the town that they were home.

Late that Saturday afternoon Peter's Elm fell.

No one knew what caused it, though several villagers heard the crash.

Some time later, when the tree was examined, it was found to be hollow, so that for years it must have stood supported only by its shell. But exactly what had brought it down on that hot, windless sunny afternoon no one knew.

When it fell the tree crashed sideways, parallel to the road, and brought down with it the only telephone wires connecting Brandling to the outside world.

There was no other line to the village. Once the wires were down Brandling became isolated.

Nor was the line immediately repairable. When Peter's Elm fell it rolled, knitting the wires into its branches, forming a tangle no one was able to unravel.

Mabel Crewe sat alone and still in the front room of the Monks' cottage. The voices had gone, the room was quiet, there was silence in her head. She was all right, she was sure. There was nothing to worry about.

But she needed time to think, to attempt to sort out the tangle of fear and uncertainty which bound her.

Everything she had avoided and put aside had returned. All the tiny signs she'd ignored were vivid again. She could no longer deny the voices she had heard or the suggestions they made to her.

And now, also, there was Deborah. The child was closer to the truth than Mabel Crewe was able to admit. She seemed to know that Mabel *did* talk to her roses and that she also listened to what they had to say. The child understood that the whispery voices *were* real and that their conversations were clear.

110

Mabel Crewe sat very still and wondered how she would ever be able to express the thoughts which filled her mind. She did not know how to begin, for they were too extreme. Nobody would believe her.

They would say she was an old fool, that she was afraid, that she'd lived too long alone.

Mabel Crewe shivered and put her hands beneath her chin, frightened by her own isolation.

Then she sighed abruptly and stood, determined to admit nothing publicly, to say nothing at all to anyone. She would not tell the others of the voices, or of the warnings they issued. Whatever had been said to her was her own business pure and simple, and she would keep it that way. Whatever meanings the roses had passed along, they passed to her alone.

The others would have to come to their own discoveries—if it was all that important they would be told also. If the danger was that close, then all the others would be included.

It was simple, she said to herself. Either she was imagining things or the voices were real. If she was imagining things then the less said the better. If she wasn't, then the others would be included in their own good time.

In the meantime she would remain silent. If Philip Monk was all that clever he would find out anyway. If Deborah knew so much then it was up to her to tell the others.

Mabel sat quietly, nodding to herself.

There was no point in stirring things up unnecessarily—no matter what had happened to her or to anyone else.

Mabel sat quietly for a while, glad she had made her decision, when she was disturbed by a knock on the door.

"Come in," she called.

One by one the Monk family entered the room, slowly, tentatively, as if reluctant to intrude.

"Come in," Mabel repeated. "I'm much better now."

"Are you?" Philip asked.

"Oh, yes," Mabel replied. "I really don't know

111

what happened this morning. It's really quite beyond me."

"Were you frightened, Miss Crewe?" Jacob asked, curious.

"Yes. I think I was quite frightened for a while. It came as such a shock." She smiled to hide her concern. "After all, the roses *did* need pruning and I didn't expect—"

"Oh, they didn't really want to hurt you," Deborah interrupted. "Not you, Miss Crewe—they like you." Her voice was serious. "They like you very much really, but they didn't want to be cut with those cutters. They didn't want to be cut at all."

"But I've done it before, often. It's—well, I know it's good for them."

"Not if they don't want it." Deborah's voice became excited. "And they didn't want to be cut, not this time. You know *that*, Miss Crewe. That's why they bit you."

"Debby—" Elizabeth's voice was softly urgent. "You mustn't—"

"She must," Philip said.

Mabel Crewe looked away. She bit her lip uncertainly.

"Philip believes the plants are trying to tell us something," Elizabeth said. She had promised not to fight him. She had promised not to resist. "It sounds strange, I know, but he really does think they're trying to talk to us all."

"They are, they really are." Deborah turned to her father. "I didn't know *you* could hear them too, Daddy."

"I can't."

"But Mummy said—"

"I can't hear them, Debby," Philip said. "But that doesn't matter, not really. But I do believe they've got something to say to us."

"They have, I know it." Deborah's face was bright with excitement. "Miss Crewe knows that too. She talks to them. I've heard her. She talks to her roses all the time."

"Perhaps I do," Mabel Crewe said evasively. She

112

had lived too long alone. "But that's different. Quite different. It's not the same thing."

"It is," Philip said. "Just because you don't *seem* to communicate doesn't mean there's no communication at all." He thought of Michael Martin. Sadness and a sense of frustration moved him. "You really have no right to *assume* they don't understand you," he said.

"Understand me?" Mabel Crewe wondered again how much they knew. "That's—well, that's ridiculous."

Mabel Crewe moved in her chair. She lived alone, she bothered no one, and she had made up her mind. The voices she heard concerned no one else.

"I think they do understand," Philip persisted. "That's why they shocked you."

"But that's impossible."

"Why?"

"Because it is, that's all. Just because it *is*."

Philip Monk walked to the window. "What do you think caused all this?" he asked, looking at the overflowing garden.

"What do you mean?"

"This. This fantastic growth. This weather." Philip's voice was hard. "You don't think it's all an accident, do you?"

"What *are* you talking about?" Mabel Crewe looked at the others. Elizabeth sat huddled. Jacob watched, his eyes round with interest. Only Deborah seemed to understand, but the harshness of her father's voice silenced her. Mabel moved uneasily. "I'm afraid I don't understand at all."

Philip turned to face the older woman. "The plants, the trees, the roses in your garden are all trying to tell us something," he said.

"What on earth"—Mabel shook her head. They'd get nothing from her—"could they tell us?"

"To behave ourselves. To stop putting the whole planet at risk."

"Nonsense." Mabel Crewe dismissed the thought. She wanted to be left alone. She needed time to think. Philip Monk had no right to question her, to intrude. "I'm quite sure of that," she said.

113

The room was quiet for a moment.

"Daddy," Deborah said suddenly. "Have we been bad?"

Philip nodded. "In a way," he said.

"All of us?"

"Well," Philip smiled. "Some more than others."

Elizabeth spoke, taking advantage of the change. "Perhaps we should let Mabel rest a little longer. She looks tired."

"Thank you," Mabel Crewe murmured.

Philip looked at his watch. "I think I'll go down to the police station," he said. "Walters may know what's wrong with the phones." He'd tried to ring Alistair Rank at the BBC, but the phone was dead. "Perhaps he's got a direct line out of here."

"Is there something wrong with the phones?" Mabel asked.

"A line down somewhere, I expect."

"Oh, dear."

"I doubt if it's anything to worry about," Elizabeth said. "It's happened before." She smiled at Mabel. "Why don't you put your feet up for a while? I'll make a cup of tea."

"That's kind of you." Mabel Crewe was grateful. "I would like to rest here a little longer."

"Of course," Elizabeth said. "Stay as long as you like."

"Will she sleep here?" Deborah asked.

"If she'd like to."

"That'll be nice," Deborah said. "We can have lovely long talks together. Can't we, Miss Crewe? Can't we?"

Mabel Crewe smiled uncertainly.

Chapter
Twenty-Four

P.C. Walters did not know that Brandling had been cut off from the rest of the world until Philip Monk appeared at the cottage which served as both dwelling and police station about noon on Saturday.

When Philip Monk knocked on the door, Walters' wife, Anne, let him in. She was a cheerful, round-faced woman, and Philip wondered, fleetingly, how she felt about Charlie Crump lying in the room that was used as the police office.

"Hello," she said, not recognizing him immediately. "Can I help you?"

"I'm—" Philip began.

"Of course," Walters' wife said. "I remember now. I've seen you on the telly. How are you, Mr. Monk?"

"Fine. Is—"

"You want Percy, don't you?" Anne Walters stepped aside. "Come in. He's got someone with him, but I'll see."

She left for a moment and returned with her husband.

Walters was a little uneasy in Philip's company. Their worlds differed, and Walters felt guilty about Michael Martin's phone call.

"Did you get the message?" Walters asked.

Philip nodded.

"I'm sorry about not giving him the number. But —well, you are unlisted."

"What?"

Walters explained. "I'm sorry," he added. "But I didn't think you'd want to be disturbed."

Philip felt sick.

He would never know what Michael Martin had

to say. He saw the tense man bending over the rows of tiny bean sprouts beneath the banks of flashing lights.

He looked at the simple, honest face of P.C. Walters.

"Did you manage to get through to him?" Walters asked.

Philip shook his head.

"I *am* sorry, Mr. Monk. But—"

"He's dead," Philip said roughly. "The man you spoke to is dead."

Walters' face sagged. Nothing would go right this day. "I *am* sorry, Mr. Monk. I never thought of anything like that. I really am."

"How did he sound? The man you spoke to?"

"Well, a bit panicky, really. I, ah, I hope you'll forgive me for saying this, but I thought he might be drunk."

"There'd be no chance of that."

"He *was* a bit . . . strange."

"That's why he rang," Philip said. He looked at the distress on Walters' face. "He did say it was the *beginning?*"

"Something like that, sir. In fact I think his words were: 'It's begun.' "

Philip shook his head sadly.

"Perhaps you'd better come into the office," Walters suggested. "Old Ted Wilkes is with me. He found Charlie this morning."

He led Philip into the office.

Ted Wilkes stood by the window, looking into the sun. The body of Charlie Crump lay covered on a table. Ted turned as Philip came in. They knew each other slightly.

"Prepare to meet thy doom?" Ted said with a twinkle in his eye as he shook Philip's hand. "That why you're here?"

Philip Monk watched the old man uncertainly.

Walters coughed. "Ted's got some idea it's the end of the world," he said apologetically. "It's that religion of his."

116

"Always knew I'd be around for it," Ted said confidently.

Philip nodded, recognizing sanity in Ted's excited eyes. The old man was not as unreal as he sounded.

"I am Alpha and Omega," Ted said, watching Philip. "The beginning and the end."

"That could apply to us all," Philip said.

Ted smiled. "Now why would you say something like that, Mr. Monk?"

"It's true enough, isn't it?"

"Do you believe it's the end of the world?"

"I don't know—yet."

Ted Wilkes chuckled. "I like you, Mr. Monk. You've got a sense of humor."

P.C. Walters coughed. "The fact of the matter, Mr. Monk, is that Ted, here, thinks Charlie's *accident*'s got something to do with them rosebushes of Miss Crewe. We found one of them had bit right into poor Charlie's leg. That's what he fell on, it seems." He shrugged. There was nothing to be gained in not informing Philip Monk. They needed to help each other. "Ted thinks Charlie was frightened by something as well."

"Frightened?"

"Look at his face," Ted Wilkes said quickly. He lifted the cover back. "He's got terror written all over him."

Philip looked. The face of the dead man was visibly distorted.

"Been running too," Ted Wilkes said. He showed Philip the hands. "Scraped to bits, they are."

Philip turned to Walters. "What's been done about this, constable?"

"I, ah, rang Taunton this morning," Walters said. "I spoke to my chief constable. But I don't think he took me all that seriously." He shrugged. "I mean, I don't know what to believe myself."

"What did you tell him?"

"Everything that's happened."

"Would you mind going over it again with me?"

117

P.C. Walters nodded. "Sit down. And I'll tell you what's gone on so far."

He began with Charlie Crump's marrow squash and the man's strange, remote behavior the night of his death. He related how Ted had discovered Charlie's body and how, together, they'd brought it here and examined it.

He paused and looked at Ted Wilkes.

"There's something else as well," Walters said. "Something Ted found this morning. It, well, it seems Charlie Crump did something to that marrow squash of his. Something strange."

"I don't understand."

"He attacked it," Ted said quickly. "Slew it. Hacked it to pieces with an ax. I found it this morning. He must've gone berserk."

"Good God."

"He offended," Ted said, his eyes bright. "And now he's paid for the offense, poor bugger. They've seen to that."

"Who are . . . they?" Philip asked carefully.

"Them." Ted's arm pointed out the window. "The creatures of the field." He walked to the window. "They're sick of it, they are. Sick of being pruned and cut and grafted. All them things we've done to them. Don't live their own lives anymore, do they? Don't have the chance." He shook his head. "Well, they got their chance now, haven't they? The weather's right for them. Their time's come. They're getting their own back for a change. Cutting and pruning some of us."

Philip watched. In the old man's words was Michael Martin's fear, and his own. A simpler fear, surrounded by older beliefs, but very much present.

Philip turned to Walters, seeing the solid, resistant expression on the constable's face.

"It's not as ridiculous as it sounds, constable," Philip said. "In fact, that's what Michael Martin meant when he told you it had begun."

"The man from London, sir?"

"Yes. He's a biologist, a scientist working at the

118

university. He thinks the same way Ted does. He believes the plant kingdom is trying to warn us that if we don't clean up our mess, they will."

P.C. Walters' expression did not alter. There was more in the room than he could accommodate.

"The only thing that surprises me," Philip said, glancing at Ted Wilkes, "is that you've come to the same conclusion."

Ted Wilkes smiled. "Don't be too surprised by that, Mr. Monk. We're close to the earth down here. We've spent our lives growing things, seeing them come up. We know what a power they are."

"Some of us more than others," Walters pointed out.

"He thinks I'm barmy," Ted said. "Most of them do. But, well, they might all change their minds now, mightn't they?"

Philip nodded, liking the old man. "There's something you've not mentioned," he said. "The sound they make. That shaking, rustling sound."

Both men's faces remained blank.

"Is it the leaves rustling?" Walters asked as if talking to a child. "Is that what you mean?"

"No. The leaves don't move at all."

Walters looked even more doubtful.

"It sounds as if the leaves are moving," Philip said. "But they're not. It's like a comment of some sort. A message."

The idea delighted Ted Wilkes. He leaned forward. "You've heard them have you, Mr. Monk?"

"Yes," Philip told him. "When I found Mabel Crewe this morning." Quickly he told them about the old lady. "The sound was all around her," Philip added. "I've never heard anything like it."

"Funny how they pick their spots," Ted mused. "Seems like that place of Mabel Crewe's one of their favorites. It's where I found Charlie, you know."

Philip nodded. A pattern was beginning to form. Charlie Crump's destruction of the marrow squash. Mabel Crewe and her roses. Michael Martin and his tiny rows of bean sprouts. Wherever there

119

was a close enough relationship, there was communication.

He wondered what Deborah was in touch with. There was nothing he knew of. But he sensed that the contact was there just the same.

"All right," Philip asked, "is there anything else?"

Walters shook his head.

Ted Wilkes predicted, "There will be sooner or later." He replaced the sheet over Charlie's body. "This poor bugger's not the last of them."

Philip spoke to Walters. "Do you have a direct line through to Taunton?"

"No, we use the same one as everyone else."

"When did you last make a telephone call?"

"An hour or so ago. When I rang Taunton. Why?"

"My phone's not working, that's why. I tried to get someone at the BBC, but the line was dead."

P.C. Walters picked up the telephone. There was no signal. He joggled the connections once or twice, then he shook his head and handed the receiver to Philip.

"It's the same as mine," Philip said. "We're cut off."

Ted Wilkes laughed. "You've got to hand it to them," he said, impressed and excited. "They think of everything."

"What?" Walters murmured.

"They've cut us off, haven't they? They've got us where they want us." He scratched his head. "They're not as silly as we think."

For a moment no one moved, aware that something seemed to be closing in around them.

"I'll go in to Taunton," P.C. Walters decided. "I'll wait till the morning, just in case the chief constable *does* decide to do something. But if I've not heard from them by then, I'll drive in myself."

Philip nodded.

"I wonder, Mr. Monk, if you'd come along too?" Walters asked. "Be a little more weight, so to speak."

"I'll see," Philip said.

Ted Wilkes looked out the window. "Won't make

no difference what you do," he told them. "Won't make no difference who comes in from outside. What we got here is ours. No one else can do anything. Our salvation lies in the palms of our own hands."

Chapter
Twenty-Five

Late that Saturday afternoon Eric Bolton hitched up his trousers and walked out of the house. Behind him the sewing machine continued to hum.

He'd not said anything more to Edith. He'd show her he was no fool. He'd prove it. It'd take more than barmy old Ted Wilkes and that copper Percy Walters to keep him out of things.

He walked down the Brandling High Street, the sun a low orange ball in the sky before him. He sneezed twice, wiped his nose with two fingers, and spat into the roadway.

It'd take more than them to fool him. He'd find out for himself what was going on at Charlie Crump's place.

When Eric Bolton arrived at Crump's cottage he stood for a moment on the far side of the road surveying the single-storied stone building on the end of the row.

Charlie and his mother had shared it until the old lady died. Then Charlie had lived there alone, going home to it nightly, drunk on rough cider, to fall into bed and drown his lonely thoughts.

Probably got something hid there, Eric Bolton thought. Whatever Charlie was, he wasn't as silly as he appeared.

If there was anything there he, Eric Bolton, would find it.

It was dim inside the house. The light bulb in the hall was burned out. Eric groped his way to Charlie's bedroom, went in, and stopped. Already the room had an unused, musty smell.

Eric Bolton turned the thin mattress, seeking he

knew not what. Beneath the mattress the sagging wire lay empty. Eric let the mattress fall back and, instinctively, wiped his fingers on his trousers.

He searched the room thoroughly, but it was pitifully bare. A dirty shirt hung behind the door. A soiled suit hung in a cupboard. There were socks and underpants and a pair of shoes, but nothing which indicated more than habitation by a single man, lonely and without direction.

There was no bathroom in the house.

In the other room, which had been Mrs. Crump's bedroom, a tin bath stood in the middle of the floor. It was half full of dirty brown water. Soap scum floated on the surface.

There was nothing of value in that room either.

Nor did the kitchen contain anything Eric Bolton wanted. The collection of dirty plates and pans was beginning to smell. As Eric entered, a rat, bent over the frying pan, lifted his head and looked at him, its small red eyes bright in the darkening room. As Eric approached, it scampered away.

Charlie didn't have much, poor bugger, Eric thought.

It wasn't until Eric went outside that he felt his search might prove to be justified. Because it was there, behind the truck, that he found the patch of turned earth beneath which Ted Wilkes had buried the remains of the marrow squash.

The earth was damp, still fresh, but already green shoots were beginning to show in the newly turned ground.

Eric Bolton moved forward to peer at the earth, greed and excitement moving in him.

The cunning sod, he thought, he had it buried out the back.

Eric Bolton stood looking down at the earth. He reached forward to tap it with his foot. Then he turned and went toward the shed at the bottom of the garden. There'd be a spade there. He'd find out just what it was Charlie Crump had hidden.

Inside the shed it was darker. Deep, heavy shadows filled the corners. A little light gleamed from the blade of the ax Ted Wilkes had cleaned and replaced. Eric Bolton's eyes searched for a spade.

He moved forward, groping, surprised how overgrown the inside of the shed was. Tendrils had forced their way in through cracks in the woodwork. New pale shoots were visible. One corner seemed totally overgrown.

Can't have used it much, Eric Bolton thought.

He saw the spade on the far wall of the shed and reached for it. As his hand grasped it he noticed a slender green tendril had wound itself tightly around the handle of the spade, binding it to the wall.

Eric Bolton took the handle of the spade and stopped, unable to remove it from its place against the wall.

He peered into the dim light, looking for something apart from the tendril which might be holding the spade in place, but there was nothing he could see.

He tugged again and this time the spade moved a little. But as it did the tendril seemed to take another turn about the handle of the spade, binding it more firmly.

Eric Bolton blinked, not believing what he had seen. He thought it was some trick of the light, an illusion. He grunted and was about to heave on the handle again when something moved. Out of the dim translucent corner of the shed a pale green arm reached gently, slowly, toward him, its whitish-green fingers seeking his throat.

Eric Bolton released the spade and stepped back to watch the arm, recognizing it as a new green shoot. But the recognition of what it was did not lessen his fear.

Instinctively he put his hand to his throat, his eyes flickering from the green shoot to the tendril binding the handle of the spade. He became aware now of the other growth; shoots, tendrils, slender leaves, all turning toward him, reaching, grasping, seeking to imprison.

124

Then he heard the sound.

It rustled around him like dead leaves shaking.

Eric Bolton placed his hands over his ears. The sound was inside his head, whispering, driving him to turn and pitch forward, running toward the arm, the shoot, the thing that reached for him from the corner, forcing him to flee.

He had never known anything like it.

He fell through the door of the shed, past the things which groped, into the fading, evening light.

Then, just as he thought he was clear, just as he'd begun to think he had escaped, he ran into the face of a sunflower.

He never knew where it came from.

As he lurched through the door it seemed to bend, swoop, glide gently down until its round yellow and black face was directly in front of his own.

For a moment it overpowered him.

It clung to his face, a huge immovable shape blotting out light and distance, direction and future. He tore the sunflower aside and ran in terror. In his ears was the sound of rustling. On his flesh he could feel the shape of the sunflower. He ran homeward, his heavy body hurtling through the dusk, his mind blank with fear.

As he neared home he slowed, gasping, peering over his shoulder to see what lay behind.

But there was nothing.

A villager stood watching him, but that was all. The street behind was empty. The rustling sound had vanished.

Eric Bolton stood on a corner and waited until his breath returned and the beating of his heart steadied. He stood for a long time until the bulk of the fear left him. What remained was its memory, its core. He would never forget as long as he lived that first sight of the pale green arm seeking his throat in the dim light, or the menacing sound.

After a while he went home and entered the house quietly.

"Is that you?" his wife called.

125

Eric Bolton muttered.

"You been out?" Edith called. "Is that right? You been out?" She listened for a moment and then continued. "Not like you to miss your afternoon kip. Where you been?"

"Walking," Eric answered, his voice unsteady. "I, ah, went for a walk."

Edith laughed. "Walking?" Her voice was incisive. "You'll be taking up golf next."

Eric Bolton did not reply.

He moved as far from his wife as he could and sat, frightened, confused, unnerved, waiting for The Bunch of Grapes to open.

He needed a drink badly.

A report came through late that Saturday evening to the P.O. Telephone Engineer's Branch in Taunton that the line to Brandling was unserviceable.

There were only two men on duty and there was little they could do until after the weekend.

"Any idea what caused it?" one asked the other.

"No, they just say they can't get through."

"Line down or something?"

"That's what usually happens."

"Wouldn't have thought anyone was worried myself," the engineer who'd received the call commented. "Nothing to talk about down there, is there?"

"You'd be surprised what goes on in a place like that," the other replied. "Open your eyes, they would, some of them villages."

"Wife swapping? Things like that?"

"Streaking, I shouldn't be surprised."

"Thought it was all muck-spreading down there."

"Same thing."

Both men laughed.

"Cut it off themselves then, more than likely."

"What you mean, you rotten sod?" the other engineer said. "Ruin your social life a thing like that."

The engineers laughed again.

"I'll put it down anyway," the first engineer decided. "The truck can make a trip that way Monday."

"Or the next day."

"Well, we'll see how busy they are, won't we?" the first engineer asked. "Like a cup of tea?"

"Might as well," his colleague replied. "Nothing else to do, is there?"

Chapter
Twenty-Six

At about the same time the telephone engineers were discussing Brandling, Harry Reynolds, keeper of parks and gardens in Taunton, also had the village in mind.

He was feeling better. The hangover which had crippled him for the early part of the day had nearly disappeared. Now he sat in the late-afternoon sun sipping a cup of weak black tea, thinking of what Chief Constable Parkhurst had told him.

He's out of his bloody mind, of course, he thought. Been far too long in the tropics. What's he think I am, a witchdoctor or something?

He sipped his tea and looked at his garden.

It was a little overgrown in spite of the fact he kept one of the department men at it full time.

I'd put the lot down in concrete if I had any sense, he thought. That and plastic gnomes.

He sat a while longer and then his wife came out and joined him. "How do you feel now?" She smiled, noting his recovery.

"A little less as if I'd been gangbanged by rattle-snakes," he told her.

"It was the whiskey," she said. "It always does that to you. I don't know why you do it."

"I'm weak."

"Nonsense."

Reynolds laughed. "Try me."

"What did old what's-his-name want?" Reynolds' wife asked after a while.

"Who?"

"Parkhurst? The chief constable."

"Well"—Reynolds shook his head—"he thinks the

128

country's about to be overtaken by flora. Have you ever heard anything like it?"

"Flora who?"

"Florabunda." Reynolds' head went back and he laughed again. Then he stopped, gently holding his head, regretting the outburst. "Florabunda, the rose," he added in a quieter voice. "We're all about to be murdered in our beds by old ladies' companions."

"Are you serious?"

"I'm not but he is."

"You're joking."

"I'll swear it," Reynolds said. "He wants me to go down to Brandling as soon as I can and investigate."

"I don't believe it."

"Nor do I, but I'll have to go. He'll call out the militia if I don't."

"Come on."

"It's true," Reynolds said. "As I sit here, it's true."

He told his wife of the chief constable's telephone call, of the man's hesitancy but final determination that an investigation be made. Perhaps, he said, it wouldn't have been so important had Charlie Crump not died, but with a corpse in Brandling someone had to go down.

"And that someone's me," Reynolds added.

"Why don't they send a detective?"

"That's what I am for the trip."

Moira Reynolds thought a moment. "Is there any chance he could have been poisoned?"

"By a rosebush?" Reynolds shook his head. "Anyway, I asked that myself."

"I don't understand it," his wife said. "I always thought that old what's-his-name was pretty sound."

"He was about as sound as a cracked bell when I spoke to him."

"Poor old thing."

"He'll get no sympathy from me."

"Not him, *you*," Reynolds' wife said. "Off on a wild-goose chase like that."

"Wild geese I can handle," Reynolds said. "It's wild *flora* I'm worried about."

Mrs. Reynolds watched her husband carefully. She knew him too well not to sense concern beneath the layer of cynicism.

"Are you really worried?" she asked.

"Don't be daft."

"Then why are you picking at your fingernails?"

Reynolds smiled, then he looked at his fingers. He'd picked at the quick of his thumb, and it was beginning to bleed.

"*Why* are you worried?" Moira Reynolds persisted.

"I'm not really," her husband said, his voice changing, some of the banter missing. "But—Well, as you say, old Parkhurst's not really an idiot, although half the time he acts like one. And the local copper down there's levelheaded enough." He shrugged. "If they're concerned I suppose they've got *some* reason to be. Otherwise there'd be no fuss—would there?"

"So you think there is . . . something?"

"I don't know what to think. All I know is that tomorrow I'll go down and have a look around." He leaned back in his chair and looked at the pale-blue evening sky. High, an invisible aircraft left twin white vapor trails, etching its way across the surface.

Reynolds sighed. "It's a funny part of the world," he said idly. "With Glastonbury just around the corner and that rich, red earth underfoot." He smiled. "I wouldn't be surprised what went on—witches, warlocks, or man-eating florabunda."

"At least you've stopped picking your nails," his wife pointed out gently.

"So I have." Reynolds stood and stretched. "I almost feel fit enough to face another drink. Join me?"

His wife smiled and together they went into the house.

Chapter
Twenty-Seven

As Harry Reynolds poured his wife a drink, Philip stood in his garden and heard a small rustling sound. He paused to listen, then turned to a cage in the corner of the garden and saw a guinea pig pushing at hay, the source of the sound.

Philip sighed and walked slowly toward the cage, squatting before the small animal.

"Hello," he said. "You must be the new one."

The guinea pig sniffed in his direction.

"None of this makes much difference to you," Philip said lightly. "You'll just go on eating whatever happens."

The guinea pig made a small squeaking sound.

Philip smiled. Slowly he reached out and undid the clasp on the side of the cage and lifted the hinged front. The guinea pig came to the edge of the cage and looked out into the sunlight.

Philip reached for the animal.

As he did so he heard the sound of feet on the grass behind him and half turned to see Deborah running toward him so quickly that he had no time to do anything else but watch as she reached in and plucked the guinea pig from the mouth of its cage.

"What—" Philip began.

"You mustn't touch him!"

"I was only going to give him a pat."

"No."

"But—"

"You mustn't touch him."

"Not at all?"

131

"No, you mustn't," Deborah repeated. "You'll spoil it."

Philip felt a moment of panic. The child was so positive, her young voice firm, cutting.

Deborah picked up the guinea pig, holding its small body close. "I can't let anyone else have him. Not now. Not just yet, anyway."

"Why can't I have him now?"

"He's not ready yet."

"Debby—" Philip reached gently for his daughter but she drew away, taking the guinea pig with her. "I'm not—"

"You don't understand." Deborah's voice rose. Color spread from her throat. "No one understands, really. Well, hardly anyone. But we've got to wait. All of us. Until it's the right time."

"Time for what, Debby?"

"Time to—" Deborah faltered, unable to find words to explain. "We must just wait until it's time to . . . listen again," she said finally.

"Listen?"

"Yes, listen." Deborah's voice revealed a touch of anger. "You know what I mean, Daddy. We've all got to listen. You know that as well as I do."

"But how does that affect him?"

Deborah's eyes moved. She looked down at the guinea pig. The animal's nostrils twitched.

"How does it?" Philip insisted.

Deborah shook her head. "I don't know—yet," she said evasively.

"What?"

"What we've got to do." Deborah shook her head vigorously. "What everyone's got to do." She looked at her father painfully. "We've all got to do something, Daddy. Even him. We've all got to . . . help. But I don't know what it is yet, really I don't. I'd tell you if I did, but I don't. So we've just all got to wait."

"Debby—" Philip spread his hands.

"No!" Deborah shouted the word and turned. "No, Daddy, you must wait. Please leave me alone."

Deborah ran, carrying the guinea pig with her.

Philip remained on the grass, chilled by the tone of his daughter's voice, frightened by her eyes.

He rose slowly, aware of a lack of warmth in the sun.

Chapter
Twenty-Eight

When The Bunch of Grapes opened that Saturday evening Eric Bolton was one of the first to enter. He walked into the sweet, beer-smelling establishment and straight to the bar.

"You're early," the barman said, reaching for a pint mug. "Bitter?"

Eric nodded. "And I'll have a rum on the side."

"Your birthday or something?"

Eric shrugged as he placed his heavy hands on the bar.

"Hear anything more about poor old Charlie?" the barman asked, eyeing the head on the beer.

"You want to ask Ted Wilkes about that," Eric said. "He's the one what found him."

The barman nodded. "So I heard." He placed the pint of bitter on the bar and turned to dispense the rum. "Shook him up something awful, they say."

Eric lifted the pint and sucked in the beer. When he took the mug away there was froth on his upper lip. "He's always been a bit barmy," he said evasively, wiping his lips with the back of his hand. "Got it from that mother of his."

"A hundred and three when she died," the barman reminisced, putting the rum down on the bar. "Read the Bible every day of her life, right up to the end." He grinned. "No wonder Ted thinks it's the end of the world."

"What'd you say?" Eric Bolton stopped.

"That's what I heard," the barman said easily. "Old Ted's been going round telling everyone to get ready for the end." He shook his head. "What was his mother, Baptist or something?"

"He's been putting it about, that it's the end of the world?"

"Suit me if it was." The barman's voice was cheerful. "Specially round closing time."

"What you mean?" Eric's voice was uncertain. "You don't think—"

"Course I don't," the barman said, pleased with his joke. "Unless you take Ted's word for it." His face sobered. "Mind you, finding poor old Charlie like that can't have been much fun."

Eric picked up his rum, his hand shaking.

"You all right?" the barman asked.

"Yes." Eric drank the rum neat. "It's—well, Charlie wasn't no special friend of mine. But it does make you think."

The barman agreed. Two more customers came in and he turned to serve them.

Eric stood alone, brooding, touched by fear.

Soon he was joined by Fred Clarke, a short, bald man whose cabbages had been one of the wonders of Brandling that summer. Enormous, they had been precursors to Charlie Crump's marrow squash.

Fred Clarke ordered a drink and then, a smile on his face, reached out and tapped Eric Bolton's stomach. "Getting rid of it at last, I see," he said. His voice was easy and slow.

Eric looked down at his belly. "What you mean?"

"Saw you running this afternoon," Fred Clarke said. "Thought to myself, he's taken up exercise, and wondered if I shouldn't do the same."

Eric Bolton gave a short laugh. Nothing was hidden in Brandling, nothing remained unknown. "Wouldn't do you any harm," he said, looking at Fred Clarke's portly figure.

"Mind you," Fred went on shrewdly, "I did think as well, that's a funny time to be going for a run, like. Usually do that sort of thing in the morning."

"Well—" Eric lifted his pint and buried his face in it. He drank, then wiped his lips. "Just thought I'd have a go."

"You *was* exercising?"

135

Eric nodded. "No other reason I'd be running through the village, is there?"

"None at all," Fred Clarke said carefully. "None I can think of, that is."

"I'll let you know in advance next time," Eric promised, "so's you can come along."

He had his pint refilled, ordered another rum, then went to sit alone at a table in the corner of the bar. Amid horse brasses and leather, copper trays, and a two-headed lamb mounted on walnut, he appeared uneasy and morose.

After a while Ted Wilkes came into The Bunch of Grapes, followed shortly after by P.C. Walters. Both carried pints of bitter to the table in the corner. Ted Wilkes sat in his seat by the fireplace and they talked quietly, their heads together, involved.

When he emptied his pint mug, Eric Bolton returned to the bar and had it filled. Then he turned, nodded at Ted Wilkes and Walters, and joined them at the long table.

"Evening," Eric said, and sat down.

Walters returned the greeting. "Evening, Eric."

Ted Wilkes smiled. "Got your house in order then? Counted the oxen and the sheep?"

Eric glanced at P.C. Walters, sipping his beer, and wished Ted were more discreet. It'd do no good stirring it up like this.

"Should've brought the wife," Ted said. "Got her a drink. One for the road, you might say."

"Get off my back," Eric said roughly. "And stop talking in them riddles of yours."

"Me?"

"Yes, you." Eric felt anger in his stomach. Ted was laughing at him. Fred Clarke had laughed at him. Even down there, at Charlie's place, they'd laughed. He could see that now. Alcohol brought him clarity. "You know what I mean," he said to Ted Wilkes. "You bloody know."

"Now, just a minute, Eric," P.C. Walters said easily. "Just tell us quietly what's on your mind." He wondered what Eric knew. What worried Walters was that there might be panic. If all of Brandling became alarmed he would not be able to control it. "What was it you wanted to know?" he asked.

Eric's eyes became cunning. "I'm not daft, you know. There's something happening here."

Ted Wilkes winked and tapped the side of his nose.

P.C. Walters didn't move.

"Something to do with Charlie Crump," Eric said. "You can't fool me. I'm onto it."

"Are you now?"

"You bet your bloody life I am." Eric's little eyes went from Walters to Ted and back again. "You can't fool me. Not bloody me."

"You got the word too, Eric?" Ted Wilkes asked in his unhurried voice. "You one of the lambs then?"

"Don't try that," Eric said quickly. "Don't give me none of that religious bullshit." He turned to P.C. Walters. "It's a trick, isn't it? To keep us away from what's going on." He leaned back, his eyes shrewd. "Had me going for a bit, it did. I don't mind admitting it gave me a scare."

"What was that, Eric?" Walters asked.

"Them sounds. That movement." Eric nodded, wanting to join in. "Bloody good, I'll give you that."

"What sounds?"

"Them, down there. You know."

"Where?"

"At Charlie's place, for Christ's sake!" Eric's voice rose. "You can't fool me, Percy. I been there, I've been down. *I heard them myself.*"

P.C. Walters put his hands on the table very carefully. "You say you've been down to Charlie Crump's?"

"Course I been down."

"And you heard—what's it you heard, Eric?"

"Them sounds, that rustling—that device you got down there to keep people away." Eric watched Walters and felt pleased with himself. He'd made it. He'd really broken through. "That had me going for a bit, I don't mind telling you. That had me fooled."

"You *visited?*" Ted Wilkes asked. He saw the mashed remains of the marrow squash and the

137

ground he'd turned to bury it, feeling again the mystery and the despair of the place. "You trod on that ground?"

Eric nodded. "There's something buried there as well."

"What?"

"I don't know." Eric looked away. "Like I say, the sounds and all that gave me a turn. I didn't hang about."

P.C. Walters glanced at the bar. No one seemed to have noticed. He looked at Eric's greedy face and wondered what he could do.

Eric stared back and gave a small conspiratorial nod. "Well?" he asked. "You going to let me in on it?"

Walters nodded also. "Well, Eric," he began slowly, taking a chance. "Seeing as how you've been down there, and you know, I don't suppose there's any real harm in telling you. . . ."

Eric leaned in hungrily.

Ted Wilkes watched P.C. Walters, a curious expression on his face.

"There's just one thing," Walters said, in the same controlled tone, his face impassive. "One little hitch, you might say."

"What's that?"

"Well, I ought to clear it first," Walters said, hoping Eric would believe him, "with Taunton. I'll be up there tomorrow and I'll tell them you're onto it. But I'd better clear it with them before I give you the full story."

Eric's face altered. They were putting him off. They'd do him out of it if they got the chance. But before he had the opportunity to speak P.C. Walters continued.

"But I'll tell you this much," Walters said. "It's—well, it's a bit dangerous like." He cleared his throat and looked around. "You know that there atomic station down on the coast?"

"Hinkley Point?"

"That's it."

"What about it?"

"Well now, that's what I can't tell you," Walters

said. "Not until I clear it tomorrow like. Not till I get the word."

Eric Bolton paused, the greed and caution still apparent in his face.

"You know what I mean, Eric?" Walters said carefully. "Things like that—well, they got to be cleared. It could be dangerous."

Eric Bolton took a deep breath. There was too much he didn't know. There was too much hidden. There *was* danger. He could taste it. He heard the sounds and felt his fear leap. He nodded slowly, admitting nothing.

"Yes . . . well . . ." he said. "If it's like that, then. . . ."

"It is."

Eric Bolton pointed a finger at Ted Wilkes. "What's he know about it?" he asked P.C. Walters.

"No more than you do."

"Is that the truth?"

"That's the truth, Eric," Ted Wilkes admired the way Walters handled Eric's greed. It was there. It was even whetted; but restrained by fear, held by something unknown. "I don't know any more facts than you."

"What you keep on talking about the end of the world for then?" Eric asked quickly.

Ted Wilkes smiled a wicked smile. "You know me, Eric," he said gently. "I'm just a silly old bugger."

Eric wet his lips. "When you say you were going to Taunton?" he asked P.C. Walters.

"Tomorrow," Walters replied with relief. "Be back sometime in the late morning."

"Well, we'll leave it until then."

"That's the stuff, Eric."

"Mind you, I won't wait any longer than that," Eric Bolton warned. "Come tomorrow I'll want to know what's going on."

"Course," Walters replied. "I know how you feel."

Eric Bolton nodded, picked up his pint mug, and found it was empty. He stood and gestured toward the bar. "I'm having another," he said. "Want one?"

Both P.C. Walters and Ted Wilkes shook their heads.

"Suit yourselves," Eric said and went to the bar.

As soon as his back was turned Ted Wilkes said to Walters. "He's heard them. The sound Mr. Monk spoke of."

"I know," Walters agreed.

Ted Wilkes nodded. There was a fear in Walters' face he'd not seen before, an awareness of a new danger.

Walters watched Eric Bolton's figure at the bar. "We'll just have to wait. I don't know what happened to him, I don't know what he's on about, but they've scared him too."

Ted Wilkes nodded. Walters was right. He watched the shape of Eric Bolton at the bar, wondering who would be next.

Chapter
Twenty-Nine

That Saturday night, with the late light softening the edges of the sky, Philip Monk made love to his wife for the first time in several weeks.

They had gone to the bedroom together, up the stairs to the beds which stood apart.

The house was quiet. Both children slept. Below, Mabel Crewe lay on the settee.

"You might think me a silly old woman," she'd said to Elizabeth when they were alone. "But I'm most grateful to you for, well, being patient with me."

"I understand," Elizabeth replied.

"Do you?"

"Yes. I think I do."

Mabel Crewe smiled and touched Elizabeth's arm. "I hope you do, my child. I hope you do."

When she and Philip went upstairs Elizabeth undressed first.

It had become her habit on those occasions when they were together to undress alone in the bathroom. She did not quite know why she did this, only that it seemed appropriate.

She put on her nightdress and came back into the bedroom to find Philip, still dressed, sitting on the side of his bed.

When he saw her he said, "Take it off," his voice strangely gentle.

"What?" Elizabeth asked, a little embarrassed.

"Your nightdress."

Elizabeth put a hand to her breast like a shield. "I'd rather—" she began.

"Please."

Elizabeth hesitated.

Philip stood and went to her. He reached forward gently and put his hands on her shoulders. Looking into her eyes, he saw wariness and caution and something, somewhere he recognized as hope.

"Please," he repeated. "It's important."

"To take my nightdress off?"

"Yes."

"Why?"

"Because we must stop hiding from each other."

Elizabeth felt her lips tremble.

"We hide all the time," Philip said.

Elizabeth nodded.

"We grow up," Philip went on. "We're educated. We go to work and we die." His voice was gentle, his eyes sad. "And for very little of our lifetimes are we really and truly honest. Or do things that we honestly enjoy, or even want. We hide from each other, Liz. We hide from each other all the time."

"Yes," Elizabeth agreed, her words whispered. "I know."

"We live our lives in the way we think other people want us to," said Philip. "Or, what's even worse, in the way we *think* they think we ought to. It's crazy but it happens all the time."

"Philip?"

Philip held his wife's shoulders. "We're not people anymore, Liz. We've become symbols, ciphers, programmed responses. Doing what we think we ought to. We're all the same. Even those who think they're rebelling follow the rules someone else's laid down. It's awful, Liz. Do you know that? It's awful."

"I know, but—"

"—you don't know how to avoid it?"

Elizabeth nodded.

"I'm not sure I do," Philip said. "But I'm going to try."

"You've changed," Elizabeth whispered.

"I know. I'm as bad as anyone. At least that's something I've learned."

Elizabeth smiled a small, hopeful smile. "Have you learned anything about us?" she asked.

"Yes."

142

"When?"

"When you said you'd stop fighting me."

"Was that so important?"

"Yes, you gave me something."

"I know it's selfish," Elizabeth confessed, "but I can't help thinking about *us*. In spite of everything—all that's happened."

"It's not selfish."

"We—all of us—are all I've got."

"I know."

Elizabeth bent her head until her forehead touched her husband's. Her hair fell about her face. "I'm frightened, Philip. I'm afraid of losing it." Her mood was delicate, sad, fragile.

"I'm afraid too. So afraid I've got to do something about it."

"You *have* changed. You'd never have admitted that before."

Philip's hand moved and the nightdress fell away from her shoulders. Philip slipped it down over her breasts and let it fall to the floor.

The room was very still.

Elizabeth waited, feeling shy again, youthful in a way she had almost forgotten.

They moved closer. Elizabeth's forehead against Philip's, her hair covering his face.

Without moving from her, without leaving, Philip undressed himself. He took off his shirt and his trousers, everything he wore, removing each garment slowly, deliberately.

Elizabeth, her head against his, watched. Looking down, she saw him in a way she had not seen in a long time. Seeing the line of him, running down; the extension of him.

Then Philip picked his wife up, carried her to a bed, placed her on it, then lay down beside her.

Elizabeth held him. "You've never done that before."

"There are too many things I've not done before."

"Will you do them now?"

"Yes," Philip said. "All of them."

"Now?"

"Yes."

The night became long and a total journey.

They were suddenly youthful, fresh, demanding, giving, innocent, exploring each other in new ways, tasting, sensing.

The light in which they lay was pink and golden, soft and endless; it covered them.

Elizabeth found a voice she had not known she possessed.

At times it rose and shouted; at times it whispered and sung. Once, when she was carried, there was a lustiness in her tongue she would not have thought possible.

Then they lay, loosely, holding each other, a little apart but together.

Philip touched Elizabeth. "What a surprise you are," he told her softly.

"Am I?"

"Who would have thought all that went on inside you."

"I didn't know myself."

"Isn't it appalling?"

"What?"

"How little we know."

"I know *you* better now," Elizabeth admitted.

"That's the sad part—*only now*. We've been as close as most people in the world, closer than most. Sleeping together, breathing together, being intimate in spite of the time we've spent apart. And all the time we've worn a veil."

"I know," Elizabeth said. "I've regretted it too."

"We've never been naked with each other before."

"I know that too—I've wanted to," Elizabeth confessed softly. "But I've never been able to."

"Are you able now?"

"Yes. I'm able . . . now." She paused. "Will it last?" she asked after a while.

"Yes."

"It's not just that we're frightened or desperate?"

"That's part of it." Philip touched her. "But now we've found each other like this, it'll last."

"I hope so."

"I'm sure of it."

Elizabeth held his face. "I love you, Philip. I love you so very much."

"It's a long time since you've said that," Philip murmured. "It's a long time since I said it also. I do love you, Liz, really."

They lay together, touching, relearning. Outside the final light dimmed and rain began to fall.

Later Elizabeth asked, "What are we going to do?"

Philip kissed her lightly. "I'm going to make love to you again."

"Yes . . . please . . ." Elizabeth said. "But I don't mean now."

"When?"

"Later, in the morning. When we've got to face it again."

Philip touched her. "Whatever we have to face will be easier now," he said.

"I know. But—"

"You worry about it?"

"Yes," Elizabeth said. "Yes, I do. There's more to lose now."

Philip nodded. "There's also more to gain." He gripped his wife and held her. "Don't ever lose sight of that, Liz. Don't ever forget that."

"Do you think I could?" Elizabeth kissed him. "Whatever happens, whatever we have to do, tonight will remain." She tightened her arms about him. "Now—make love to me again," she commanded happily.

Chapter
Thirty

Eric Bolton woke up sweating.

Sweat matted him and he felt cold in the night air. He lay, not knowing what sound or movement had wakened him, aware only of his own penetrating fear.

Beside him Edith snored loudly in the bed. She lay on her back and her cheeks shook with her snoring.

Eric Bolton considered waking her. He wanted something to hold, someone to whisper to, but he could not. She would sneer, she would deride.

He lay, sweat rolling in little cold streams down his body, and waited.

Then he heard the noise.

It was a low, grating noise, harsh and grinding, reminding Eric of fingers scraping across a blackboard at school. He shivered.

Slowly, steadily, the noise was repeated.

Eric Bolton was suddenly too afraid to remain inactive. Fear urged him to move slowly from the bed and stand trembling in the darkness. He held his hands together before him like a supplicant, waiting to be further impelled.

Edith turned over when Eric moved. Her snoring ceased.

"Whaa . . ." she mumbled sleepily.

Eric Bolton was unable to reply.

His wife moved again and resumed her snoring.

Eric waited and then he heard the low, grating noise again. It came from the back of the house.

Slowly, automatically, aware only of his isolation and the need to respond, Eric Bolton began to move toward the sound. It was hyponotic; it drew him; he was powerless to avoid it.

He stood in the hallway, feeling the clamminess of his body and the fine wires of terror which held him together. There was nothing in his mind but tension and the certainty that he had to follow the sound.

He walked down the hallway to the kitchen and stopped again.

The sound had ceased.

The house was suddenly still and empty. Outside a gentle rain fell. Inside the air was heavy. Eric Bolton listened, wondering if he had imagined the sound, knowing that he had not.

He opened his mouth and made a dry, clacking sound, then moved his feet. They felt numb on the linoleum floor.

He turned uncertainly to look in the direction of the bedroom and then he heard the sound again, this time from the kitchen. It was suddenly loud, gnawing at him.

Eric Bolton held his hands together and for a moment his fear was so oppressive he thought he would void himself. His stomach turned and rocked as he waited, breathing as little as he could, trying not to bolt and run.

In the corner of his mind there was a green arm moving, a thin rustling sound. He saw himself lurch and turn and run from Charlie Crump's shed in primitive fear, as he relived yesterday.

The sound grated again.

Eric Bolton turned toward it. This was not the same sound as yesterday, neither as sudden nor as unexpected. He put his hand on the kitchen door and quietly turned the handle.

The noise paused, then resumed, louder.

Eric Bolton felt for the kitchen light, and just before he turned it on, in that moment between terror and the inability to resist seeking, he wondered if he would be able to control what the kitchen contained.

Then he switched on the light.

On the kitchen table, gnawing the bone of the chop he had eaten earlier in the day, was an old, scruffy, tortoiseshell cat. Its teeth scraped on the bone, making a dry, grating sound. Its eyes, in the light, were round with fear.

As soon as it saw Eric Bolton the cat began to move.

Eric moved also.

In anger, in outrage, in relief, he reached for the nearest object and threw it at the cat. It was a teapot and it struck the cat on its back and knocked it to the floor.

The cat cried out in fear and pain and leaped again.

Eric Bolton reached for it and for a moment caught it, but the cat, even as it was caught, turned and scratched Eric Bolton's forearm, leaving three long clawmarks in the flesh which immediately began to bleed.

Eric lashed after the cat, but it was gone. It sprang through the window and into the night rain, raced a few yards, and then, hearing no pursuit, stopped and looked behind. After a moment it slowly limped away.

In the kitchen Eric Bolton examined his arm.

He swore as he wrapped a tea towel around the bleeding, picked up the teapot, and replaced it, feeling a small wave of relief that it had not broken. He looked at the tea leaves spilled on the floor and slowly wiped them up.

As his fear left him it was replaced with a simmering anger.

Bloody cat, he thought. Bloody mangy cat.

He looked at the scratches on his arm. He should've known what it was from the beginning.

He stopped suddenly and a small, knowing grin appeared on his heavy face. It was probably the same last night, down at Charlie Crump's. Probably some simple explanation for all that too, if only he'd stayed and had a good look. Probably nothing to be scared of at all.

He was glad now that the cat had frightened him.

By pursuing it he had seen how meaningless his fear was, how simple the explanation had been.

Then his grin broadened.

"I'll be—" he said aloud and shook his head in admiration.

He was sure now why the arm had moved in the gathering green and why the thin, soft, rustling voices had whispered. It *was* a device to frighten. It *had* been planted by Ted Wilkes or Percy Walters or whoever it was who had something to hide. When he had confronted them earlier in the evening he had only been guessing. But now he was sure. It was a sort of scarecrow, and he admired its installation.

Well, they wouldn't fool him. He was smarter than that. It didn't matter what they got up to, he'd see through it. It'd take more than them to get the better of him. Whatever it was they had down there he was going to get his share. They'd have to do better than a scarecrow to cut him out.

Eric Bolton wiped his arm again and switched off the kitchen light.

Then he went back to the bedroom and climbed into bed.

Edith grunted and turned over.

Eric lay listening to the silent night. He smiled, secured by his knowledge. Percy Walters better have a good story when he returned from Taunton. After a time Eric drifted to sleep, happy now, contented, confident in the cocoon of his greed.

Chapter
Thirty-One

Ted Wilkes woke on Sunday morning cheerful and alert, at his usual time, just after five. He dressed, went to the kennel, and released his dog, William, who was waiting for him. He licked Ted's hand then urinated in a corner of the garden.

"Another day, William," Ted pointed out. "Another morning."

At eighty, Ted Wilkes felt each day measured another small victory against time. He savored time, knowing that however long he remained active there was relatively little of it left.

He lifted his eyes to study the early sky. It was pinker this morning, more tinted. There was something about the color of it which made Ted look at it carefully. He sniffed the air, suddenly aware that there was a difference about the day. Something special. He could read it in the sky.

Ted Wilkes smiled. The morning was young, still clear. Later, the haze would spread, shimmering the valley. But now a layer of freshness hung over Brandling. And there was a difference in the air.

Ted Wilkes watched a falcon hover overhead.

He felt that somehow his life had altered.

He did not know where the knowledge had come from, he was only aware that change was all about him.

"Today's the day, William," he said. "That's what they said, the sun became black as sackcloth and the moon became as blood." He looked at the pink sky. "That's the blood sun, William. It's the sign we've been waiting for."

William sat, looking up, eager to be off.

150

"Don't make no difference to you, does it, dog?" Ted Wilkes rubbed William's ears. "Beginning of the world or the end of it, you still want your walk."

William wagged his tail and together they set off.

The night before, in The Bunch of Grapes, after Walters had told Eric Bolton of his intention to drive to Taunton, Ted had said, "There's nothing Taunton can do for us. What we got to do down here we got to do ourselves."

Walters shrugged. "I only told Eric that to keep him quiet."

"But you're off to Taunton just the same?"

Walters nodded.

"Won't get no help there."

"What you suggest I do then?" Walters asked, his concern strong. "You got any bright ideas?"

Ted Wilkes shook his head. "I got no real ideas. If it's written, it's written. If it comes to pass—well, now, that's another matter."

"You don't believe that stuff."

"I do and I don't," Ted wavered. "All I'm sure of is that it's up to us, down here. No one from outside's going to do us any good."

Walters sat back, his honest face worried. "You think there's anything in what Mr. Monk says?" he asked. "I mean all that stuff about mankind, all that?"

"Yes and no."

"What you mean, yes or no?"

"I was down the coast some weeks back," Ted Wilkes said, his old voice calm. "I was walking along the shingle, me and William, and I came across a penguin, one of them little fellers, covered with oil slick." Ted Wilkes shook his head. "Poor little bugger couldn't move hardly. Nearly dead it was. Stuck together with bloody oil, thick with it." He sighed. "I thought to myself then, what a lot of muck we make. What a lot of trouble we make. Just being untidy. Just by making a mess." He looked at Walters. "So that feller Monk might have something. All them creatures of the fields, all them plants and things, got a right to live, you know. They got the same right we have.

So if they're sick of it and if they're letting us know, then it don't surprise me at all." He watched Walters' face as he spoke. "I wrung its neck," he said finally. "That's the best I could do for it."

"The penguin?"

Ted Wilkes nodded. "Not much help, was I?" he asked sadly.

"Put it out of its misery."

"That don't seem the way to save the world."

"Well," Walters said, "I'm going in to Taunton."

"You'll find nothing there."

"We can't just sit round waiting."

"That's true enough," Ted replied. "But, well, maybe we should try to let them know we've got the message. Maybe we should try to get through somehow."

P.C. Walters stared at Ted Wilkes. "Funny how you and Mr. Monk keep on about that."

Ted grinned. "It'll take all kinds. The rich and the poor, the halt and the lame. All of us, together."

"What do you mean?"

"Don't know exactly." Ted Wilkes scratched his chin. "But maybe that's why they selected us, here in Brandling. Because I'm here. Because Mr. Monk's here. Because poor old Charlie Crump was here. That marrow squash of his was looking for someone to understand, I reckon. Someone to what Mr. Monk calls 'communicate with.'"

P.C. Walters shook his head in disbelief.

"It could be," Ted said.

"What you think they want us to do?" Walters asked.

"Got no idea really," Ted Wilkes had said, a shrewd expression in his eyes. "Unless we piled up all the automobiles we got and set fire to them. That'd be a start." He chuckled. "That'd be a start all right. That'd be a real start."

"That doesn't make sense."

"Makes good sense to me," Ted Wilkes said. "Get rid of a lot of muck, it would." He chuckled again. "Get rid of all them pale riders, as well."

Walters shook his head. "I don't know," he said. "I don't know what to do." He stared into his beer.

"You ever thought of praying?"

P.C. Walters looked up quickly.

"Might help," Ted had said. "Might get through."

"I—" P.C. Walters could not accept anything that naïve, that simple, any more than he could really accept that the plants were responsible for their actions. Such things were beyond his imagination. "I— I'd rather go to Taunton. Someone there must have some idea what's going on."

"You'll find there's nothing there."

"If I go in I'll be sure."

Ted Wilkes watched him and sipped his ale. There'd be nothing in Taunton, of that he was certain. It had begun in Brandling and it would either end in Brandling or spread until the whole country was affected.

Strangely, he didn't mind what the outcome was.

Now, as he walked in the early light with William, Ted Wilkes wondered. There must be a way, he thought. There must be something someone could do.

He walked a little out of the village, enjoying the fresh, early air, looking with his old eyes at the new light. He found he looked at things a little longer these days, held them in his gaze a fraction more. Getting from them all he could in the time that remained.

He walked past a gate, twisted on its hinges, and crossed a field while William chased a rabbit. Ted Wilkes stood watching the dog racing after the white-tailed rabbit, savoring the excitement of the chase and the vigor it contained.

The rabbit disappeared into dense greenery and William returned, his pink tongue hanging, his breath gushing.

"Damned fool," Ted said kindly.

William wagged his tail.

On the edge of the field a massive oak grew.

Ted Wilkes often walked to the oak, its simple

153

majesty never failing to give him pleasure, its size and age a source of comfort.

"Hello, tree," Ted said, standing beneath it, admiring its size and shape against the early pink sky. "All right today, are you?"

Ted Wilkes always greeted the tree; it was one of his small rituals. Usually he spoke to it and passed on but this morning he paused, staring up into the nest of branches and the rich green leaf. Then he turned and sat beneath it, making a cushion of the thick grass and leaning his back against the massive trunk.

He sat, feeling the strength of the tree behind him.

Before him the green field stretched and above it a plowland revealed its red earth to the morning.

A strange feeling of peace began to fill Ted Wilkes. Reaching back, he placed the palms of his hands against the rough bark of the tree and rubbed softly, listening to the slurring noise he made.

He leaned his old head back and rested against the body of the tree, not knowing why but acting with the same instinct that had made him bury the remains of Charlie Crump's marrow squash.

He looked out across the field in which he sat, seeing William sniffing in the grass. He felt strangely, simply content. It was as if the tree enfolded him, took him within its massiveness so that he began to feel part of it. He belonged. Its flesh was his flesh. Its arms and branches his.

And then suddenly he knew where the solution lay.

The communication was simple. It was old and simple and natural. All it required was enough of them believing to make it possible. Enough of them together to make it work.

He pressed his head into the tree, achingly aware of the strength of it behind him. He touched it with the palms of his hands. He knew that between them something was passing. Some message, some transmission, something of hope.

He knew also that it would work for all of them

154

as long as there were enough who were honest enough to make it possible.

The tree understood.

The plants would understand.

There was no mystery, no barrier; all that was needed was faith.

Ted Wilkes sat for a long time beneath the great oak, feeling the spirit passing between them, filling him, giving, taking nothing away.

After a time he got to his feet feeling reborn, simplified, renewed.

He would have liked to say something but knew his voice would betray him. It would not be enough.

He turned and walked away, William trotting beside him.

Ted Wilkes cleared his throat and spoke to the dog. "I don't know how I'm going to get it over to them, William," he said. "They think I'm barmy enough as it is."

William wagged his tail at the sound of the voice.

Together they walked back to Brandling.

Chapter
Thirty-Two

Later that morning P.C. Walters knocked on the door of the Monks' white, thatched cottage. When Philip came to the door Walters said, "I'm off to Taunton now, Mr. Monk. I wondered if you'd thought any more about joining me."

Philip looked at the constable, noticing the lines of worry under his eyes, and felt guilty as he saw the concern on the simple face.

"I mean, you're known, Mr. Monk. They'll have seen you and your science talks on the telly. They might take more notice of me if I had you along backing me up."

"I'm sorry," Philip said. He had decided not to leave Elizabeth and the children. "I can't go. I think I should remain here."

"They'd listen to you."

"They'll listen to you too, constable."

Walters nodded, his face blank. "I see, sir," he said. "I'm sorry I troubled you. I didn't know you'd changed your mind."

"It's not that," Philip said quickly.

P.C. Walters turned away. "I understand."

"Do you?" Philip's words were sharp.

Walters paused. "Well, when you came along yesterday, Mr. Monk, I thought you were going to help, that's all."

"I will," Philip promised, "but—"

"You won't come to Taunton?"

"No."

"You're a funny feller, Mr. Monk," Walters said, his frustration, his need for help, showing. There was too much he didn't understand. "I don't know that I get you at all." He shrugged. "Was you after something for one of your telly talks when you came along yesterday?"

"You know better than that." Philip's words were harsh. "You knew that when Michael Martin called you."

P.C. Walters swallowed.

"We're being given a chance, constable," Philip tried to explain. "Here, now. I'm glad you're going to Taunton—someone's got to try to make them understand what's happening here. But most of us have got to stay. To face, here, whatever there is to face."

P.C. Walters looked away.

"What are you going to tell your chief constable?" Philip Monk asked.

Walters shook his head. "What can I tell him? What can I tell him he doesn't already know? I covered the facts yesterday."

"About Charlie Crump?"

"Well, yes. There's no one else dead is there? I mean, he's not going to be interested in an old lady who got knocked over by a rosebush, is he? Or some old man in the village who's got religion." Walters' appeal was moving. "Ask yourself, Mr. Monk. What's he going to think of me? I don't know myself what to believe." For a moment he was tempted to tell Philip about Eric Bolton's greed and the man's visit to Charlie Crump's, the sounds he'd heard and the fear they had instilled. But he couldn't bring himself to do so. Last night, in the company of Ted Wilkes, it hadn't seemed so incredible. This morning, in the sunlight, it would sound insane. Walters looked at Philip Monk. "I'll probably get the sack," he said. "They won't take me seriously at all."

"I know," Philip said.

"You know, sir."

Philip nodded.

"Then what's the point of my going at all?" Walters looked about him. "I mean, Mr. Monk, how am I going to tell them you heard those roses across the way making a noise? I mean, really, sir. They'll lock me up."

157

"I know," Philip repeated. "That's our trouble. We keep avoiding evidence until it's overwhelming. And then it's usually too late."

"So what do I tell them?"

Philip thought. "There's a man in America, New York I think, called Backster. Get in touch with him if you can. Or get someone to call him. Today, if possible."

"Telephone America, sir?"

"Yes, International Directories should be able to find you the number. Or someone at London University'll have a contact."

"I don't think I could telephone America, sir."

"Then get someone else to do it," Philip suggested. "Persuade your chief constable to get in touch with this man. You remember the name?"

"Backster?"

"Yes. If there's anyone who might get that chief constable of yours to take what you've got to say seriously, Backster should be able to."

Walters nodded. "What else have I got to say, sir?"

"Tell them about Mabel Crewe as well," Philip went on quickly. "Exaggerate her condition if you have to. Tell them about Michael Martin. His death will add something. Make it clear to them that, however incredible it sounds, we are being contacted by the plant kingdom. And what's more, we'd better respond. Otherwise they might just decide to grow right over the top of us. That's a prospect anyone must take seriously."

"I hope so, sir."

"So do I." Philip's voice softened. "And, I'm sorry," he added.

"What for?"

"Not coming with you. I'm staying here. Whatever happens, I'd like to be with my family."

"I understand. I'm sorry I can't do the same."

"Just get to Taunton and try and make *them* understand."

P.C. Walters nodded, turned, and walked down the village street, looking out of place in his dark uniform in the hot, flat sunlight. Philip watched him go, thinking how lonely he appeared.

As Philip went back into the cottage he stopped by the door, bent, and peered at a small yellow flower growing by the doorway. He reached for the flower, hesitated, then picked it and looked deep into its yellow heart.

Philip smiled a small, bewildered smile. "It is absurd," he said to himself. "It's ridiculous."

When he went indoors he took the flower with him.

Chapter
Thirty-Three

That Sunday morning Harry Reynolds, the keeper of parks and gardens, was about to get into his car in Taunton when his wife called to him. The chief constable was on the phone, she said. He wanted a word.

"Oh, God." Reynolds moaned. "What's he want now? Has a budgerigar run amok or something?"

His wife laughed. "I think he's checking."

Reynolds went into the house and picked up the telephone. "Hello. Reynolds here."

"Ah . . . Reynolds . . ."

"Yes?"

"Just wondered what you were doing about the Brandling business." Chief Constable Parkhurst sounded slightly embarrassed. "Today, I mean?"

"I'd be on my way now if it wasn't for this phone call," Reynolds said sarcastically.

"Oh . . . good, good."

"Is that all?"

"Well no, not quite." The chief constable cleared his throat and Reynolds raised his eyebrows in despair. "There *is* something else."

"What's that?"

"I understand the lines are down—the telephone lines to Brandling. I wondered if you'd be a good chap and keep your eye open for, well, anything that might indicate the cause."

"Like a fallen telephone pole?"

"That's the sort of thing."

Reynolds sighed. "What's the Post Office doing?" he asked peevishly. "Isn't that their line of country?"

"It is really. But, well, you might be able to help." The chief constable coughed. "As a matter of fact I tried to ring that constable chappie down there . . . Brandling. I wanted to let him know help was on its way. That sort of thing. When I couldn't get through I rang the exchange and they told me the lines were down."

"What do you want me to do?" Reynolds asked patiently.

"Keep your eye open, that's all."

"I really think the Post Office should do their own dirty work."

"Their chaps are awfully busy. There's been a lot of it this summer, you know."

"A lot of what?"

"Lines down, that sort of thing."

"All right," Reynolds agreed. "I'll keep my eye open. Is that all?"

"Yes. I think so."

"No burst water mains, that sort of thing?"

The chief constable hesitated, then chuckled. "Damned good that," he said. "Damned good."

"Thank you."

"And as far as the other matter's concerned, do have a good look round, won't you? See if you can find out what's behind it."

"You mean the florabunda?"

"That's it. Don't want London to think we've done nothing about it." There was concern beneath the geniality. "Got to do our bit, you know."

"Yes." Reynolds paused. "You're worried about this, aren't you? I mean, you think there might be something in it?"

"Well, there's no smoke without fire, you know." The chief constable coughed again. "I mean, if London's involved . . ."

"Don't worry," Reynolds told him gently. "I'll look into it."

"Lived too much of my life amongst—" The chief constable hesitated. He doubted if Reynolds would understand. There were mysteries that did not survive explanation. "What I mean to say is, I shouldn't be surprised what's going on. All we can do is have a look around. See if there's anything in all this."

161

"All right," Reynolds said. "I'll see what I can do."

"There's a good chap."

The chief constable's voice went away. Reynolds hung up and went out into the sunshine again, wondering.

The chief constable was more concerned than he was prepared to admit. His interest in the telephones was only a way of emphasizing his worry. Reynolds remembered that the man had spent most of his life in some colonial administration or other.

Probably thinks it's voodoo, Reynolds thought as he went to his car.

His wife called, "Everything all right?"

"Perfect."

Reynolds paused before he got into his car and looked at a rose bloom hanging heavy in the heat.

"What's it going to be today?" he asked. "Rape? Arson? Murder?"

But the sarcasm was gone from his voice.

Chapter
Thirty-Four

P.C. Walters drove out of Brandling just after nine on Sunday morning. The air was thick with sunshine, the countryside rich and green and fulsome.

White butterflies and bees, dragonflies and wasps, hummed and buzzed among the wild flowers.

It was a lovely day, vibrating with lush growth.

P.C. Walters was too aware now to ignore its presence. Every single blade of grass seemed alien, and he understood why Philip Monk remained with his family. He wished he'd been able to do the same.

Walters drove slowly from the village, through the green and golden countryside, until he turned the corner and found Peter's Elm lying entangled with telephone wire by the side of the road.

Walters stopped the car and examined the tree.

He tugged at the broken line but there was no way he could release it. The exertion caused him to sweat and he removed his jacket. He stood in his undershirt, looking down at the mess of wire. There was nothing he could do.

He climbed back into the car and drove on.

It'd be some time before they got that sorted out, he thought. It was just as well he'd decided to drive to Taunton.

After a while Walters frowned as he drove, then shook his head. Peering out of both sides of the car, he wondered if he was imagining things.

The road seemed to be narrowing. The vegetation on both sides of the road appeared to be creeping in, filling it. It was as if the little country road were being invaded, grown over.

The farther Walters drove the thicker the vegetation became. He was sure of it now. It wasn't his imagination. The road was becoming narrower.

Growth came in from either side, heavily, densely. At times both sides of the car scraped against leaves and branches. Once or twice Walters was forced to slow down.

It was some weeks since Walters had used the road to Taunton; then it had been almost normal. A little overgrown, perhaps, but nothing like this.

Funny no one's mentioned it, Walters thought.

He wiped his brow with the back of his hand and drove on slowly, avoiding the growth as much as possible.

But as he progressed the way became more and more impassable. For a moment Walters had the wild idea that the vegetation was actually closing in around him, moving steadily over the road in front to prevent his progress.

Glancing into the rearview mirror, he saw the wall of green behind him and for a second his mind was stilled with fear. He was being encased.

Walters shook his head, jarring the thought.

Don't be a bloody fool, he said to himself.

But the fear persisted as the way ahead became denser.

A branch flicked off the front of the fender and caught Walters across the arm, whipping him and leaving a red weal across his flesh. Walters wound up the window quickly and then reached across and closed the other, sealing himself in the car.

Immediately the heat engulfed him. Sweat soaked his undershirt. His back stuck to the plastic seatcover.

This is bloody ridiculous, he thought, as the car came to a stumbling halt. The back wheels locked and the motor stalled.

P.C. Walters sat behind the wheel, his hands white where they gripped it. The air in the car was thick with heat. As he breathed, Walters felt it, like cotton wool, clogging his lungs. He was suddenly aware of the rapid beating of his heart.

Come along, he said to himself as levelly as he could. Get moving again.

He pushed the starter and felt immense relief when the motor caught. He accelerated and heard the revolutions build. But when he let the clutch out the back wheels remained locked and the motor stalled again.

In that instant P.C. Walters came close to panic.

He pushed the starter once more, clumsily, missing it the first time and stabbing again with his finger until the connection was made. Then, accelerating wildly, he heard the motor race.

Blue exhaust issued from the car.

This time P.C. Walters let out the clutch very slowly. Forcing the motor, listening to it roar, he eased out the clutch pedal a fraction of an inch at a time and tried to force the car to move.

The clutch began to engage.

The motor felt the pull on it and slowed. Walters forced the accelerator and kept the clutch pedal in the same position. The motor held, more exhaust issued, and he felt the wheels begin to take the load.

He let the clutch out a little more and felt the wheels respond.

Sweat ran down his face now, hanging from his eyebrows, stinging his eyes. His heart raced like a sewing machine.

He let the clutch out further, felt the strain on the wheels. He pushed the accelerator down as far as it would go and, in the tunnel of sound the motor made, let the clutch engage.

The wheels began to turn and the car lurched forward.

The motor roared and thundered. It strained, the wheels turned, moved, began to gather momentum. Then blue, oily smoke suddenly filled the car as the clutch burned and the car was stationary again.

Walters pushed the accelerator. The motor raced but the clutch was dead. Smoke poured forth and a rattling sound began to shake the car. There was no forward movement.

165

He turned off the motor. Smoke filled his lungs, and he couldn't breathe. Clawing, he pulled at the door handle. It opened two inches and then stopped, halted by the growth on the side of the road.

P.C. Walters knew then with certainty that he was going to die.

He heaved against the car door, thrusting and clawing. He forced the door open and burst out of the car, gasping for breath, his face distorted by sweat and fear.

He would not have believed he could have been so afraid.

He pushed against the car, heaving, looking for some way through the tangle of branch and leaf, stalk and tendril, that seemed to surround him. He fought his way along the body of the car and looked at the back wheels.

They were completely locked by greenery.

Jesus, he thought, how could it happen? How could it all have got there?

He turned his head, still seeking a way out.

And then he heard the sound.

In the still, sun-filled, windless morning the sound of the plants seemed to come from nowhere and yet from all around. It filled P.C. Walters' ears, invading him.

He twisted, seeking the source, but there was nothing. He pushed against the car and turned his body, looking for something he could focus on. But there was only the sound, silvery, sinister, pervading.

Then he began to feel the pressure.

Slowly, inexorably, the pressure of the green all about him began to increase. Walters pushed out an arm. It disappeared into grass and leaf and branch. He pulled it back and pushed again and again there was no resistance. He could feel the plants encroaching.

He stood with his back to the car and fought them.

But nothing he did made any difference.

The wall of green invaded, held him, overrode him. Then, slowly, it began to smother him. P.C.

Walters uttered a loud, hopeless cry, lost among the steady rustling of the plants.

Nothing resisted and nothing ceased. His arms became bloodied with their encounter with branches, torn and shredded by the tiny twigs they broke and pushed but failed to stop.

Slowly the wall of greenery engulfed him.

He fought for as long as he was able, calling out, struggling until there was no longer strength in his body. He survived for as long as he could.

Then he sank into the greenery.

Why me? he thought, as the blackness overtook him. What have I ever done to them?

The plants covered his body almost completely. One bloodied hand emerged from their embrace, but that was all.

And then the plants were silent.

A blackbird flew out of the sun. It perched on the top of P.C. Walters' car and looked at the bloodied, helpless hand.

Then it flew away.

Chapter
Thirty-Five

Deborah was with her father when she became aware that P.C. Walters was dead. They stood in the garden behind the white, thatched cottage, feeling the heat of the sun, when Deborah stiffened suddenly, putting her hands over her eyes.

She did not say anything, made no movement, and it was a moment before Philip realized that anything was wrong. Then he turned, seeing her standing stiff, unnaturally, her little feet together, her hands pushed tightly over her eyes.

Philip moved to her.

"What— Debby?" he asked. "What—"

Deborah shook her head; silent, unseeing, then she shuddered.

"Debby?"

Philip reached for her hands to remove them from her eyes, but they were like iron. He put his hands on her shoulders, feeling her shuddering, wondering what he could do.

He thought of Elizabeth and was immediately glad she was not there.

"Debby—" Philip kept his voice steady, holding the child. "It's all right. Listen to me. It's all right. I won't let anything hurt you. I won't."

"It's—not—me," Deborah said, her usually quick voice wooden. The words came separately, slowly, "It's—a—man—in—a—car."

"What man, Debby? What car? Where?"

Deborah shook her head.

"Try, Debby. Where?"

She shook her head vigorously.

"Who is it then? Do you know who it is?"

Deborah stilled. "It's—the—man—"

"Who?"

"From—"

Philip put his face close to his daughter's. He had no fear for the child; he did not think she was in any danger. But she was communicating with something, somewhere, and somehow she was getting through. Philip held her. When he spoke his voice was gentle but intense.

"You've got to try, Debby," he said. "You've got to try and see who it is and what's happening. You'll be all right, I know that. You must believe that no harm will come to you. But try and see who it is."

"I—am—all—right."

"Yes, yes, I know that. But—"

"It's—the—man—from—the—police—station."

"Walters? Constable Walters?"

Deborah nodded.

Philip's voice faltered. He knew. "What's happened to him?"

"He's—fighting—them."

Philip held his daughter. "My God. He mustn't, he mustn't fight them. That's the last thing he must do. Can you tell him that, Debby? Can you tell him not to fight them?"

"No."

"He mustn't."

"He—is—fighting."

"He'll lose," Philip said sadly. He could see the solid, dark figure walk away from him; the confusion in Walters' eyes and the determination to do something no matter how little he understood. "He mustn't fight them," Philip said, to Deborah, to himself. "That's not the way."

"They—are—covering—him," Deborah said. "They—are—"

Her voice died, the tautness left her body; her hands remained pressed over her eyes but she moved closer to her father, leaning against him.

"Debby?" Philip asked gently. "Can you see what's happening now?"

"He's—covered."

169

Philip Monk held his daughter as she began to cry. It came as a small, frightened wail and grew until tears ran down her cheeks and she sobbed uncontrollably. Philip took her in his arms and held her as the sobbing subsided. "Are you all right, Debby?"

"I had a nasty dream, Daddy."

"I know, but it's over."

"I wasn't asleep, Daddy. I wasn't in bed. But I had a nasty, nasty dream. It was—" She remembered suddenly and buried her face against her father. "It was awful."

"I know."

"You know?" Deborah lifted her face and looked at Philip. "How do you know? Did you dream it too?"

"You told me about it when you were dreaming," Philip explained. "You talked in your sleep."

"Did I?"

"Yes, I know what it was about."

"It was awful." Deborah sniffed, recovering. "He shouldn't have fought them, should he, Daddy? They're our friends really, aren't they? All of them, they're our friends."

"Yes," Philip said sadly, picturing the lonely figure on the country road, dying for reasons or causes or motives which were beyond his understanding. "Yes, they *are* our friends, if only we knew it."

Deborah studied her father's face and its sadness. "It *was* a dream, wasn't it, Daddy?" she asked carefully. "It *was* only a dream."

Philip pushed his daughter gently from him, aware of the total innocence in her eyes. She knows more than any of us, he thought. She's closer to it than we are. Closer than Ted Wilkes and his simple belief. Closer than Mabel Crewe and her fears. She knows, he thought, otherwise she'd never have asked. But he was afraid of her knowledge. He had no way of knowing how well she would be able to control it. How much reality she could bear.

"I mean," Deborah went on, "it *could* have happened, couldn't it? Things like that do happen sometimes, don't they, Daddy?"

"You know they do."

"Do *you* know it too?"

"Yes," said Philip, "I do. In fact," he added slowly, "I don't think it was a dream at all. I think you saw it happen. I think what you saw was real."

Deborah nodded. "I think so too," she said simply.

"Does that happen to you very often?" Philip asked, carefully, delicately denying importance. "I mean, do you often have those funny, sort-of-real dreams?"

Deborah nodded again. They were images to her, sights which passed before her eyes. Sometimes, when they were nasty, they frightened her, the way they'd done this morning. But usually she enjoyed them. They were more real than her normal dreams, more colorful. Their content did not worry her. Death belonged to another world, a part of being grown up.

She peered into her father's face. "I often have funny dreams when I'm not in bed," she confided. "Do you, Daddy? Do you?" she asked, persisting innocently.

"Not the way you do."

"Oh." Deborah was disappointed. "What a shame. You should have them, you know. They're nice, really they are. Well, *most* of the time they're very nice." She smiled suddenly, openly, fully. "Sometimes when I'm feeling a bit sad I have them and then they're wonderful. I love them, I really love them. That's all right, isn't it? It's not naughty or anything?"

"No, never." Philip held her, emotion moving him. "No. You must never even think anything like that. They're good, Debby. They're very good."

His daughter smiled, delighted.

They remained together a little longer and then walked slowly into the house, hand in hand, out of the sunlight.

As they went indoors Philip thought of Walters. His death was so unnecessary.

Philip wondered what would happen next. Perhaps he should seek out Ted Wilkes and tell him. The old man would understand. Perhaps together the old man and Deborah, between them, would know what to do. Nothing seemed unlikely any more; nothing too extreme.

Philip suddenly remembered Ted Wilkes' voice, distant and whispering. "I am Alpha and Omega," it had said, "the first and the last."

Inside the house Elizabeth waited.

She seemed more at ease this morning, more relaxed. There was still apprehension in her eyes and concern accompanied her, but there was now peace between them.

Philip told her nothing of Walters' death or of Deborah's vision. Deborah did not speak of them either. She didn't remain long with her parents, but ran off, quickly.

Philip kissed Elizabeth gently. "It's going to be all right," he said soothingly.

"Is it?"

"Yes," Philip said, "it is."

He went upstairs. There was a cupboard in Jacob's room full of his son's old toys, pieces of elementary scientific equipment, collected junk.

Philip searched through the cupboard and finally found what he was seeking. An old army field telephone unit and battery. He examined the telephone, hoping it would work and that there was enough charge left in the battery.

He left the house, carrying the field telephone, and walked up through the village in the direction of Peter's Elm. Here, he'd heard, was where there was a break in the line.

The sun was hot; the sky faintly milky.

Chapter
Thirty-Six

On that Sunday morning Mabel Crewe woke early. She had slept on the Monks' settee more securely than she had for weeks. There was something about not being alone which comforted, and she lay for a long time after she opened her eyes, contented and at peace.

After a while there was a gentle knock on the living room door.

"Yes, come in," Mabel Crewe called.

The door opened slowly and a tray appeared; Deborah followed. "Would you like a cup of tea?" she asked carefully, walking slowly, trying not to spill anything. "Mummy thought you'd like a cup of tea so I said I'd bring it in to you. Did you have a nice sleep?"

Mabel smiled. "I slept very well."

"Mummy thought it might be a bit bumpy."

"No, it wasn't bumpy at all." Mabel Crewe reached for the tray and took it. There were two cups on the tray. "Are you going to join me for a cuppa?"

"Yes, please," Deborah said. She sat beside Mabel on the edge of the settee and waited, her small hands folded on her lap, her bright face expectant. "Can I have two lumps of sugar, please?"

"Of course you can." Mabel poured tea and passed Deborah a cup. "There you are, two lumps."

Deborah took her tea and held it. "Are you going to stay with us for a long time?"

"I don't know," Mabel replied carefully. "Would you mind if I did?"

"I'd love it," Deborah said eagerly. "That'd be lovely." Her face was happy. "We could go for walks and things and I could show you—" She paused for a moment, looking capricious. "I could show you the sunflowers."

"The sunflowers?"

Deborah nodded, her eyes mischievous and secret.

"I didn't know there were sunflowers in the garden," Mabel said, watching the child. "I've never seen—"

"They're not in the garden," Deborah told her. "They're, well, they're somewhere special really. It's sort of a secret."

"A secret, Debby?"

Deborah hesitated. "Promise you won't tell." She held her tea very carefully, her body tense with excitement. "You must promise you won't tell," she went on, "because it really is a secret. Jacob's the only one who knows about it except me, although"—her face clouded a little—"although he nearly told. He nearly did. He told about me talking to them anyway."

"That wasn't very nice," Mabel sympathized.

"It wasn't, was it? He promised not to, too." Her dark eyes were piercing. "But you wouldn't, would you? If you promise not to tell."

Mabel Crewe waited. She lifted her cup and sipped tea. As she brought the cup close to her lips she noticed her hand trembling slightly.

Don't be absurd, she thought. She's only a child.

"You wouldn't, would you?" Deborah repeated. "You've got to keep secrets, haven't you? If you promise not to tell, really promise, then you mustn't, must you?"

"No," Mabel agreed, "you mustn't."

"That's what I said. That's what I told Jacob. But he told, you know, he told Mummy about—well, about them, and now everyone knows." She looked steadily at Mabel. "Now they know about talking to the sunflowers. But they don't know *where* the sunflowers are. They don't know that."

Suddenly Mabel Crewe felt tired. The peace of the morning was beginning to disappear. "You'd better drink your tea, Debby," she said, and paused to consider. "It'll be getting cold." She watched the child smile innocently and lift the cup to her lips.

"Anyway," Deborah went on, as if the old lady had said nothing, "you're the only one who knows about listening to them. Jacob's been with me when I've heard, but you're the only one who really knows about listening."

The simple words disturbed Mabel Crewe, uncovering everything she was trying to avoid. "But we've all heard them now, Debby," she said uncertainly. "We've all heard the sounds they make." She held the cup steady on the saucer.

"But we hadn't before," Deborah persisted. "Before they started to talk to everyone. Before then it was only us, wasn't it? We were the only ones who'd heard them, then."

"You seem very sure that I had heard them," Mabel said. She replaced her cup on the tray. "I mean, my dear, I mightn't have heard them at all, might I?"

"Oh, you've heard them all right," Deborah told her happily. "I know you've heard them. I know."

"Do you really . . . *know?*"

Deborah nodded emphatically.

"How do you . . . know?"

"They've told me, that's why." Deborah appeared delighted with the game. "They told me a long time ago, ages ago really. That's why I came to see you the day you were going to cut them."

"That was only yesterday," Mabel said in a tired voice.

"It seems much longer ago than that," Deborah said.

Mabel Crewe looked at the child sitting on the settee. "When you told me about . . . listening." She chose her words carefully. "You told me you didn't understand what they said." Deborah didn't move. "Why did you say that, Deborah? Why did you tell me a lie?"

"It wasn't a lie, really."

"What was it then?"

"Well, you know—" Deborah's face remained unchanged, the innocence of her expression unaltered.

175

"*You* know, Miss Crewe, *you* know what secrets are like."

"Secrets?"

"They said it was a secret."

"Who did?"

"The sunflowers, of course."

"Of course." Mabel Crewe's voice was quiet. "The ... sunflowers."

"Would you like to see them?" Deborah continued. "I will show them to you if you like. Only you must promise not to tell."

Mabel Crewe sighed. She was too old. She had lived too long.

"Promise?"

Mabel Crewe hesitated, then slowly nodded. There was no point in hiding any longer. The innocent demand of the child was too strong. She might just as well go along with Deborah. There seemed nothing else left to do.

"Promise?" Deborah repeated.

"I promise."

"All right then." Deborah's voice grew conspiratorial. "We can go and see them. Just you and me. We'll go down and see them on our own." She paused then, remembering. "Except we'll have to take the new guinea pig, too. We used to take Mr. Snuffles but he died. So I think we'd better take the new guinea pig with us."

"Is that necessary?" Mabel Crewe asked in a dry voice.

"Oh, yes. I think so."

"Why?"

"The sunflowers liked Mr. Snuffles very much. They were so sorry when he died. I think they'll like the new one, too. I haven't given him a name yet, but I think they'll like him, too."

Mabel Crewe looked out the window. The hard sunlight seemed to burn her eyes. I should have been honest with Philip Monk, she thought. I should have told him. Only there's no point to it, she thought. There's nothing we can do. If they really decide we're not worth another chance, there's nothing we can do

176

at all. She sighed, watching the sunlight burn with green.

"Would you like another cup of tea?" Deborah asked.

Mabel Crewe blinked.

"There's more in the pot if you'd like some," Deborah said. She drank the remains of her own cup. "There's lots more left."

Mabel Crewe could not take her eyes off the child's innocence.

"We could go later on this morning if you like," Deborah suggested. "It's not far at all. It doesn't take very long."

Mabel Crewe did not know how to reply. She opened her mouth to say something but was interrupted by Elizabeth's sudden entrance.

"Hello, you two," Elizabeth said; she too seemed more at ease this morning. "How are you getting on?"

"We're talking," Deborah said.

"I hope she's not bothering you," Elizabeth said. "I know she chatters once she gets going." She turned to Deborah. "You've not been making a nuisance of yourself, have you, Debby?"

"No," Mabel Crewe answered quickly. She'd decided now. She knew. There was no purpose in putting it off any longer. Sooner or later she must face it and be sure. "No, she's been very entertaining. In fact we've decided to go walking together later on."

"Oh." Elizabeth's voice showed a touch of concern. "Is that wise?"

"It's not far, Mummy," Deborah said. "I've been there before and it's quite safe really."

"I'm sure it is," Mabel Crewe said.

"Well, if it's not too far," Elizabeth said, remembering her promise to Philip. "With all that's going on, I shouldn't go too far."

"We won't."

"All right, then." Elizabeth turned to Mabel. "Is there anything you want?" she asked. "I mean, you know where the bathroom is and all that sort of thing."

"I'm fine. I'll get up soon."

"There's no hurry. Stay there as long as you like." She turned to go. "And if our daughter gets on your nerves just ask her to run along and leave you alone."

"You've no need to worry about her," Mabel Crewe told her. "She and I are getting along famously."

Deborah smiled a slow secretive smile as her mother left the room. She turned to Mabel Crewe and looked at her. Mabel could not hold the child's gaze. She moved her eyes and looked out of the window at the hot, burning sun.

She wished she had said more to Philip Monk. She wished she could be more positive about the voices. She wished she could be sure that they *were* all in her head.

Chapter
Thirty-Seven

Harry Reynolds drove out of Taunton. The Sunday
morning was bright and clear, the sky a colorless blue.
Surrounding him, the green and rolling hillsides disappeared into a shimmering haze.

Reynolds drove on steadily.

The heavy, hot air moved about him sluggishly.
He opened windows and loosened his tie.

After a while he began to whistle.

There was nothing about the day which was in
any way depressing. He could not share the doubts
the chief constable had entertained. They seemed
distant now, remote, removed from the lovely, flowing landscape. He was glad he had been pressured
into making the journey. He couldn't think of a nicer
way to spend the day.

What a load of cod's wallop, he thought. Fancy
grown people acting like that. Bloody ridiculous, the
things we do.

As he drove, the warm summer air dispelling his
concern, he studied the healthy growth on either side
of the road.

We live in a sick society, he told himself. My God,
most of us would give our left ball to be able to produce fruitfulness such as this.

Smiling he turned at a crossroad, following a sign
which pointed to Brandling.

He drove on steadily, watching the countryside,
the green hills roll past, observing that the telephone
wires were intact.

He smiled, shaking his head.

He was still smiling when he turned the corner

and came upon the tangled remains of P.C. Walters and his car.

Reynolds stopped, unable to believe what he was seeing in the sunlit morning. He half closed his eyes as he peered at the blood-encrusted hand protruding from the greenery. He opened his mouth, stupefied, then glanced about him, seeking someone to confirm the visual travesty.

He began, very slowly, to walk toward the arm emerging from the green; frozen in its final appeal for help.

The air was quiet now. The plants had ceased their rustling. The only sound was the noise of Reynolds' dragging footsteps as he walked toward Walters and the green which held him.

Reynolds could not believe that the day had altered so brutally. The sunlight was unchanged. The countryside remained. But what Reynolds walked toward was alien.

He approached the car, pushing aside the tangle of branch and leaf. It moved easily, neither resisting nor menacing. Reynolds peered into the overgrowth and saw Walters' dead face. Fear was stamped on it like a brand, and mixed with that fear, intermingled with it, disbelief and astonishment, the inability to accept what was happening.

"My God," Reynolds whispered, his voice harsh in the silent sunlit morning. "I don't believe it."

He released the greenery and the growth slipped back, once more covering Walters' tortured face. Only the hand remained.

Reynolds moved past Walters and the car, his eyes not leaving the beckoning hand, and stood on the country road looking back at it and the growth, then at his own car.

He would have to go on foot now. There was no way to drive past Walters' remains and his car.

Reynolds turned, tearing his gaze from what lay in the road, and began to walk steadily toward Brandling; pushing aside the quiet growth where it lay across the country road. He stopped once to glance back, seeing for the last time the green mound and the hand and the black shadows in the hard sunlight. In spite of the heat he shivered, wondering if the greenery would close in behind him.

He went on, down toward the valley in which Brandling lay.

The sun was hot on his bald head and, after a while, he took a handkerchief from his pocket, knotted the corners, and fitted it over his head.

When he came to Peter's Elm he stopped to examine the twisted wires caught in the branches. This phenomenon, at least, he thought he understood.

Then he looked down toward the village, at the peaceful collection of buildings, their slate roofs sparkling in the sunlight. His short figure, capped with the knotted handkerchief, trudging along, seemed absurd somehow in the sun-drenched morning.

No cynicism remained in him now, no sarcasm. There was nothing to sneer at. If his lips were to utter anything, Reynolds told himself, it could only be a prayer.

Chapter
Thirty-Eight

Philip Monk was walking out of Brandling toward Peter's Elm, the sun above him high and clear, when he saw Harry Reynolds coming toward him.

Philip stopped, stunned by Reynolds' tortured expression and the absurd tied handkerchief cap he wore.

"You're—" Reynolds said, recognizing him. "I've seen you before. What in God's name is happening here?"

Philip wondered how much the man knew. Behind him the High Street was almost deserted in the heat. Two women stood on the far side of the road talking in the shade. A man rode by on a bicycle. Everything appeared normal.

"What do you mean?" Philip asked. He swung the field telephone behind him, pushing it out of sight, curious as to why Reynolds was so agitated. "There's—"

"There's been an accident," Reynolds said quickly. "On the road some distance back. My God."

"Is it bad?"

"Shocking. A man's dead. I've never seen anything like it."

"Who was it?" Philip asked, already knowing.

"I don't know. A policeman, I'd think, but there wasn't—"

"Walters," Philip told him quietly.

"What?"

"Nothing," said Philip. "What happened?"

"My God." Reynolds turned away. "He was—he was mauled. It was unbelievable. Torn to pieces."

"Mauled?"

"Yes." Reynolds' face came close. "You won't believe this, but he was mauled by a hedge. Believe it or not it just grew into him. What the devil is going on down here?"

"Don't you know?"

Reynolds shook his head.

"What are you doing here?" Philip asked.

"I wish to God I knew that also."

"Who sent you?"

Reynolds explained. "I'm with the Agricultural Department. In Taunton. Parkhurst, chief constable there, had a call from—" he paused. "I suppose it was him I found back there, saying something odd was going on. I was asked to come down."

Philip closed his eyes. How ironic, he thought. The chief constable *had* taken Walters seriously after all. There had been no need for the man to drive to Taunton.

"I didn't believe it," Reynolds was saying. "I thought old Parkhurst was touched or something. Voodoo, I think he thought it was. I thought it was some sort of joke. I mean, I didn't expect to find something like *that* on the road."

"I know."

Reynolds' hands flailed at the air. "My God, the man was torn to shreds. It was horrible."

"Something extraordinary *is* happening here," Philip said. "I can't explain it properly because I don't understand it." He couldn't begin to go into detail. Explanations would take too long and the solution was too remote. "But we've got a chance," he promised. "You've seen what they can do. Walters is the second man to die here. But I believe we've got a chance if only we can get in touch with them."

"*Get in touch with them?*" Reynolds waved a hand. "Them? What do you mean, them?"

"The plants."

"My God, you don't mean it!"

"I mean it, right enough. There *are* people who can communicate with them. My daughter's one. She—"

"Communicate with plants?" Reynolds looked

about him. Behind them the village was quiet. The two women in the shade talked on. A dog lay sleeping.

"I don't believe it."

"You should," Philip said evenly. "I knew about the death of the constable before you did. My daughter saw it happen."

Reynolds didn't move.

"She has these—visions," Philip continued. "She says she can hear what the plants are saying. She saw Walters die. I was with her when it happened. That's how I knew."

"My God, man. What are you saying?" Reynolds closed his eyes. "That's witchcraft."

"Not necessarily."

"What else would you call it?"

"Living," Philip explained simply. "A recognition of the fact that we're all alive."

"*Seriously?*"

"Seriously."

Reynolds shook his head. The morning, the day, changed, and he himself, he knew, would never be the same again.

"All right," he said, trying to accept. "Let's assume, just assume, there's something in what you say. Where do we go from here?"

Philip Monk lifted the field telephone he held. "I was going to see if this'd work. The lines are down."

"I know, I saw them. Who would you ring?"

"There's a BBC announcer I know. I've spoken to him before about this. He might have something new."

"He takes it *seriously?*"

"He did last time we spoke," Philip explained. "He introduced me to it all." He began to walk along the road.

"Do you mind if I come along?" Reynolds asked.

"Of course not."

"It's just that—"

"I know."

Harry Reynolds and Philip Monk climbed the hill toward Peter's Elm, silently. When they arrived at Peter's Elm the two men examined the tangle of wires bound about it. There was no way they could unwind it.

Philip took a pair of pliers from his pocket and found wires which led toward Taunton. He cut and attached them to the terminals of the field telephone.

Reynolds watched silently.

Philip glanced up. "I hope this works," he said.

"What good will it do? I mean"—Reynolds spread his hands—"what do you expect anyone to do? Bring in defoliants. Burn everything in sight? Call in the—"

"No." Philip's voice was sharp. "Nothing like that."

"What then?"

"Somewhere there must be someone who understands. The way Debby understands. But someone older, who's done it before."

"You're talking witchcraft again."

Philip shrugged, turned the handle on the field telephone, and waited. Nothing happened. He rang again and waited; again there was silence. Then he changed the wires on the terminals and rang a third time. This time a faint voice answered.

"Thank God," Philip whispered. In a louder voice he asked, "Who's that? Who's speaking?"

"This is Taunton exchange. What number were you calling?"

"The BBC London."

"What number are you calling from?"

"I'm not." Philip looked at the old gray telephone. "This is an emergency. The lines are down. I'm using—"

"What number are you?"

Philip took a deep breath. "Listen," he said, his voice controlled. "This is a genuine emergency. Please don't waste time but put me through to the BBC London. I need to speak to Alistair Rank. He knows me. My name is Philip Monk. Just ask him—"

"I'll have to see if they'll accept the charges first," the operator said briskly. "All this is most unusual. Emergency calls normally go to the police. Are you sure?"

"I'm sure."

"Very well then. But it is most unusual."

There was a click in Philip's ear and he took the receiver away. Reynolds watched him. They sat together in the sunlight, not speaking.

After a while there was another click and the operator said, "The BBC will accept charges. Go ahead, please."

"Alistair?" Philip asked.

"Who was it you wanted?"

"Alistair Rank."

"I'll see if I can find him."

Finally Alistair Rank came to the phone.

"It's Philip—Philip Monk. I've been—"

"Oh," Rank said. "Those letters. Look, I'm awfully sorry about all that, but—"

"It doesn't matter. This is more important."

"But it's not! I mean, it couldn't be." Alistair's voice was cautious. "They've put a block on everything. I'm surprised you haven't been told."

"Told what? What block?"

Alistair's tone became confidential. "All this stuff about plants and growth. All that. The Minister's put a block on everything. We're not to mention it."

Philip Monk looked at the tangled wreck of wires wound around the fallen Peter's Elm, then at Reynolds waiting in the sunlight, finally at the old army field telephone between his feet. It all seemed out of place.

"Do you understand?" Alistair's voice continued. "The whole place has been cautioned. There's talk of the Official Secrets Act."

"When did this happen?" Philip asked.

"This morning, officially. But there've been rumors of it for days." Alistair paused. "I'm not even sure I should be telling you anything."

"You've got to."

"Got to? Jesus, Philip, this is serious. The Prime Minister's involved. You know what it's like when the word gets round here. The whole place flaps."

"Listen." Philip's voice hardened. "You've got to tell me everything you know. Yes, I heard what you said. But at the moment I'm sitting on the side of the road outside Brandling. I'm talking to you on a field telephone my son used to play with. The wires are down and there's no other way of getting in touch. The roads are overgrown and I've got with me a man named Reynolds—yes, Reynolds. He's the keeper of parks and gardens in Taunton and this morning he found our local constable torn to pieces by plants. Yes, torn to pieces. Dead. He was on his way for help when it happened. It's bloody urgent, Alistair."

Philip stopped. On the other end of the line he could hear the tension in Alistair Rank's breathing.

"Jesus," Alistair said finally. "Dead?"

"Yes. He's the third."

"I heard about one other."

"There's Michael Martin as well." Philip tried to keep his voice steady. "Dr. Martin of the London University. He was working on plant memory. His death is tied in somehow, too."

"What do you know about him?" Alistair asked quickly.

"He was a friend."

"Did you know what he was doing?"

"Yes, I saw the work."

"Jesus." The announcer was tense. "That's what really put the lid on things." His voice raced. "You know about the letters and all the reports we were getting. Well, no one really took all that much notice of them. But when they found the wreck at the lab, and those plants all over the place, that's when the shutters really went up."

"Has anybody any idea what they're going to do?"

"Not yet." The announcer's voice dropped. "I mean, there are *rumors*, Philip, all that sort of thing. But at the moment everyone's got their head in the sand hoping it will all go away."

"It won't."

"I know."

"Something's going to happen," Philip said. "Down here."

"What?"

"Some sort of communication. Some sort of contact. Here, in Brandling. I know it."

"Contact?"

187

"Yes."

"You mean you're going to *speak* to them or something?"

"God knows."

"Jesus . . ." the announcer's voice trailed away.

"It's going to happen."

There was a silence on the other end of the line.

"And if it works," Philip went on, his voice steady, "if we do get through then I think we'll be all right. I mean, I think they'll understand."

"By God, that's more than I do."

Philip went on eagerly. "If it works here it'll work everywhere. They'll tell each other. They *can* communicate that fast."

"Jesus," the announcer said again. "You're talking about them as if they were—"

"—intelligent creatures," Philip finished.

"Yes."

"They are. Don't ever forget it."

"All right," Alistair Rank said, after a pause. "What do you want me to do?"

"Tell the Minister. Ask him to get hold of the best plant experts he can. Get him to fly them down in a helicopter."

"When?"

"As soon as you can."

"It may take some time."

"Do your best."

"Anything else?"

"Yes," Philip said. "There's an American named Backster who knows more about this sort of thing than most people. Get hold of him too if it's possible."

"All right." Alistair Rank's voice was brittle. "I'll do what I can." He put down the telephone and noticed his hand was shaking. It all began with a bloody marrow squash, he thought. You never know where you are these days.

Philip summarized for Reynolds the detail of the communication. "Let's go back to the village," he suggested, "and talk to the others."

"Others?" Reynolds questioned. "What others? How many down here think the way you do?"

188

"There's only one," Philip admitted. "Ted Wilkes, and most of the village thinks he's a religious nut."

"My God."

"Come along." Philip picked up the telephone.

Reynolds walked a pace or two beside Philip, then asked, "Why are you so damned relaxed about all this? What's happening is sheer bloody murder. How can you take it so easily?"

"Because something *is* happening," Philip replied. "For days there's been uncertainty; we've all been afraid. But now that something's actually happening, well, it's easier to take somehow."

"You sure about that? I mean, that it really *is* happening?"

"You saw for yourself back there on the road. There's been nothing like that before."

Reynolds swallowed and was silent.

Chapter
Thirty-Nine

Eric Bolton sat in The Bunch of Grapes. It was almost noon on Sunday and there was no news of P.C. Walters. Taunton wasn't that far away. If Walters had left early enough he should be back by now.

Eric Bolton sipped his pint of bitter and watched the door. Each time someone new entered he jumped. If Walters didn't arrive soon Ted Wilkes would. He always came in for a pint about midday.

Fred Clarke, the farmer, had come in earlier for a hurried drink. "You know the telephone lines are down?" he'd asked the barman. "Been down since yesterday."

"So I heard."

"What's the trouble?"

"Peter's Elm went over." The barman poured a drink. "Took the lines with it." He grinned. "What you worried about? Expecting a call from Raquel Welch?"

"Need weedkiller," Fred Clarke said. "That back wheat of mine's fighting a losing battle against ragwort. I was expecting some down Friday but it's not turned up. I want to be sure about tomorrow."

"Some of the stuff I pass across the bar's pretty deadly," the barman said. "Any good to you?"

"Couldn't afford it." Fred Clarke grinned, lifting his glass.

"Well, if you change your mind."

The barman went away. Fred Clarke glanced across at Eric Bolton. "Didn't see you at it this morning."

"What's that?"

"Jogging round the village."

"Oh, that." Bolton's voice was uneasy. "Don't want to overdo that sort of thing."

"Don't blame you." Fred Clarke finished his drink. "If you hear of anyone going into town let me know," he called to the barman.

The barman nodded. "Don't let the nettles get you down."

Fred Clarke waved a hand and left.

Eric Bolton waited.

Earlier that morning when Edith had asked him why he was looking so secretive, he'd not replied.

"Look like the cat that just swallowed the cream," she said. "I hope you know what you're doing. Lose another job in this place and there'll be no one left who'll have you."

Eric Bolton stared back at her. Her heavy arms were folded over her stomach and there was scorn in her eyes.

"Don't you worry about me," he said. "I'm onto something."

"Only thing you've ever been onto was a pint of bitter."

"Now . . ."

"Now nothing. You're not going to sit round under my feet all day. Go off and make your fortune somewhere else."

"You don't believe me, do you?"

Edith laughed.

"You'll see."

"I've seen before." Edith laughed again. "And a lot of good it's done me."

Eric Bolton hitched his trousers about his thick waist, looked at his wife, and turned away. He left the house and went out into the hot, flat sunlight and walked slowly toward The Bunch of Grapes.

A little after noon Ted Wilkes entered the public house.

He came in slowly. At his back he could still feel the strength of the oak. He went to the bar and waited while the barman poured him a pint of bitter from the wood.

"There you are, Ted," the barman said as he set the beer down.

Ted drank. "First today," he reported. The early, pink morning seemed very close. The day had for him a special touch. "Let's hope it's not the last."

"Knowing you? No chance."

"I hope you're right."

"I'd lay money on it."

"Never bet on certainties," Ted cautioned. "It's the best way I know of losing."

The barman grinned and moved off. Immediately Eric Bolton was at Ted's elbow. "Any news?" There were beads of sweat on his heavy forehead.

"Any news of what?" Ted asked, looking into Eric's greedy eyes.

It would not be easy, Ted knew that. No one was prepared for what he had to say; no one else was as ready as he to accept the strength of the oak and the simple solution it offered. They thought he was mad enough as it was. He only hoped that when the time came he would be able to convince enough of them.

"Percy? Is he back yet?" Eric persisted.

"I've not seen him."

"He did go to Taunton?"

"That's what he said."

"Listen." Eric's face moved closer. "You're not going to cut me out of it. Not now. Not after Percy told me about it last night."

Ted Wilkes sighed.

"Don't try bullshitting me now," Eric pressed on. "I've been down there, remember. I see what's buried there. I heard that—the device you set up to scare people off. Percy as much admitted—"

"There's nothing there, Eric," Ted said carefully. Sooner or later Eric had to be told the truth, and it might as well be now. "Not the sort of thing you think anyway," Ted added.

"I've seen it." Eric hissed the words. "With my own eyes. I heard them sounds. I saw the place."

"What you saw was the remains of Charlie Crump's marrow squash," Ted said. "What you heard—"

192

"Bullshit."

"It's the truth."

"Charlie Crump's squash? You expect me to believe that?"

"You've got to."

"What you rig up that scarecrow thing for, then?" His voice rose. "What was all them *sounds* I heard?"

Ted Wilkes shook his head. "I'm not sure, Eric," he said gently. "But I think you heard the voices of the creatures of the field."

"No."

"Yes."

"Bullshit." Eric Bolton repeated, but the force had gone from the word. He remembered the whispering; he saw the green shape move. He shook his head. "What you mean, creatures of the bloody field?"

"Charlie had some sort of turn," Ted explained, "the night before he died. He took an ax and cut that marrow squash to pieces. I found it, drying in the sun, smashed all over the back of that truck of his. So I buried it. I put it back where it came from. It seemed the decent thing to do."

Eric Bolton licked his lips.

"That's what's buried there, Eric. That's what you found."

"I don't fucking believe you."

"Like to go and dig it up then?"

Eric Bolton swallowed.

"There's nothing there except that marrow squash," Ted said gently, "back where it belongs."

"But—" Eric put both hands on the bar; something had been taken from him, something had been removed. "What's that got to do with Hinkley Point—that there atom power station?"

"Nothing."

"But Percy said—"

"I know," Ted said. "He was putting you off, Eric. He was trying to keep you quiet."

"Why?"

"Well—" Ted drank a little beer—"that's something different, Eric. That's something different altogether."

"Listen." Eric's voice rose again. "You're not bloody—" He turned. There were other faces involved now, others listening. "There must've been something. If there wasn't, what was Percy putting me off for?"

Ted Wilkes sighed. "Percy went for help," he said. "He thinks he'll find it in Taunton."

"Help?"

"Yes."

"What for?"

"Us, all of us."

"What you on about?" Eric stepped back, his eyes cautious. There was too much he didn't understand. "What you telling me all this bullshit for?"

"I got a lot more to tell you, and none of it's bullshit." Ted raised his voice. "I got a lot to tell all of you. I was hoping it could wait until Percy got back but it looks as if I'll have to try on my own now."

"What's this," the barman asked, "something to do with Hinkley Point? I always said that atom station should never have been built down there."

"It's got nothing to do with that," Ted said.

"What's it got to do with, then?"

"Hard to say in a few words," Ted replied, glad it had begun. "But I suppose you could say it started with that marrow squash Charlie Crump found in his garden. It sort of began with that."

"What did?"

"Everything," Ted said simply.

The men in the pub edged closer. They began to listen. Ted Wilkes could not have chosen a better starting point, for everyone had seen Charlie Crump's marrow squash, most had touched its bulk. These men lived by the soil; they were close to it; what the soil produced they trusted. But they had seen the changes the summer had brought and now they listened to Ted Wilkes as he began to try to explain what he believed the changes meant to them all.

"What happened to Charlie?" someone asked.

"He—" Ted began.

Eric interrupted. "He went berserk or something.

194

He chopped that marrow to pieces. That's what Ted says, anyway." He turned to the others. "That don't sound right to me," he added. "It's not like Charlie."

"Not like Charlie to drink lemonade," the barman pointed out.

"Not like—"

"Listen to me, all of you!" Ted Wilkes raised his voice. "Charlie's dead. He cut that marrow to pieces and he's dead. Now I got a few ideas about what happened to him and what's happening to all of us."

He looked at the eager faces, hoping he would be able to convince enough of them.

"I got a few things to say to you, all of you. I was going to wait till Percy Walters got back from Taunton but I reckon the time has come."

"What's Percy gone into Taunton for?" someone asked.

"He's gone to tell them what I'm going to tell you," Ted said. "The telephone wires are down so he drove in this morning."

"What you got to tell us that's so important?"

Ted smiled. "All I ask is that you're patient with me. I know most of you think I'm a daft old bugger. Well, all of you might after this."

"You're not going to tell us it's the end of the world again?" said the barman, making an effort to keep his voice light. "None of that crap?"

"You'll have to make up your own mind about that." Ted Wilkes picked up his pint of bitter and walked to the long table by the fireplace and sat in his seat in the corner. "Why don't you all come over here?" he suggested. "Be easier if you're sitting down."

"Well . . ."

Some hesitated, but there was something about the day which involved them all, and they had nothing else to do.

Eric Bolton was the last to join them. He hitched his trousers about his heavyset body and waited. It didn't matter what Ted Wilkes said to the others, he wasn't fooled. There was more in Charlie's garden than a marrow squash. He was still convinced of it.

The men at the table sat quietly. No one spoke. They'd give old Ted Wilkes his chance. They'd do that. He might even be good for a laugh.

Ted Wilkes looked at them all, feeling suddenly peaceful, wise, and somehow prepared. It was as if he'd come a long way for this and he was glad he had finally arrived.

He began to speak and the men at the table listened.

Only the barman remained leaning on the bar, listening also.

Outside the sky altered; deepened and grew darker. The sun turned to red and a band of light began to spread along the horizon as Ted Wilkes talked of the plants. And how he believed the plants were watching them all.

Chapter
Forty

As Ted Wilkes expounded on his theory in The Bunch of Grapes, Deborah Monk led Mabel Crewe away from the village.

They walked steadily along a country lane deeper into the valley in which Brandling lay.

Mabel Crewe felt vulnerable, exposed. It was the first time she'd been out of the house since the rosebush had thrown her to the ground. She walked carefully, her upright old figure a little behind Deborah's.

Deborah walked eagerly, looking down toward the green, overgrown, rolling valley and the little stream which ran through it. She knew what she would find when she came to the stream. She'd been there often, mostly alone, but once with Jacob.

There was a stone bridge at the bottom of the lane which spanned the sparkling stream. From the bridge a narrow path ran along the bank toward a clearing in which the sunflowers grew.

Deborah didn't know where the sunflowers came from or if anyone had planted them. All she knew was that they'd been in the clearing all summer and that they were her special friends.

She walked eagerly toward them, her brown and white guinea pig cuddled in her thin arms.

Hesitantly, Mabel Crewe followed, a little afraid. She would be faced with it now. Until Deborah had approached her that morning she had almost been able to deny the voices and the things they told her. She had been able to put the phenomenon down to age or an aberration of hearing. But the bright eager eyes of the child and the innocence of her voice had disarmed the old woman.

197

Mabel Crewe's worst moment had been yesterday when Philip had tried to tell her what he thought was happening. Then fear had overwhelmed her and all she'd been able to do was hide.

But now, as she walked down the country lane, she became aware of a growing sense of companionship. This precocious child was suddenly very dear to her. Around her she was intensely aware of the presence of everything which grew.

Even the guinea pig in Deborah's arms seemed part of her now.

Mabel Crewe marveled, her step quickening. In the sunlight, among green leaf and wild flower, between butterflies and bees, walking with the simple child holding her tiny pet, Mabel Crewe felt as if she were becoming more complete, were beginning to feel closer to everything around her than she ever had before.

"Is it far now?" she asked.

Deborah looked up. "No, it's not far now." She walked another pace or two, moving steadily, concentrating on her progress, then she asked, "Would you like to carry the guinea pig for a while?" She lifted the small animal and held it at arm's length. "He's not very heavy."

Mabel Crewe took the guinea pig. "I'd be delighted to."

"We really should give him a name, shouldn't we?" Deborah suggested. "It's not fair to let him go too far without a name, is it?"

"No, it doesn't seem right."

"I mean, we all have names, don't we?"

"Yes, we do." Mabel Crewe rubbed the guinea pig's snout and it pressed against her fingers. "Do the sunflowers have names?" she asked.

Deborah shook her head. "No. They don't have names. They don't need them, you see. They're *special* friends, so they don't need names at all."

Mabel Crewe nodded. There seemed nothing further to say.

As Deborah guided Mabel Crewe to the sunflowers, her father led Harry Reynolds into The Bunch of Grapes.

When they entered, Philip thought at first that the public house was empty. Only the barman stood at the bar, and for the moment or two it took his eyes to accustom to the light, he did not see the group at the long table in the corner.

Ted Wilkes looked up as Philip and Reynolds entered; conversation ceased. Ted wondered what the baldheaded man with Philip represented. He hoped it was help, some kind of cooperation. He was convinced that belief and understanding were needed now; faith, not science or rationalization, might get them through the long, slow process of communication which lay ahead.

At the long table he'd spoken to the others of the danger he believed they all faced. He told them of Philip Monk's involvement and how Monk believed that the plants were trying to warn them all of their own insanity; of the risk that mankind as a whole ran if the pollution and waste and disregard for the planet continued.

He explained how both he and Monk felt it was up to them all to answer the plants, to try to communicate.

As he spoke to the sunburned faces, lined with weather and time, Ted Wilkes felt a definite response. It was slow, almost laconic, but these men *had* seen what the summer had done. They'd witnessed growth which had amazed them, and in some cases the amazement had been mixed with awe.

So, as they watched the face they'd known for years and listened to old words put together in new ways, they became acutely aware of the old man's belief and his conviction.

Yet it would take more than Ted's beliefs and convictions to persuade them that their lives were in actual danger or that the shape of their own knowledge had changed so abruptly.

It was into this atmosphere of uncertainty and mixed belief that Philip Monk and Harry Reynolds came, adjusting their eyes to the gloom. They stopped when they saw the group at the table and turned toward it.

"Come over," Ted Wilkes invited. "I've just been telling the lads what's going on down here."

The faces at the table watched Philip and Reynolds approach; the outside world had entered and now that outsiders were involved the circumstances seemed somehow more official.

Philip introduced Reynolds.

Reynolds looked down at the men. This gathering in The Bunch of Grapes appeared almost as unreal to him as the hand emerging from the foliage on the country road.

"What exactly have you told these men?" Philip asked Ted Wilkes.

"Just about everything I know."

"Do they believe you?"

"Hard to say." Ted sighed. "I think most of them are sure I'm as daft as I sound."

"They've got to believe you."

"*Got* to, Mr. Monk?" a voice queried.

"Yes. Your constable didn't and it killed him."

The brutal words had their effect; faces hardened, eyes turned away.

"Percy?" someone asked.

"He's dead," Philip told them. "He didn't get through to Taunton. Mr. Reynolds found him on the road. He'd been torn to shreds."

"For Christ's sake!"

Philip described what Reynolds had found, and as he spoke he watched the expressions on their faces alter. Something primitive, something ancient, had entered the barroom.

"Poor old Percy," Ted Wilkes said finally. "I told him not to go."

"What do you mean?" Eric Bolton asked quickly. "What do you bloody know about this?"

"Like I said, I told him."

"You knew it was going to happen?"

"No," Ted answered evenly. "But I knew there

was no help in Taunton. I knew that what we had to do, we had to do here, ourselves."

"Listen"—Eric Bolton stood and leaned on the table—"I've had enough of this. I've had enough bullshit. I want to know what's really going on. I want the real truth."

"The truth?" Ted's voice was suddenly sharp. "Is that what you want, Eric Bolton? The truth?"

"Course."

"Would you know it if you heard it?"

"Course I would."

"Tell us about it, then." The old man leaned forward. "Tell us about the *truth*, Eric."

Eric Bolton's resolution waned. There was a sound he did not understand, a movement which did not belong.

"Come on," Ted Wilkes persisted. "You faced it, Eric Bolton. You were there. Greed, gluttony, Eric— that's your sin." His voice softened. "The way Percy's was pride."

"I don't know what you mean." Eric cleared his throat. "I don't know what you're on about."

"You've seen the truth, Eric," Ted told him evenly. "When you were down there at Charlie Crump's place."

Everyone looked at Eric Bolton.

"You were down there and you *saw* the truth, Eric," Ted continued. "Tell us about it. Tell us what you saw, and heard."

"Listen—" Eric's voice was uncertain. "I didn't—"

"*Tell us what happened.*"

Eric Bolton's heavy face sagged. Ted Wilkes' words were cutting. The eyes of his companions stripped him bare. "You know what happened." Eric begged Ted Wilkes. "I told you."

"I want you to tell everyone, Eric. I want them to hear what you've got to say." Ted's voice rose in pitch. "You were there; you *visited*. You know what happened. It's important that you tell us all." He smiled. "In a way you're a chosen one, Eric. You've heard the voice of the God of the earth. Now, tell us what it said."

Eric Bolton swallowed and began in a shaky voice to tell of his visit to Charlie Crump's and what he found there. The others listened. It was easier for them now. Where Ted had outlined a belief, Eric Bolton made it real. He had been there, motivated by reasons they all understood.

Philip Monk listened closely. Everything Eric Bolton said confirmed Michael Martin's earlier fears. It was all there. It had all happened. It was as if one of Martin's experiments had become vocal, bearing witness, relating.

Reynolds shook his head in disbelief. It was impossible. Yet it had occurred. I am part of this now, he thought. I am a protagonist. If I hadn't found Walters they wouldn't be taking this as seriously. Good God, it's medieval.

Everyone listened as Eric told of the sound, the green arm moving, and the fear.

"Then I ran," Eric said. "I didn't know what it was. I ran. It scared me."

The men at the table saw his fear, heard it in his voice. It was with each of them for a moment in the bar.

"I've never seen nothing like it." Eric's voice trembled. "Shit, I just run."

"We'd all have run," Ted told him.

"It was the sound they made."

"I know," Philip Monk said quietly. "I've heard it too."

Others turned toward Philip Monk, this stranger, the man who came to their village when it suited him.

"When I found Mabel Crewe," Philip said. "I heard it. Mabel heard it too."

"And this—sound," someone asked, "what you make of it? You do all the science stuff. You should know."

Philip looked at the speaker. He was tall, with a hooked nose, a man seeking someone to blame for what he could neither explain nor reject.

"I don't know what it is," Philip said. "But my

daughter says it's the sound the plants make when they're talking."

The men murmured in unison, grateful for a scapegoat, glad to have found someone to blame. Here was an opportunity to turn their fear into scorn.

"I thought you knew about science?" The hook-nosed man scoffed.

"Load of—" someone else agreed.

"His *daughter?*" the man with the hooknose added. "Who's he think he is?"

"—living in London—"

"It's us down here that matters, Mr. Monk," a steadier voice said. "Us, in the village here. We *live* here, we're—"

"Alpha and Omega," Ted Wilkes commented quietly. "An old man and a child." But no one seemed to hear.

Then Reynolds broke in. "*Stop it. The lot of you. Stop it,*" he shouted, amid the anger and the babble. He had brought the news which confirmed their fear. He would use it now to restore order. "*Stop this . . . chaos,*" he cried.

The voices diminished.

Reynolds suddenly had great presence.

"I don't understand what's happened here," he told them. "I only know what I've seen. Here. Today. This morning. And let me tell you if any of you had seen what was left of that man, of his face—nothing but that hand sticking out. If you'd seen it, none of you would be shouting now like children. You'd all be listening. If it happened to him it could happen to you. Because it was bloody murder."

The barroom was silent.

"It's not only Brandling," Reynolds went on quickly, pointing to Philip. "He got through to London. It's beginning all over the country."

He reported on Philip's conversation with Alistair Rank. "They've no idea what to do." Reynolds added, "They just don't know how to fight it." The men looked at each other, then away.

"But—" someone began, uncertainly.

203

"There are no buts," Reynolds interrupted. "There are only facts. I've seen one of those facts and it's changed me. In all my life, in all the years I've worked with all sorts of fauna, I've never come across anything like this. You've got to believe me," he urged them. *There's never been anything like this before.*"

"We've been selected," Ted Wilkes said simply.

"Selected?"

"Yes, it's up to us now. We must bear the burden."

"Do *you* know what to do?" Philip Monk asked gently.

Ted Wilkes nodded. "Yes."

"What?"

"Believe."

"Believe?"

"All of us, together, must believe in the creatures of the field," Ted said. "Make them understand." He looked about the table. "I know what you're thinking. You think I've got religion." He shook his head. "Well, it's not like that at all. Believing is our only hope."

"It's our only chance," Philip agreed, and sat at the table, joining the others. "We mustn't fight them and we mustn't resist. We must just let them tell us what we've got to know."

"That's stupid," someone said. "Just because that girl of yours—"

"That girl of mine is closer to all living things than you or I will ever be," Philip answered.

"Is she?"

"Yes."

"She is," Ted Wilkes confirmed. "I *know.*"

"What *do* you know?"

"I know that today there will be a sign."

"What do you mean, a sign?" the man with the hooked nose asked.

"I felt it this morning and I know it will come today," Ted replied.

"How do you know?"

"How do I know anything?" Ted Wilkes leaned toward the speaker. "How do I know the sun will shine in the morning or darkness will come tonight?

Not because it's happened before. Not anything that simple. I *know* there'll be a sign," he repeated. "And if you doubt me, go outside and look at the sky."

For a moment no one moved.

Then one or two went, consumed by curiosity and fear and something close to awe. Finally they all obeyed. There was a look in Ted Wilkes' eye which directed them. There were foreign forces at work which compelled. There was their own basic unease at the summer and its power which forced them to go outside and look up at the sky.

It was pink now and the sun was darkening, growing blood red and heavy. The day had altered. The long, blue, cloudless sky they'd known all summer was slowly changing before their eyes.

"What is it?" someone asked.

"The beginning," Ted Wilkes said. "Or the end."

"It's—"

"We must all gather," Ted Wilkes said. "We must all get together." He knew he had to collect them. "Go home. Gather your wives and families. Bring them here."

"Why?"

"What for?"

"Go and collect them," Ted Wilkes commanded. He looked at their faces and there was a smile in his eyes. A glint of something close to laughter. "*And lo, there was a great earthquake and the sun became black as a sackcloth of hair and the moon became as blood,*" he quoted. "Go now, while you've still got the chance."

Slowly the men began to dispel, reluctantly, uncertainly most of them because they did not know what else to do.

Only Reynolds remained with Ted Wilkes, the barman, and Philip Monk. They stood in a small group watching the others walk away.

Then the barman spoke. "I'll have to bring her down," he said, referring to the landlady who lay upstairs. Elderly, blind, incontinent, she'd not been down the stairs of The Bunch of Grapes in almost five years. "She can't be left alone."

"She'll be all right," Ted Wilkes said.

"Not if what you say's true."

"Then bring her down."

"I can't manage on me own."

"I'll help you."

"She'll want to go to church though," the barman told them. "She swore she'd not come down those stairs unless it was to go to church." He looked at Ted. "Why don't we all go there, to the church?"

"It's empty now," Ted said. "The vicar's been gone for years. They only hold a service on feast days. Some stranger comes and talks to us and it's opened for the day. Rest of the time it's locked shut, lad. You know that as well as I do. This place'll suit us fine."

"If you say so," the barman said uncertainly.

"I do."

Ted Wilkes and the barman went inside.

Philip Monk turned to Reynolds. "I'll go and get Elizabeth and the children," he said, aware of a twinge of fear.

"I'll stay here," Reynolds offered. "God knows why, but I'll stay here."

"The others will be back soon."

"Will they?"

Philip nodded. "They've no alternative."

Philip Monk walked up the High Street toward the white, thatched cottage. Something was going to happen which made him suddenly sure. This was what they had all been waiting for and its imminent presence was awesome.

Philip hurried. His scalp prickled and his fear grew. He had an immediate need to be with Elizabeth and the children. They seemed suddenly vulnerable, far away.

Philip hurried, wondering where his fear came from. It was not like him to panic.

Chapter
Forty-One

"Where's everyone gone?" Jacob asked Elizabeth as he dumped his books on a chair. "The place's deserted."

Elizabeth looked up from the bed she was making.

"Daddy's gone out." Jacob answered his own question. "Debby and Miss Crewe've gone too. It's all a bit preposterous."

"Debby's gone," his mother began, then remembered. "Oh, yes—she and Mabel went for a walk."

"A walk?"

"Yes." Elizabeth tucked in a corner. "That's what they said."

"I wonder where they've gone?" Jacob mused. Walking to the window, he looked out at the changing sky. "They'll get wet if they're not careful."

"Wet?"

"I think it's going to rain."

"I'd like to believe you, Jacob," Elizabeth said, shaking out a pillow. "But rain's something that happens at night these days."

"Well, it *looks* like rain."

Elizabeth smoothed a sheet, then joined her son at the window. The pink sky and the blood-red sun startled her. The blue she'd become accustomed to was gone.

"It *does* look funny," she agreed.

"A sky like that's the sign of something," Jacob said easily. He folded his arms and looked at his mother. "Where did you say Debby and Miss Crewe had gone?"

"Oh—" Elizabeth shrugged. "Not far. They said they wouldn't go very far."

"Well, I think it's all *very* strange."

"What is?"

"The fact that they've taken the new guinea pig with them," Jacob said. "I find *that* very odd."

"Oh?"

"I went down to have a look at him a little while ago," Jacob explained, "and he wasn't there. The cage was empty so I can only conclude they've taken him with them."

"What's odd about that?"

"Well, the only time Debby ever takes the guinea pig out—she used to take Mr. Snuffles down there quite a lot—was when she went to talk to the sunflowers."

Elizabeth stopped. Something alien had entered the peaceful room. She felt suddenly close to panic. She looked at Jacob, at his small, serious face.

"That's the only time I've ever *known* her take Mr. Snuffles out, anyway," he said.

"Why—" Elizabeth began, but the words would not come. She patted the already made bed and attempted to pull herself together. "Why would they go down there?" she managed to ask.

"To see the sunflowers?" Jacob wondered. "You know what Debby's like about them." His voice was distant, not quite even. "We talked about it the other day, don't you remember?"

"In the kitchen?"

"That's right. When she said it was—" Jacob hesitated.

"—a secret?" Elizabeth's head came up. The moment of panic had passed. Replacing it was a deeper fear, something old, buried, half forgotten. "Is that what you mean? When Debby said you'd a secret?"

Jacob shrugged uneasily.

Elizabeth walked toward her son and took his hands, holding them hard, seeing the reaction in his eyes and recognizing in them a distant concealed fear of his own. He had not spoken casually. He had mentioned the sunflowers with thought and purpose.

"Tell me about the sunflowers, Jacob," Elizabeth said as calmly as she could. "What's so important about them?"

Jacob suddenly looked very young, very vulnerable, very much a child.

"I've got to know, Jacob. It's very important."

"They're special sunflowers," Jacob said uneasily. "They grow down by the Old Bridge. There's a space there they grow in."

"Why are they a secret?" Elizabeth felt the edge in her voice. She disliked what she was doing and the fear it created in Jacob's eyes. But she must persist. There was something urgent in the room now. The light was changing. The day was turning. "Tell me, Jacob," she insisted. "Why are they a secret?"

Jacob looked at his mother. "Don't you know?" he asked.

Elizabeth shook her head.

"But I—we've told you how Debby talks to them."

"But that's just games."

"And they talk to Debby too," Jacob said, his words gathering confession. "You know that too. We told you that."

"Games—weren't they just games?" Elizabeth's voice faltered. There had been too many conversations. There had been too much said. The voices of the children, the sounds of the garden. The conversations with Philip. The deaths and the entrances. It was more than she could accommodate any longer.

No, she told herself abruptly. *I must hold on to what sanity remains. I must not lose touch.* She looked into her son's eyes. They were desperate for help. "Games?" she repeated. "Weren't they just games?"

"No."

"What were they then?"

"Oh, Mummy." Jacob broke. He held himself stiffly, then began to cry, silently, feeling the tears run down his face. "Mummy," he said. "They frighten me —the sunflowers. . . . I don't understand them the way Debby does."

"Why is Debby . . . different?" his mother asked, forcing the words.

"She says they're her friends."

"Friends?"

"Yes." Jacob sobbed, a deep choking sob. "They tell things to her. She says they tell her things." His voice broke again. "She says they tell her things about other people."

"What things?"

"I—I don't know," Jacob said. "I—I don't know what they say to—to her. I don't like it down there with the sunflowers. They frighten me."

While the blood sun hung in the darkening sky and her daughter walked down the country lane, Elizabeth knew then she must hurry.

"I'm sorry." Jacob reached out for his mother and held her. "I didn't think there was anything wrong."

"There's nothing wrong."

"But you're cross with me."

"No," Elizabeth said. "I'm not cross with you. I'm not cross with anyone. But I must know what Debby's doing. I must know why she's gone down to the sunflowers—now." She bit her lip. "I must know why she took Mabel with her."

"She said—" Jacob began.

"What?"

"She said the sunflowers told her to." The words spilled out. "I promised not to say anything about that too. I said I wouldn't. But they did—that's what she told me. They told her to take Miss Crewe down there. She said—they said—they wanted to see her."

"*They* . . . said that?"

"That's what Debby said."

"Why?"

"I don't know." Jacob's voice broke. He pushed his head forward, holding himself against his mother. "I don't know, Mummy. Really I don't. Please, I don't know anything about them. It's Debby who knows."

"Do you know where they are?"

Jacob nodded, moving his head against Elizabeth.

"Then you must take me there."

Jacob held his mother and said nothing.

"You must." Elizabeth was surprised at her own calm. She would go now and find what there was to be found. She was responsible. There was no alternative. "You must show me where the sunflowers are, Jacob,"

she said. "We must go down and find them. Now—
we must go now."

"All right." Jacob rubbed his cheek against his
mother's. "All right, then."

Elizabeth took her son by the hand and allowed
herself to be led from the white, thatched cottage.
The fear she had known was receding, changing, becoming a force she could use.

Just before she and Jacob left the house, Elizabeth scribbled a note to Philip on a pad by the telephone in the hall.

We've gone to the Old Bridge, she wrote. *Please
come down if you possibly can.*

She dropped the note on the floor by the front
door and then she left, led by Jacob. Going out into
the huge, darkening day.

She did not know exactly what it was she was
seeking or what she would find, merely that now, she
was doing something positive. She neither wept, nor
questioned, nor despaired, and suddenly she felt very
much alive.

Chapter
Forty-Two

Deborah and Mabel Crewe sat in the small clearing in which the great sunflowers grew.

It was an isolated clearing, separate from the green lushness that surrounded them.

Behind, the small stream thrust its way silently between a growth of waterweed. Above, the pink sky showed between leafy overgrowth. About, there was a tangle of aspen and willow, a net of leaf and creeper, vine and tendril; wild flowers and nettles grew in profusion.

But where they sat, beneath the sunflowers, the clearing was spare, open, and inviting, and the sunflowers reigned.

There were seven tall, majestic creatures with strong green leaves and enormous blades and yellow faces. Faces which now turned down on their stately necks to the group seated below.

Deborah sat easily, her legs crossed, holding the guinea pig on her lap. She smiled happily at the flowers towering above.

Mabel Crewe sat stiffly on the rich grass, wishing she were able to relax the way Deborah relaxed and regretting it was impossible. Relaxing was something she had never achieved. Throughout her long, lonely life, she suddenly realized, she had never been completely at ease.

Mabel watched Deborah's bright, upturned face. You don't know how lucky you are, she thought. You don't know how exempt you are from so much adult anguish.

Mabel watched the sunflowers and saw them

move. The tall stately plants seemed, fractionally, hardly at all, to turn, to nod in greeting.

Mabel Crewe put a hand to her mouth; she watched the gentle movement again. It was delicate, fragile, and Mabel wondered why she was not more afraid, more disbelieving. She felt curious, almost enchanted, but not afraid.

She was aware of the innocence and delight on Deborah's upturned face.

"It's all right, Miss Crewe," Deborah said. "They like you."

"Do they?" Mabel Crewe found herself whispering.

Deborah nodded, her face radiant. "Yes, they're very gad you've come. They like my new guinea pig, too. They like us all very much."

Mabel Crewe sat very still. There was nothing she wanted to say, she felt peaceful and strangely elevated. She thought about the curious process which had led her to where she was, and she regretted she had not shared her emotions.

She wished she had been able to tell Philip Monk more about her own experiences, but there were too many barriers. When she'd heard voices or listened to the sounds her plants made, or, if she was truthful, the sounds she *thought* they made, she'd dismissed them. She'd pushed them aside. It was her age, she told herself; it was because she'd lived too long alone.

The only thing she'd ever done to admit the existence of the voices was to write to the BBC about Charlie Crump's marrow squash. But that was only because they'd been so persistent. Only because they'd told her again and again that she must write, that she must do something. Finally she had written, and was glad about it. It had relieved her to write it all down on a piece of paper, seal the envelope, and post it off.

Even when she'd seen those ponies on television, trapped by the overgrowth in the New Forest, and the voices told her that her own kind was being warned, separated, judged, she'd done nothing about it. It would have sounded silly, she knew. No one would have taken her seriously.

She understood, of course, why the rosebush had shocked her. It wasn't because she was about to prune it; or, it wasn't only that. It was because she'd not passed on the messages; she'd not told anyone else what she knew. She had been chosen and she had been informed, but she'd failed the test. And she knew it. That was why the rosebush had retaliated. She should have done what they'd asked her to do from the beginning.

Well, anyway, she thought, I'm here now. That's something. At least I've come this far, now.

"They haven't said anything yet," Deborah explained. "Sometimes it takes them quite a long time before they begin. And sometimes they don't say anything at all." She smiled at Mabel Crewe. "Isn't that funny. Sometimes I just sit here and listen and listen but they don't say anything at all."

"Have you ever brought anyone else down here?" Mabel asked.

"Only Jacob. He was quite odd about it," Deborah said, sitting very straight, holding the guinea pig on her lap. The animal sat huddled, hardly moving, its black eyes steady. "He thought it was all a joke at first and he laughed at me. But later on, when they moved, he got a bit frightened and wanted to go home. He really did." Her smile was mischievous. "He really got a fright."

"They don't frighten you though, do they?"

"Of course not—they're my friends."

"Of course."

"He said he wasn't going to tell anyone about them," Deborah went on. "But he did. He told Mummy. Even though he said he wouldn't. It was going to be a secret between us, but he told."

"That wasn't very nice."

"Well," Deborah said forgivingly, "I don't suppose it's his fault really. He's a boy. Boys can't keep secrets the same way girls can."

Mabel Crewe smiled.

"But I hope they'll talk to us today," Deborah

went on. "They like you and they like the new guinea pig so I suppose they will. I hope so, anyway."

"So do I."

"Although I must say it's a funny-looking day," Deborah said. "Can't you see? The sky's gone quite pink, and the sun's gone a funny color as well. It doesn't usually look like that."

Mabel Crewe hadn't noticed how the sky had changed and the color of the sun had deepened, becoming that of blood. She stared up, past the stately sunflower heads, wondering if there were anything specially significant about the color of the sky.

There must be, she thought. I can feel it.

What it was that surrounded her she did not know. What was about to overtake her she could not imagine. She merely knew that as surely as she sat on the grass beneath the sunflowers, something was about to occur, and that she was part of it.

The sunflowers continued to move, arcing their delicate necks in a stately bow to the people below. They began to tremble slightly, delicately, so that their leaves and petals made the faintest, rustling sound.

"Listen!" Deborah said excitedly. "They're talking to us."

Mabel Crewe waited.

She glanced at Deborah and saw the enchantment on the child's face; it radiated peace and innocence.

The sunflowers rustled, moving their great yellow and black faces.

"Can't you hear them?" Deborah asked, her voice high with excitement. "Miss Crewe—can *you* hear what they're saying?"

"No." Mabel shook her head. There was something wrong somewhere, something out of place. These were not her voices, not the sounds she had heard, not the messages she'd received. She felt suddenly alien. "No," she whispered, "I can't hear what they're saying at all."

"You must listen very hard."

"I am."

"They like you."

"Are you sure?"

Deborah nodded.

"But I can't hear them!"

"Oh, what a pity."

"Why can't I hear them, Deborah?" Mabel Crewe felt lost, deprived. Somehow the illusion that she held of joining the child, of sharing her simplicity, was dying. She was uncertain now of her feeling of peace. There was harm somewhere, danger. She felt an outsider. "Why can't I hear them?" she repeated.

"You're not listening hard enough," Deborah said confidently. "You've really got to listen very hard, Miss Crewe. Very hard with all your ears."

"No." Mabel Crewe shook her head vigorously. "I can't."

"Yes, you can."

Miss Crewe listened to the delicate rustling of the plants as it increased, turning her head this way and that. The rustling sound rose. There were no words among it, no voices. Only the steady sound of leaves shivering. And something else. There was a smell in the clearing now, a delicate musky odor, floating in waves, accompanying the sound.

"They're sorry you can't understand them," Deborah said. "They're very sorry about that. They know how disappointed you must be but you've got to know them a long time, a very long time, to really understand them." She smiled a wise smile. "They say it's different with your roses. You know them a lot better, that's why you can hear them."

"My roses—" Mabel Crewe stopped. "They know about my roses?"

"They know about everything. There's nothing they don't know," Deborah confided, pleased, proud, part of their spirit. "They're very sorry about you and they want you to be patient."

Mabel Crewe waited.

"They want something else," Deborah said, responding in a new way. She was watching the heavy black and yellow faces make their fragile maneuvers.

216

"I'm not quite sure what it is yet, but they want something or someone."

"Someone?"

Deborah nodded. "Yes," she said, "I think it's someone they want, but I'm not certain yet."

Mabel Crewe stared at the child. "Are you sure?"

"Well, I think it's *someone* they want," Deborah said, concentrating.

The sound was spreading now, widening; other plants began to move.

"They've had people before," Deborah said. "They've told me about *that*."

"What people? Where?"

"There was that man outside your place." Deborah glanced at Mabel Crewe, giving her a look that was knowing, wise beyond all time. "The one that died there."

"Charlie Crump?" Mabel Crewe whispered.

"He did something terrible," Deborah said. "Very, very wicked. He chopped up something with an ax. They were very cross about that, very cross indeed."

"Is that what they told you?"

Deborah nodded.

"What else did they tell you?"

"About the policeman," Deborah said. "They told me about him this morning."

"Walters?"

"Yes."

"What happened to him?" Mabel Crewe asked, knowing already, sensing the answer but forcing the question. "Tell me. What happened to him?"

"He died too," Deborah said. "He was fighting them and he shouldn't have been fighting them. So he died too." She sighed. "They were sorry about that because they liked him, but he was fighting them and that's wrong."

"My God." Mabel Crewe's voice trembled. "What do they want now?"

"It *is* a pity you don't understand them."

"Tell me what they want now?"

"They want someone who'll go with them," Deborah said slowly. "Someone who will go with them on their own. Someone they don't have to take."

"No—"

"Because they don't like taking people, Miss Crewe, unless they're wicked."

"Yes, yes," Mabel urged. Danger had come now. It had spoken. "But—"

"—but they do want someone," Deborah continued. "They want someone who will go with them. Someone who will go with them and stay."

"Why do they want this, this atonement?"

Deborah did not understand the word.

"Why do they want—someone?" Mabel explained. "Why, Debby? Have they told you why?"

Deborah nodded. "If someone goes to them, on their own," she explained, "then they'll know we understand them. They will, won't they, Miss Crewe?" she asked. "They'll know, then, that there's more than just me listening. They'll know that there's more— more people who understand."

"Is that what they've said?" Mabel Crewe's voice was a whisper. "Are you sure that's what they want."

"Yes." Deborah was confident. "That's what they want."

She lifted her head to the sunflowers, listening to what they had to say, fascinated by each movement. She smiled and her young face was calm.

Mabel Crewe shivered, aware of a distant fear and at the same time of a strange responsibility. Her gaze went past the sunflowers to the changing sky and slowly she became certain that she had spent all her life waiting for this unusual day.

So they remained, unaware that behind them Elizabeth and Jacob were following the same route, or that soon Philip Monk would also be drawn to the sunflowers.

When Philip Monk arrived at the cottage he was concerned to find it empty. He'd hurried from The Bunch of Grapes convinced that somehow on this incredible day a threat surrounded them all.

218

Although he did not know what it was, he was aware of its enormous presence and of a sudden need to be with his family.

When he arrived he went around the side of the cottage, hoping to find the children in the garden or Elizabeth in the kitchen.

Both places were deserted, and it wasn't until he'd been through the house itself that he found the note by the front door.

We've gone to the Old Bridge. Please come down if you possibly can.

The writing was hurried, scrawled, obviously urgent.

Philip frowned, not certain where the Old Bridge was. There was the stream skirting the village and the lane which led to it, but was there a bridge? Then he recalled—the yellow stone bridge and a clear, bright stream running beneath it.

He looked at the note again. It did not tell him enough. He imagined that all four had gone to the Old Bridge together, but he couldn't think why. He was aware that his hands were shaking.

It doesn't make sense, he thought.

He looked out, up at the sky filled with a blood-heavy sun.

Liz is frightened, he thought, like I am. Philip crumpled the note and dropped it. He opened the front door and went out, then paused, wondering for one absurd moment whether or not he should take something—a weapon, a tool, something for protection.

Then he shook his head. The idea was ridiculous.

He left the cottage, running. He did not know what he would find. He only hoped that whatever it was he would arrive before it became active. He couldn't remember ever having experienced such fear before.

Chapter
Forty-Three

While Philip Monk ran toward the Old Bridge, the villagers of Brandling gathered at The Bunch of Grapes.

They came in twos and threes; some in family groups, some alone; slowly or quickly; silently or making their voices heard. They gathered, looking toward one another for some hope or explanation, but primarily they came to share their fear.

Some had come readily enough, accepting that the long, hot, bursting summer precursed such a day as this. Others looked at the changing sky and were afraid, wanting to hide, to remain behind with the doors locked and the windows closed. But reluctantly or with readiness, all finally began to gather at the public house.

Some came emptyhanded. Others brought with them some small possession. A vase, a picture, a plastic radio, some token of the security they had known and wanted desperately to retain; something that confirmed who they were; something that told them everything would be all right.

Each and every one of them had his own personal fear.

They came with their children and their aged.

They held or carried or helped those who were unable to walk unaided, arriving as a community for the first time in all the years any of them had lived in the village. They assembled in a way they had never done before.

They all came, every villager in Brandling was drawn to The Bunch of Grapes that Monday under the reddening sky and there they waited, patiently or impatiently, with peace or ill will, until their number was complete.

There were thirty-seven inhabitants of Brandling gathered at the pub that day. All came except the Monks and Mabel Crewe.

Harry Reynolds, in disbelief, watched the villagers gather.

Ted Wilkes had convinced him that some aspect of a community feeling was needed. But he would not have believed that the village itself would respond so readily.

My God, he thought, it's either a miracle or some gigantic folly.

He stood by as they gathered at The Bunch of Grapes, filling it, spilling out, standing about the doorway beneath the sign, waiting.

Ted Wilkes and the barman brought the old lady who held the license for the pub down the low, twisting stairs and seated her behind the bar.

She was confused and petulant. "Is it church?" she asked in a wavering voice. "Is that why you've brought me down?"

"Yes," Ted Wilkes told her evenly.

"Where's the vicar?"

"He'll be here soon."

The old woman shook her head and looked at all the waiting faces. "Well, there's a good turnout," she observed. "The best I've seen for ages." A smile crossed her face.

"Yes," Ted Wilkes agreed. "It's the best it's ever likely to be." He watched the waiting faces, listened to the chatter. He was satisfied. It couldn't have been better. The absence of the Monks and Miss Crewe didn't distress him. Theirs was a separate solution. This was his. "Yes," he confirmed, "we're all here now."

"Where's the vicar?" the old lady persisted. "We can't start without the vicar."

"He's coming," Ted said softly. "He is nigh."

The old lady looked away, then began sucking the edge of her shawl.

Ted Wilkes eased his way through the crowd.

221

When he came to Eric Bolton and his wife, Edith, he paused. Eric had been closer to this phenomenon than most. "I'm glad you came," he said.

Eric Bolton grasped Ted's arm. "What's going to happen?"

"We'll all know soon enough," Ted replied. He removed Eric's fingers from his arm and moved on through the crowd, stopping here, talking there. Telling them all to be quiet and patient, asking them to believe.

In what? they asked. And how?

"We'll find out soon enough," he said.

A woman's lips trembled. "Someone said it's the end of the world." Her face was like chalk. "Is that true? Tell me, is that true?"

"What if it was?"

The woman closed her eyes.

"Wouldn't you be glad you were here for it?" Ted Wilkes asked gently. "Be better than missing it."

"I don't want to die," the woman whispered.

"Who said anything about that?"

"If it's the end of the world—"

"If it is, then you're lucky," Ted Wilkes said simply. "You've got a fighting chance."

He moved on. He came to Harry Reynolds, standing apart from the crowd.

"Well, you've done it," Reynolds said. "You've got them here. God knows how. But you have."

"They wanted to come."

"Why?"

"They wanted to come, Mr. Reynolds, because *they wanted something to believe in*. They don't know it yet, and maybe they won't ever know it really. But that's why they're here."

Reynolds looked at the old man. "You're taking an awful chance, aren't you?"

"I know that."

"Why?"

Ted Wilkes smiled. "I'm doing it because I believe in it, Mr. Reynolds," he said simply. "I think they need us as much as we need them."

"Who—the plants?"

Ted Wilkes nodded.

Reynolds shook his head. "The plant kingdom doesn't need us."

"That's where you're wrong," Ted corrected. "You and Mr. Monk both. We all need one another." His voice was calm.

"I wish I shared your belief."

"Well, Mr. Reynolds," Ted Wilkes said easily, "by the end of the day you might do that. You might come round to believing that yourself."

"Why are you so sure something's actually going to happen?" Reynolds asked.

"I *know* it."

"How?"

For a moment Ted was tempted to tell Reynolds about his experience with the oak that morning, but he could not. I'm done with talking, he thought, I've got to show them now. That's the only thing that's left.

"I just know it will. It's natural—that's what it is, natural."

"When?"

Ted Wilkes looked up at the sky. It was growing darker. Redness spilled up from the horizon. A dark rim surrounded the sun. "We'll know soon enough," he said. "That's natural also."

It began with a jingling of horse brasses. Then The Bunch of Grapes began to shake, gently, steadily, awesomely. The whole building quivered. And inside, on the dark, low-beamed walls, the horse brasses jingled. Their sharp, urgent, clearly insistent sound silenced everything else.

The muttered conversation stopped; the murmurs of indecision and the small sounds of fear died. Everyone was still, quiet, not knowing immediately where the sharp metallic sound came from, only that it indicated the beginning of the event they had gathered to attend.

When they realized what was causing the sound their voices lifted in agitation. Some called out; some

223

whimpered. Then they all began to move outside, away from the steady jingling of the brasses and the slow, fearful shaking of The Bunch of Grapes.

They pushed one another out of the way, scrambling for the door. The sounds they made rose as their activity increased.

A child began to cry on a high, loud note.

The woman who had spoken to Ted Wilkes put her hand to her face and whispered again, "I don't want to die . . . please . . . I don't want to die." She clung to the quivering wall.

A man with a baby in his arms and a woman, also bearing a child, pushed through the doorway simultaneously. They struggled against each other, jamming the low-beamed doorway. Behind them those still inside pushed and, in the space of a few seconds, panic grew as they struggled and thrust, insistent on escape.

Then Ted Wilkes' massive, old man's voice cut through all the other sounds, silencing them.

"Don't be bloody fools!" Ted cried. "Don't throw it all away. This is what you've come here for. This is why you've gathered. It's happening, don't you see? It's happening."

The villagers of Brandling paused and some of the panic subsided.

"Go outside," Ted Wilkes said. "Go slowly. Don't be afraid. Everything will be all right."

Gradually the villagers began to obey.

The steady jingling of the horse brasses continued. With it now, gathering, gaining, and spilling over, came the rustling sounds of the plants, filling their ears.

Eric Bolton was the first to recognize it. "That's it," he said, panic in his voice. He called to Ted Wilkes. "That's the sound I heard down at Charlie Crump's." Holding his arms, he resisted an overwhelming desire to flee.

Ted Wilkes nodded. "It's the beginning."

"But what's—" Eric looked at The Bunch of Grapes and the gentle, steady movement it made. "The shaking?"

"I know the answer to that," Ted Wilkes said, rais-

224

ing his voice, informing them all. "But I want you all with me. I can't do it on my own."

The Bunch of Grapes was empty now except for the old woman sucking the edge of her shawl behind the bar. She sat with her head bent, listening to the sounds. Slowly, she began to sing the fractured, untuneful memory of a hymn.

Outside, the villagers looked at Ted Wilkes. He was their leader now, the only one with sufficient faith.

Slowly, surely, Ted walked around The Bunch of Grapes, beneath the hanging sign to the back of the white-plastered building with its beams and its thatch and the horseshoes nailed above the door. He walked steadily and the crowd followed.

Behind the building, pressing against the back wall of The Bunch of Grapes, grew an immense espaliered peach tree. For generations its arms and branches had been trained along the wall so that now it embraced the whole of it. The back wall of The Bunch of Grapes was entwined in its grip.

The tree was shaking now, pulsing like a live muscle along the wall of the building, its power immense.

Where it was nailed to the wall, plaster fell and a crack appeared at the corner of the building. Upstairs a window shattered and glass sprayed. Inside, the two-headed sheep on its mount of walnut over the bar fell to the floor.

A woman screamed when she saw the peach tree shuddering. She ran, then fell, her skirt riding up over her thigh. She continued to scream, lying on the grass beside The Bunch of Grapes.

Ted Wilkes turned as he heard her. He saw her fall. He went to her and, kneeling beside her on the grass, said soothingly, "It's all right. Don't be afraid."

The woman's eyes opened and she put a hand over her mouth. The sound of her screaming wrung the air. Somewhere a child began to cry in sympathy. The other women whispered, their own fear a tangible thing.

"Quiet," Ted said to the woman on the grass. "There's nothing to fear."

225

"I—" the woman began, saliva bubbling from her lips. "I want to go home. I want to get away."

"You must stay."

"No." The woman's terrified eyes turned to the peach tree. "It's the devil."

"No."

"Yes." The woman's voice rose. "You can see it. Look! It's not natural. It's the devil himself."

Ted Wilkes shook his head.

"It *is*."

"It's not the devil," Ted Wilkes told her calmly, raising his voice to include them all, the men with their amazed and cautious faces, the women with their murmurings and their palpable fear, the crying children. "It's not the devil," Ted Wilkes repeated. "It's the creatures of the field among us, making us hearken, telling us what to do. Advising us. Showing us the way."

"No." The woman rolled away, attempting to climb to her feet. "No—it's the devil. He's come to kill us all."

"Quiet."

"Look at the sky."

Ted Wilkes lifted his eyes and saw the red and vermilion darkening sky, aware of the light along the horizon.

"It's not right," the woman babbled. "It's evil."

"Listen." Ted Wilkes lifted his voice again, trying to calm the frightened faces, attempting to calm them all. "It's not evil. Or the devil. It's not wrong and there's nothing to fear. You must remain, be calm. This is our opportunity to believe and to show we believe. If we lose it now we are truly lost."

The woman became still, compelled by the sureness in Ted's voice.

The others paused. The child's crying was hushed and every villager stood and listened.

"You've all got to understand," Ted Wilkes went on. "The creatures of the field are waiting for an answer. We've got to speak to them. We've got to tell them what they want to know."

"And what's that?" a voice called.

"That we believe in all living things," Ted explained. "The house of God has many mansions. We've all got a place."

"Don't give us none of that."

"It's not me what's giving it," Ted interrupted, pointing to the shaking building. "You can see that for yourself."

"But—"

"But nothing. The time is nigh."

The heads of the villagers turned uneasily to and fro between the old man standing beside the woman who had screamed, and The Bunch of Grapes, shuddering beneath the strength of the peach tree.

It was a delicate moment, hanging precariously between an abyss of disbelief on one side and a valley of fear on the other.

"All right then," a man said, his voice breaking the tension. "Supposing we do believe you. Now you got us here what are you going to do?"

An immense sense of relief filled Ted Wilkes, comforting him. He breathed deeply. Whatever happened now, whatever the outcome, at least together, as a unity, the village was beginning to respond.

"Well?" the man persisted. "What you got in mind?"

"I'm going to try," Ted Wilkes replied.

"Try what?"

"Watch me." Ted Wilkes moved toward the peach tree, to the source of the power shaking the building. "Open your eyes and see."

The crowd waited. They had no choice now but to trust Ted Wilkes.

He walked toward the peach tree, extending both hands. Where the tree was thickest, above the point its roots entered the ground, he held it in his work-roughened hands and clung to it. He placed his forehead among its leaves. Slowly, gently, steadily he began to vibrate with the tree.

The tree seemed to move him as it moved the building, making him part of the force which flowed upward from the earth.

Pressing his forehead against the tree, it was as

though he sought the exchange of spirit he'd known earlier that morning beneath the oak. He felt the beginnings of transmission stirring him. As he clung to the tree, he believed for a moment that he alone would be enough.

Subdued, awed, the villagers watched as very slowly the vibrations increased in magnitude.

The building shuddered and a drain pipe fell to the ground. Dust rose from the thatching. The noise of the plants increased in volume.

Ted Wilkes lifted his head. His presence wasn't going to be enough, he knew that now. The others needed to become involved as well. They too must join.

"You've got to help me," he called. "I can't do it on my own."

No one responded.

"Come over here," Ted's voice urged. "Take hold of it the way I have. Join."

No one moved.

"Come on!"

The vibrations pulsated, the sounds deafened, dust motes swirled in the blood-dark air.

"Come on, all of you! You've all got to join."

Eric Bolton was the first to move. He approached Ted Wilkes slowly, uncertainly, rubbing his hands on his trousers. Then he stood beside Ted and took hold of the peach tree.

The power he felt throbbing through his fingers was so immense it stunned him. His impulse was to draw back. He looked into Ted's eyes, revealing his fear, and waited for the old man's calm, reassuring voice.

"I'm glad it's you," Ted said.

"Jesus, I'm scared!"

"Don't be. Stay with me."

"It's so bloody strong."

"I know. But hang on, Eric. Just hang on. Go with it."

"I can't."

"You can, Eric, you can." Ted's voice encouraged

him. "But don't fight it. Don't try to stop it. Put your head against the trunk and let it take you."

Eric Bolton put his head among the green peach leaves and tried to do what Ted Wilkes had asked him to do. He felt the tree's power absorb him and then, very slowly, he felt it take him, draw him in. He felt his fear dissolving into the tree. He felt at peace, at one with the tree, the earth, all life.

The villagers watched Eric Bolton, saw the ritual, and then they began to follow.

Edith stood beside her husband, lifting her heavy arms to take hold of the leaves and the branches.

The others came, moving slowly to the peach tree and placing their hands on the branches, their heads against the rustling leaves. For a moment they stood, quivering with the movement from the earth, forming a network, a filagree of hands and arms, leaves and branches, about The Bunch of Grapes.

"Believe," Ted Wilkes told them. "Just believe."

He looked at the figures, the bowed heads, as they felt themselves being drawn in, belonging.

"If you believe enough," Ted said, "the plants will know. If you're honest enough, they'll understand." His voice was steady. "If we all believe that we need one another, that there's room for us all, that we're all creatures of the field and that we all belong, they'll understand." He lifted his head from the peach tree. "It's dignity you've got to believe in," he said simply. "Dignity and truth and sharing."

Harry Reynolds watched, spellbound.

"Dignity," Ted Wilkes repeated, "and truth, and sharing."

Then Reynolds joined the villagers. He never knew, then or after, what made him do it. But, slowly, like a man in a dream, he moved to the tree and joined it.

This is—he thought, but that was all.

The movement began to recede.

Slowly, almost imperceptibly, while the villagers held the tree, and Ted Wilkes lifted his voice to the sky, the peach tree became still. The quivering stopped, the branches of the tree against the building relaxed. The hands of the people were no longer shaken. The rustling of the leaves ceased.

No one spoke now. No one moved. They stood together as the peach tree grew completely still and the dust in the air settled.

Ted Wilkes was the first to move. Lowering his hands, he told them, "It's over now. They understand." Traces of his west-country accent were clear in his voice.

They all began to move away silently, unable to give voice to the experience they'd shared.

Some remained holding hands; some went with their heads still bowed. An old lady cried and a child suddenly laughed.

"Go home now," Ted Wilkes said. "Go to your home and live your lives and remember what happened here today." He looked at all the faces. "We're all creatures of the field," he said. "That's what you must remember. We all need each other. We've all got a place on the earth."

The villagers began to disperse, in twos and threes, in family groups. None of them left alone.

The barman went into The Bunch of Grapes looking for the old lady. She sat behind the bar sucking her shawl, untouched by everything that had happened around her.

She looked up as the barman entered. "Is the service over?" she asked in her quavering voice.

The barman nodded.

"Has the vicar gone?"

"Yes," the barman whispered.

"Oh, what a pity," the old lady said. "I did so want to talk to him." She smiled, twisting the edge of her shawl.

Outside Ted Wilkes stood with Reynolds, watching the villagers walk away.

"Is it over now?" Reynolds asked, his voice strangely dry. "Really over?"

Ted shook his head. "It'll never really be over," he said. "But it's begun, Mr. Reynolds, it's begun."

"Is that all then for now?"

"Who knows?" said old Ted Wilkes.

Reynolds looked at the dispersing villagers. "You think it'll make any difference?" he asked. "The thing that's happened here today?"

"Yes."

"I hope so."

"Well," said Ted, "we've understood, haven't we, sir? And if we can, everyone can. It's up to all of us."

Reynolds nodded.

"I only hope the others are all right," Ted added as an afterthought.

"The others?"

Ted Wilkes nodded. "Them that wasn't here to share—the Monks and Mabel Crewe."

Chapter
Forty-Four

Philip Monk ran toward the Old Bridge, glancing at the changing sky, his footsteps sounding heavy in the hot air. Cottages rushed past as he ran from the village, past the church which stood deserted and shut, through the narrow lane. He saw no one.

Philip turned out of the town, then came to the turning before the Old Bridge. Around the bend in the lane he suddenly saw the yellow stone bridge and the clear running stream. Beyond it, about to follow the tiny overgrown path beside the riverbank, were the figures of Elizabeth and Jacob.

They turned when they heard his footsteps, waiting until he caught up with them.

"What—" Philip began, out of breath. "What's wrong?"

"Wrong?" Elizabeth queried.

"Yes—your note." Philip was surprised at his wife's calm. "I thought you were frightened."

Elizabeth shook her head. "No, not anymore." She touched Jacob's hair. "Jacob's taking me to where Deborah is. Where the sunflowers are."

"What sunflowers?"

"Deborah's. The ones she listens to."

Philip was confused. "What's all this about?" he asked uncertainly.

"They're Debby's," Jacob said. "She talks to them. She says they tell her everything. They frighten me a bit. I've only been down there once before. But they frightened me when they moved."

"You actually saw them *move?*"

Jacob nodded.

Philip glanced up at Elizabeth's calm face. "You

knew about all this?" He found it hard to accept her total involvement while he remained, somehow, an outsider.

"Yes, Jacob told me."

"And you still wanted to come down?"

"Yes."

"What's happened to you?" Philip stared at his wife, struggling to understand aspects of her he hadn't known before. Somehow he managed to keep his own fear in control. "What's changed you?"

"I'm still the same."

"You're not afraid anymore."

"No."

"Jacob is." Philip looked down at his son. "You can see it."

"I was too," said Elizabeth. "But I'm not now." She smiled. "Perhaps that's what they want. Perhaps that's how they'll touch us. They'll make us afraid and then they'll make us understand. It's their way of beginning."

Philip looked away. Her comprehension was beyond him.

"Are you coming with us?" Elizabeth asked, taking charge. "To the sunflowers?"

"Yes, of course."

"Come along then," Elizabeth said. She took Jacob's hand and they moved along the little path beside the stream. "Let's all go together."

Philip followed.

They walked together beside the stream and, slowly, growing out of the gentle sounds of the summer afternoon, they became aware of the rustling of the plants. It spread about them, whispering its menace.

When he heard it Philip stopped.

Elizabeth turned, her hand in Jacob's. "It's all right, Philip," she told her husband confidently. "It really is. Come on. I'm sure there's nothing to be frightened of."

Jacob swallowed and held his mother's hand.

Philip hesitated. "How can you be sure?"

"I'm sure."

"But—"

"You must trust me," Elizabeth said. The source of her confidence was a puzzle to her. She only knew that from the moment she'd left the cottage and begun to search for whatever it was that had to be found, her fear had begun to diminish. "Please, Philip." She smiled. "Don't fight me."

Philip nodded. There was no other way.

He followed as Elizabeth led them into the small clearing where Deborah and Mabel Crewe sat on the grass, seven large sunflowers reigning above them.

Deborah turned as she saw them, an expression of surprise crossing her face.

She spoke, briskly. "Shh—something's happening. Don't upset them now."

Her father reached for her. "Debby, are you—"

"Shhh."

"Philip—" Elizabeth sat on the grass, drawing Jacob down beside her. "Sit down, Philip."

"Something very important's happening," Deborah repeated. "Miss Crewe and I've been listening. We've all got to sit down and listen. They say so."

Philip did not move.

"Sit down," Deborah ordered crossly. "We *must* all listen.

Slowly Philip Monk sat down on the grass in the clearing.

He looked at the sunflowers, watching them move their stately heads, feeling himself tremble as the great black and yellow faces seemed to fasten their gaze on him. He listened to the sounds they made, feeling chilled, smelling the dry, musty smell in the clearing. None of this bore any relationship to anything he had ever known. Except for his family and Mabel Crewe, nothing in the clearing had any reality for him. He had no experience of it.

This is the difference, he thought, between an idea and its execution.

He glanced at the others seated about him. All held their faces up to the sunflowers. All were still and silent, totally enraptured.

He wondered why he alone appeared to be afraid and did not know the answer.

He studied the faces of the sunflowers and couldn't help thinking how appropriate the name was. Huge and beautiful sun symbols, eaten in some parts of the world, worshiped in others.

"Something's happened," Deborah said suddenly in urgency. "They're saying something's happened in the village." She tilted her head, listening. "They think we should all be there. That's what they want. All of us together."

"What do they want us for, Debby?" Elizabeth asked. "Do they say why?"

"No." Deborah listened. "Anyway, it's too late now. We can't go with the others. It's too late."

"Where are the others?" Mabel Crewe asked, speaking for the first time since the others arrived. "Do they say where they are?"

"In the village."

"I should be there, too," Mabel decided. "I should be with them."

"No." Deborah shook her head. "It's all right for you to be here with us. They say that. Anyway, it's too late to be anywhere else."

"Then I'm glad I'm here," Mabel said.

"But something *is* happening," Deborah repeated emphatically. "Something that's very important to everyone. All the people in the village are together, and they're all—" She sat, her eyes tightly closed. "Oh, I wish someone else could hear them too. I don't understand it all."

"What don't you understand?" Elizabeth asked softly. "What is it?"

"It's something about—they're holding hands and helping—helping each other. And all of them are trying to—talk to each other. They're trying to—"

"Communicate?" said Elizabeth.

"Yes. That's it. Comm—" Deborah opened her eyes and looked at her mother. "Can you hear them too?"

"No," Elizabeth replied. "I can only hear you."

"I'm not so frightened anymore," Jacob said suddenly. He swallowed loudly. "Perhaps I was a bit inexperienced before."

"Shhh," Deborah told him. "They're saying something else."

The sunflowers bent their heads, swooping low over the five figures seated beneath them. An odor of musk invaded the air.

"They—want—someone," Deborah said, sitting very still, her eyes closed, her voice the wooden voice Philip had heard in the garden. "They—want—someone—to—go—with—them."

Philip Monk felt his scalp prickle, Mabel Crewe's frail body seemed to sink deeper into the grass.

Jacob's serious eyes never left the sunflowers. Elizabeth felt a great sadness begin to well up inside her.

"They—want—someone."

"No," Philip whispered.

"Yes," said Mabel Crewe, sure now there was nothing left to hide. Everyone knew now. "Yes, they do. They've said this before. They want an atonement." She moved her fingers over the earth. "Earlier, before you arrived, they were talking to Deborah about it."

She forced the words from her lips, suddenly overcoming a lifetime of inhibition and reserve. They might not be *her* voices that had spoken to the child, but she believed them. They might not have uttered *their* requirements to *her*, but she was now prepared to serve.

"They want someone to *give* themselves," she explained. "They want a sign of—commitment."

"What sort of sign?" Philip asked, fear tightening his throat.

"Someone to die for them."

"No. *No.*"

"Yes."

Philip Monk closed his eyes. Michael Martin had been right—so right. The condemnation of the plants against all mankind *was* a moral one.

"Who?" asked Elizabeth.

"One—of—us," Deborah answered in her wooden voice. "At the village—they all—understood. Now one of us—must say—we—understand too."

The motion of the sunflowers increased as they

swung lazily above the seated figures, the rustling of their leaves growing louder, the odor of musk all-pervading.

Above, the sky was blood colored; the sun dark-rimmed and gorged. Around the length of the horizon was a band of golden light.

"Now," Deborah continued. "Now."

"No." Fear gripped Philip like a band. "No."

"It's what—they want," Deborah said emphatically. "Someone who understands—someone who—will *give* themselves. Someone they—don't have to—*take*."

"Take?" Philip whispered. "What do you mean, take?"

"The way Charlie Crump was taken," Mabel Crewe explained. "The way they took Walters."

"You know about Walters?"

"I know about them all now. Debby's told me. The sunflowers told her."

"The others—were—bad," Deborah went on. "They—did bad things. They—fought them—they hurt them. Now—they want—someone good."

"Must they really take someone?" Elizabeth asked.

"Yes—someone good."

Jacob turned to his mother and took her hand. "Mummy?" he asked. "Is there anything I can do to help? I've been good. I have."

"No," Elizabeth said, her voice trembling. "Just being here is enough, I'm sure. That's what they're really saying, isn't it?"

Philip looked at his family, then got to his feet.

"It—must be—now," Deborah told them. "Now—now—now."

"No," her father said, standing among the sunflowers, looking down at his daughter. "Not—*you*."

Deborah smiled, then opened her eyes. "You know it must be me, Daddy," she said, no trace of fear in her voice. "You know that, don't you? It's me they want."

"No." Philip reached out for her. "I won't let them."

"I don't really mind," Deborah confided. "I'm not afraid at all." She motioned to the sunflowers. "They're my friends. They'll look after me. They promised they would. I don't mind going with them at all."

"Oh, Debby," Elizabeth's voice was thick with sadness. "Must it be you?"

"Yes, Mummy."

"Oh, Debby." For a moment Elizabeth felt tears beginning. The peace she had felt was shattered, all her beliefs were faltering. "Oh, Debby . . ."

"Yes." Deborah looked at her mother, her eyes full of an ancient, infinite wisdom. "I don't think there *is* anyone else."

Elizabeth felt the tears on her cheeks. I am being asked, she thought, and I cannot respond. I need my daughter's strength.

"No." Philip moved to stand before the sunflowers, spreading his arms. "Don't take her. We need her. If someone must go, take me."

The clearing was filled with new waves of sound.

"Philip!" Elizabeth called out.

The sound of the plants rose in a crescendo, shattering the air.

"Yes!" Philip shouted. "Leave her. I'll come with you."

"No, Daddy!" Deborah cried out. "You can't hear them. That's very important. You can't hear what they're saying."

"But I can," Mabel Crewe told them. "I can hear them. I'll go."

Deborah smiled at the old woman.

"They like me." Mabel Crewe's voice grew fainter. "I can go."

"Yes. They told me they like you very much," Debby agreed.

"Then, it *is* all right for me to go with them?"

"If you'd like to," Debby told her.

"Yes, oh, yes," Mabel Crewe decided. "I'd like to very much."

"And you *can* hear what they're saying now?"

"Yes. Every word."

"Then it must be all right, mustn't it? If they like you and you can hear them, it must be all right, Miss Crewe."

"No one else spoke.

Mabel Crewe smiled. "Thank you," she said, simply, her voice a mere whisper.

She seemed to float toward the sunflowers. They bent as though enfolding her. Lifting her tired, careworn face to them, she was aware of their own yellow and black faces surrounding her. She placed her hands together and the stalks of the sunflowers curved about them. Tears flowed from her eyes and she felt lighthearted. Gradually the great flowers covered her and in one long, endless moment, she disappeared into them completely.

She seemed to be sinking among them, and then she was gone. When the villagers came for her later, there was nothing of her that remained. Her clothing lay on the ground along with her glasses and an old gold watch. But of the woman herself nothing was ever seen again.

Slowly the sunflowers ceased their movement; their rustling sound grew fainter. Then the sky began to clear.

Philip Monk felt his heart resume its normal beat. He felt the fear leave him. He took Elizabeth by the hand and she stood, Jacob beside her. They all looked at Deborah.

Deborah smiled. "They did like her," she said. "And they really, really wanted someone to go with them. Isn't it nice she could go?"

"Yes," said Elizabeth. "It is."

Deborah got to her feet, holding the guinea pig. "I think we should go now."

"Yes," said Philip, his voice uneven. "I think we should."

Deborah led them from the clearing along the riverbank and over the yellow stone bridge toward the village.

No one said anything. There were no words that seemed appropriate.

Philip and Elizabeth and Jacob followed Deborah back to Brandling under the lightening sky.

Deborah led them to the center of the village, to The Bunch of Grapes.

On the way they passed groups of villagers in twos and threes. On all the faces they saw peace and something of communication. No one spoke to them but all passed enfolded in the understanding that something had been shared.

When they reached The Bunch of Grapes, Deborah stopped.

Ted Wilkes and Harry Reynolds stood outside the public house. Deborah approached Ted Wilkes and handed him the guinea pig.

Ted Wilkes took it in his work-roughened hands, holding it gently. "Now what have we got here?" he asked in his easy voice.

"It's a present," Deborah said. "I thought you'd like to have it. It hasn't got a name yet, but I thought you'd like to have it all the same."

"He hasn't got a name, you say?"

"Not yet." Deborah smiled. "But that doesn't matter, does it? You don't really have to have a name, do you?"

"No, my girl, you don't." Ted Wilkes tapped the side of his nose with his forefinger, knowledgeably, with relish. "You and I know that now, don't we?"

"Yes," Deborah agreed. "We do."

She turned and began to walk home, toward the cottage. The others followed. Philip and Elizabeth and Jacob caught up with her and they all walked together, leaving Ted Wilkes and Reynolds alone.

Reynolds shook his head. "Don't quote me on this," he said slowly. "But I think I've just seen a miracle."

Ted Wilkes smiled as he fondled the guinea pig. "You haven't seen one, Mr. Reynolds, but you've lived through one."

He lifted his head and watched the Monks walk away, together, united, safe.

Ted Wilkes couldn't explain where it had really begun or where it would end. He only knew that Brandling would endure.

He felt a cool breeze on his cheek and smiled. It

240

was the first he had felt for weeks. He lifted his head and sniffed the air. It was gentle air, clean, wholesome, refreshing.

Thank God it happened here, he thought. Where we understood. An old man and a child.

Chapter
Forty-Five

After the Events in Brandling, as they came to be known in the press, were over, the Endless Summer turned.

The breeze Ted Wilkes had felt on his cheek blew across the entire country. From the beaches in northern Scotland to the cliffs of Cornwall the heat dissipated and was blown away.

The long hot days cooled and the persistent evening showers spread and scattered. The weather pattern returned to normal and the overgrowth of plant and vegetation diminished.

No one could explain the change. Almost everyone welcomed it. Hay fever was reduced and allergies lessened. The pollen count dropped to almost normal. Familiar gray English skies became common again.

"At least it's a bit cooler," people said. "At least you can get your breath."

The country began to forget the Events in Brandling.

By the time the telephone lines were up again and the road cleared, other news filled the pages of the newspapers. The three deaths in the small village in Somerset no longer seemed important.

Even the BBC relaxed its vigilance.

There continued to be, for a while, isolated reports of the incidents. A magazine ran an article on Anne Walters, wife of the dead constable. But as no one had seen him die, there was little interest in his death.

One of the more sensational London papers reported an incident of biodynamic interference from outer space. But that was all.

The villagers of Brandling proved to be unresponsive. They gave little to reporters who visited the village.

The experience was their own, they felt, too personal to share. The outside world would laugh at them if they related what really had happened. The plants had understood and that was enough.

Brandling did not welcome outsiders.

However, in Taunton, at the insistence of the chief constable, a committee was set up to report on the Events in Brandling.

Harry Reynolds, a former keeper of parks and gardens, was asked to attend, but as he had applied for a transfer shortly after the events themselves, he was not able to do so.

At the moment the committee is still investigating the Events in Brandling and to date their report is still unpublished.

ABOUT THE AUTHOR

KENNETH McKENNEY worked for some years as a geologist in Australia and Fiji. By then he had had enough of rocks, and his interest in writing led him to advertising as a copywriter. He is now an advertising executive in Britain. *The Plants* is his first novel to be published in the United States.

RELAX!
SIT DOWN
and Catch Up On Your Reading!

Bantam Book Catalog

It lists over a thousand money-saving best-sellers originally priced from $3.75 to $15.00 —bestsellers that are yours now for as little as 60¢ to $2.95!

The catalog gives you a great opportunity to build your own private library at huge savings!

So don't delay any longer—send us your name and address and 25¢ (to help defray postage and handling costs).